MATCHES

ALSO BY ALAN KAUFMAN

Memoir
Jew Boy

Poetry
Who Are We?

Anthologies
The Outlaw Bible of American Poetry

*The Outlaw Bible of American Literature
(with Neil Ortenberg and Barney Rosset)*

*The New Generation: Fiction for Our Time from
America's Writing Programs*

MATCHES

A Novel

ALAN KAUFMAN

BACK BAY BOOKS
LITTLE, BROWN AND COMPANY
New York Boston

Back Bay Books / Little, Brown and Company
Time Warner Book Group
1271 Avenue of the Americas, New York, NY 10020
Visit our Web site at www.twbookmark.com

First Edition: October 2005

This is a work of fiction. I lived through and witnessed many events during my service as an Israeli combat infantry soldier. These events inform my fiction. I have changed all names, modified identities, and consolidated events and people to create my characters. Certain real locations and public figures are mentioned, but all other characters and the events described are imaginary.

Grateful acknowledgment is made to the *San Francisco Chronicle* for publication of an earlier version of "The Orchard" and to *McSweeney's* for publication of an earlier version of "G-Beat."

The author is grateful for permission to reprint "In Memory of W. B. Yeats," copyright 1940 & renewed 1968 by W. H. Auden, from *Collected Poems* by W. H. Auden. Used by permission of Random House, Inc.

Library of Congress Cataloging-in-Publication Data

Kaufman, Alan.
    Matches : tales of an Israeli soldier / Alan Kaufman. — 1st ed.
       p.   cm.
    ISBN 0-316-10664-X
    1. Israel — History, Military — Fiction. 2. Soldiers — Fiction.   I. Title.

PS3561.A827M38   2005
813'.54 — dc22   2005002592

10 9 8 7 6 5 4 3 2 1

Q-FF

Design by Renato Stanisic

Printed in the United States of America

For Joseph Herlicy, Allen Tannenbaum, and Fred Jordan

In the Israeli army, a unit commander reporting from the field will refer to the soldiers under his command as "Matches." The term, taken from Hannah Senesh's poem "Blessed Is the Match" — a hymn to valor — is the IDF code word for a soldier. Among the troops, it has come to mean someone who strikes, burns, and dies.

CONTENTS

MATCHES

Prologue
THE ORCHARD

That morning, when it was done, when we were sickened unto death, and curfew reigned, we tore our helmets off and sped through the riot streets of shattered glass over blood-spattered flagstones. Past bullet-punched walls we flew. The boiling black smoke pillars of burning tires stalked us like the desert God. Our wheels scattered spent shells, crimson rocks. Here and there, one of our "cousins," as we called the locals, curled in a doorway, defiant, weeping with rage, his kaffiyeh clenched in his teeth.

The air reeked of camel shit and dread. My sleepless eyes drifted shut: on their side six shot, no telling how many dead, and from our end two wounded, bad, and one, curly-headed Reuvi, the newlywed, bagged for a grave. Only twenty-four he was, the boy. A mob-tossed hand grenade mangled his guts. A bad scene.

My mouth yawned wide to gulp the morning air, and my filthy fingers pried my eyes apart. I was no boy and needed strong mud coffee. But we did not stop. We could not. Neither did we take the patrol route back to base: we fled town. Good riddance. Fuck them all!

The blurred green-black road trembled, the sun risen over us with an ill-sounding birdsong. Sometimes a song can sound diseased. We stopped our ears. I put my fists to mine. I shook. Then the armored car swerved sharply and Brandt shouted something indecipherable and we rumbled through a vineyard into a clearing. At the end of the road it was, in a grove of olive trees. Right there, we pulled off the red clay and onto thick brown grass and stopped.

Brandt and Uri jumped out, dropped their guns to the ground, shrugged off their gear, threw themselves down, and passed out, clutching the grass like a woman's hair. Groggily, I followed suit. The last thing I saw before sleep was a giant black fly stropping its legs on my hand.

I was the first who awakened to see the old Arab squatting there beside our guns. A Palestinian. My eyes snapped from him to the weapons and back. He held out apples, said whatever: I didn't care to know. Climbing casually to my feet I walked with a fiercely pounding heart to the guns, shouldered mine, and, collecting the others', deposited them next to my sleeping comrades, whom I brought awake with sharp kicks. The Arab took in all this.

When Uri talked to him in perfect Arabic, the old man listened carefully, his black clotted eyes mucal with age. His thin frowning face had a prominent square jaw, covered with gray thistles. His apricot-colored skin was mapped with a thousand prehistoric wadis. An aura of bandoliers and virgin brides hung about him, and scores of grandchildren playing in his ravines. He wore a white kaffiyeh with a black agal, the traditional headdress; a long white Shillahat robe with billowing sleeves and turquoise sirwal pants. He was a ragged old rake. He had rope sandals on his thickly callused feet. In his worn leather belt was that short

Bedouin knife they use to cut the throats of game birds. When a breeze stirred the kaffiyeh, it revealed large sculpted ears delicately inlaid with fine white hairs. Finally, Uri finished and the old man thought.

Then he spoke, his hands gesturing with strong, graceful motions that trembled for age. When he finished, he looked around at us and nodded to each emphatically, slapping the back of one hand against the palm of the other, again and again.

"He says," Uri began, "that his name is Jamal Abu-Da'ud. That we are guests on his farm. That we are in an orchard here, planted by his own hands with the help of three sons and ten grandchildren. His wife is dead. His daughters all married. He has lived here since infancy. Wants we should eat his fruit. Ours to eat, he says. Says that we have nothing to fear."

Uri paused. Then: "And he says that he knows that our peoples are at war. That he has seen what his own people do and he knows the war they make is cruel. And he has also seen Israeli soldiers like us come and go and what we do. He thinks that everyone has gone very crazy. But that is out there, he says, beyond the orchard, and not here. And yes, if they ask him to, he will join them to fight, because he is a patriot. Then, yes, he too will make war on us. But not here, he says. Here we are not Arab or Jew, but only men eating fruit. He encourages us to eat our fill before we go. He wishes us a good rest. There is no rush. He'll bring water to refresh ourselves with." And with that, Uri nodded and the old man rose and walked off.

"Eat up quick, and let's get the fuck out of here before he returns with 'friends,'" said Brandt. He spit in the dust. And added: "Murdering old son of a bitch!"

Hurriedly we filled our helmets with apples, jumped aboard the armored car, and roared off. They all had guns hidden someplace. Even an old man like that.

5

"How good is your Arabic?" Brandt snarled at Uri, whom we knew to be a real peacenik. "I think you made up that old shit's speech!"

We laughed, Uri too. We were so dead tired. True or not about Uri's little speech, we all feared our return to the city of graves, where more rioting loomed. But even as we laughed in despair, we peered back hard at the old man's groves. We no longer searched for his gun's muzzle flash, but watched his trees recede, growing smaller and smaller, his world disappearing, and even now, long after it has vanished altogether, still we glance back to there, or what we think is there, so far away. We look with a sense of longing and regret, though that too is fast fading.

PART 1

THE JEWISH WARS

This was in the Gaza Strip: a long, secret, protracted agony of daily attack and counterattack that turned our days and nights into a flare-lit shadow dance with skulls, on head-nodding patrols in areas where even the wild pariah dogs shunned to go.

We were a reserve unit of combat-trained Israeli armored infantry but minus our big, boxy personnel carriers — long ago we left them buried to their hatches in scorpion-infested sand somewhere out in the camouflaging desert — and sent here to quell "unrest," some general's euphemism for armed Palestinian revolt.

In exchange for our TOW shoulder-held tank blasters and other sorts of dangerous toys that we took pride in handling well, we were issued rubber bullets, body armor, riot helmets, shatterproof shields, and nasty-looking crowd control batons, but the men never used that junk except for the bulletproof ceramic vests. They left the rest rattling in heaps in the corners of our fast-moving steel-plated patrol trucks, or Noon Noons, as they were called.

Because some of us yet thought of ourselves as soldiers. And some of us still thought that we just couldn't be down here forever, though by now the service had dragged on over years.

But again and again they sent us down to Gaza, and the more we operated down here, the more we hated the work, but also the better at it we got until counterinsurgency became our pet calling. It was an ugly little pet indeed, and we had to walk it every day and keep it fed on blood and tears.

We learned as we went, methods strictly unconventional, no big hardware set piece battles but dry, dirty games of small arms and concealable explosives, informers and smugglers, and suspects hauled in for attitude adjustment by the Sheen Bet Security Services. Some of us couldn't even remember how to load or shoot a TOW anymore, let alone recite the code for purity of arms, but we could blow a terrorist safe house sky high in nothing flat and unearth an arms factory where you thought you saw only a dress shop.

Tonight some sort of wide-scale action was in motion throughout the Khan Yunis sector. Other patrols had gone out in a big hurry, but since no one had summoned us — which as far as we were concerned was just fine — Brandt, Avi, and I had just stayed in the garrison club room, with its scarred Ping-Pong table with the shredded net and a battered TV set with reception so bad that the picture looked like transmissions from Mars.

This TV, by the way, had a wire clothing hanger antenna, and part of the ritual of watching it involved jumping up from your seat to fiddle with it in a futile quest for the exact invisible spot for good reception. There was a way, though, to get it good enough that you could watch the Jordanian broadcast of the American sitcom *Three's Company,* with its girls in tiny shorts and the emasculated male roommate bumbling around issuing bland punch lines.

It was the closest thing to sex we had, and we sat around staring at it numbly, our unshaven cheeks sagging in insomniacal frowns.

Brandt nodded at the blond TV star with the ponytail. "How sweet is that ass?"

Avi shrugged. "She looks like Goldie Hawn. Falk, here, he likes that — right, Falk? Falk eats that bony Goldie Hawn tail."

"Like lobster." I grinned.

"Lobster's not kosher," Avi said gravely.

"Bullshit," snapped Brandt. "Blondes are kosher. Besides, I eat lobster. With plenty of butter. Huh, Nathan? You like that butter sauce?"

I nodded happily. "You know it. I like it blond and buttery."

"Falk," said Avi. "What kind of Jewish name is that?" to which I replied, "It's New York City Yiddish for 'Go Falk Yourself,'" and we all burst out laughing.

We teamed well together, we three — liked each other a lot, got along. Which meant your back got watched when you went out there knocking on Arafat's door. It gave you something close to peace of mind.

Brandt, our handsome squad leader, was only a reservist corporal but was treated like an officer by the staff because looks-wise he was movie-star caliber; he worked as a ground maintenance supervisor for El Al airlines and so not only had unlimited access to a constantly replenishing supply of Israel's most beautiful stewardesses to fuck, but flew anywhere in the world he liked, cost-free.

And as if to etch our envy with hydrochloric acid on Sinai stone, God had also arranged that Brandt should happen to be a professional soccer referee as well, who was quite often seen on national broadcast, officiating in major league play. And while the rest of us in civilian life scrambled for bleacher seats to the playoff games, the lucky SOB saw any match he liked; just turned up at any stadium and walked right in.

Even Brandt's divorce was enviable. Not to go on too much about him, but this Brandt, you see, his ex-wife was a former Miss Israel, a ten named Mariana, the daughter of multimillionaire plastics manufacturers, the famed Borzoys of Haifa. She was Brandt's best friend and close confidante and had not only waived child support but even given Brandt full access to his kids, who could stay with him whenever he liked. She actually even entertained, I was told, some of the girlfriends he brought home.

He had a certain cynical charm, our corporal, a wry confidence that women found absolutely devastating. They fell for him like axed trees.

Some who had gone with him into Tel Aviv on twenty-four-hour leaves could attest to how he entered a club and ten minutes later left in the escort of not one but two bombshells. His secret? He regarded all things with a sneering curl of his upper lip, a disdainful gleam in his eye. He beheld alike, with equal contempt, generals, beauty queens, soccer stars, politicians, policemen, tax collectors, and terrorists. He had, as I said, this little smirk. Only a corporal, yet he wielded a captain's influence. When high-ranking officers glanced his way for approval, he smirked and it leveled their self-esteem.

Our unit commander was Lieutenant Yitzak, who strolled around in the freezing cold garrison in a wife-beater T-shirt and bling-bling gold chains, his spoiled, rich-boy voice whining in our ears. Here was an officer who stepped from his barrack each dawn with his hand thrust down the crotch of his bleached white BVDs, lovingly scratching his balls and yawning like a pimp on holiday in Cancún. So it was not exactly Yitzak we obeyed, but rather the hulking, begrizzled Sergeant Dedi, who implemented Yitzak's "orders," though only in his own way.

In action, this Sergeant Dedi, who was built like a wrestler, had the darkstaring focus of a Ninja tenth-degree black belt. He called clear shots when things got tough and he got you through in one piece. When Dedi spoke in his low, measured way, everybody listened up. We were all agreed, even Yitzak, on one thing: this Dedi was a good boy. Had a bright head too. In civilian life he was finishing up a graduate art history degree. Van Gogh's no help in a fight, but when the rocks and bullets flew, Dedi's the one you wanted in there, dropped to one knee with weapon cradled in his arm, his calm hand signals directing you to cover.

But also, as I had learned on one of my first times out with this unit, in a really tight spot often you needed a fast way out, and for that there was Avi, working the gas and the brake pedals of the steel-plated Noon Noons.

Avi had the deadpan reflexes of a mobbed-up getaway man; could spin-turn in a kasbah alley, under fire, a two-ton armoured car.

Bullets didn't even make him flinch. He drove with a kind of dour defiance. Avi even sort of looked gangland, with his swarthy, hard-boned face, lanky build, kinked nap, and laconic air.

A Fez-born Moroccan, he had smuggled himself to Israel as a teen and now owned and operated in civilian life a paid-up Mercedes Benz limo taxi that made shuttle runs beween Tel Aviv and the Holy City of Jerusalem.

I was the anomalous American, to most Israelis something strange: a New York Jew who had actually acquired Israeli citizenship in return for the dubious privilege of getting called up to serve in the most dangerous army on earth, the Israel Defense Forces.

For in so doing I had bucked what had become, after years of ceaseless warfare and endless terrorism, the primo fantasy of so many sabras born behind the Green Line, Israel's traditional borderline: complete your army service, and then jet straight out for the fleshpots of Berlin, Amsterdam, New York, or L.A., there to live by your greencarded wits, make a killing in bucks, not blood, and, more so, to thrive immersed in Coppertone and Disney World, SUVs, Costco, and Cost Plus, neck-deep in fluffy towels, CDs, skateboards, laptops, wide-screen TVs, and Betty Crocker cake mix.

Most Israelis who fled the Jewish State wanted never ever to have to don a uniform again, or fire a .05 machine gun, or numbly roll through an Arab refugee camp exposed to hidden black-masked jihadists with shoulder-held RPG waiting to turn your jeep into a Jerry Bruckheimer fireball.

So all through my two years of regular army service and now as a reservist I was asked, again and again, by grinning, incredulous troops: "What brought you to this insane mess? Why join the army if you don't have to?"

The best I could come up with was that during my time in America I'd lived pretending to myself that the non-Jews didn't really think I was a Christ-killing, world-dominating, media-controlling kike — pretending to myself that they really didn't chide my Jewishness behind my back. But after all, they often did. And always, there was this ice-cold separateness. They never let you forget not so much that you were a Jew but that they, bless their Christmasy asses, were not.

I figured the one place on earth where I could really feel free of all that shit was in Israel. I wanted, for once, to be just generally human, immersed in a kinky-haired majority. To whatever soldier asked me about my strange presence I held up in my hands the assault rifle, the Colt automatic rifle, or CAR-15, that we carried: "See this?" I said. "Truth is, once I saw you Israeli soldiers, Clint Eastwood Jews with big guns in your hands, man, I couldn't even pretend that I didn't want to serve. Fuck my feminine side. Are you kidding? You know how proud you guys made me feel? It brought the man right out in me!" They always laughed and clapped my back for saying this.

But not Avi. Disposed to gloom, he didn't seem amused. He went right past my shtick, snorted, and said disdainfully: "You're full of shit. Majority? What majority? I ask you, Nathan: what majority? You know how many Arabs are out there? Do you?" His hand jabbed toward the "out there" of the whole Middle East, at Gaza, the West Bank, Jordan, Syria, Lebanon, Egypt, Iran, Algeria, Libya, Iraq, Saudi Arabia, Kuwait, and sheikdoms I didn't even know the names of. A couple hundred million Arabs, an ocean. "And now they hate you even more as an Israeli then they would have hated you as an American. You wanted to escape the difference and the hate? But now you are really hated. No one in the world is hated by Arabs more than us Israelis. We are the 'difference' that they are born to hate."

Now Udi, the radio man, leaned his bespectacled face in the club room door. "*He* himself wants to see you." Meaning: Yitzak. We groaned to our feet, trooped past Udi's insolent smile.

The lieutenant met us with his boots planted on a wall of the communication room; rocked back and forth on the chair's rear legs, headset on, his hand shooting out to adjust the transmitter's dials.

When he saw us he removed the headset and studied us with a weak smile as though we were his long-awaited salvation. "I have special work," he said, his free hand making a nervous adjustment to his gold chain. "And I want you three in there. To go to a settlement. But not just any settlement. These are true believers. There are known conspirators among them. They're not just playing. They kill Arabs. If they could, they'd blow up the Temple Mount.

Several of them from this settlement have been in and out of jail for various serious activities. You can guess what those are. They are very to the right. Religious fanatics. Of all the groups, these are known to be the most extreme. They have had it hard, where they are. Many attacks against them. Also, they feel betrayed by us. After all, we let them in there in the first place. They know that when the time comes, the army will arrive and throw them out of there. It's just a matter of time before the government strikes some deal with the 'cousins.' And they have lived with constant hostilities. They are bitter, believe me. A number of them have lost family . . . a few children, a couple of infants, newborns — you understand. A wife. A sister. A boy. All killed by the Palestinians. And so on. Not good. Not good."

"You're talking about Neve Parsha," said Brandt.

Yitzak nodded. "Yes. Go there and take a look. Just a look. Nothing special. See. Just see. That's all. Just have a look around."

"Tell me, Yitzak," said Brandt, "why is it every time there is something in Neve Parsha, you send us and you make this same fucked-up little speech as though we never heard of the place?"

Yitzak's face and ears reddened. His chair's front legs and then his boots struck the floor hard. "Because Falk here is still somewhat new to your squad and, uh, he, uh, he has not been there. Isn't that true, Falk?"

"I've been with the unit for two years. But I guess in a way it is."

"And so, I, uh, I want he should understand. He is not born here, remember. He should know."

"Know what?" I asked.

Yitzak looked at me disdainfully, using his eyes to transfer onto me the shame that Brandt had laid on him. I stared back coldly, deflecting the transfer. His eyes retreated, grew small, narrow, lonely. Yes, lonely. This surprised me.

"It's not a piece of Israel that you have maybe come across before. These are poor moshavniks, not wealthy. They are Yemenites. They came here in the Magic Carpet airlift. They were treated badly in Yemen. Persecuted. Killed. The Israeli Air Force flew them out, rescued them. So, these folks have no especial pity for the Arabs, the Palestinians, or for Yemenites for that matter, or any other kind of Arab whatsoever. To them, it is all the same. Because they had no country in Yemen, and they were not just treated there like second-class citizens but murdered. Then they came here and were safe, yes, but not much else. We gave them jobs as low-wage laborers and janitors. To improve their prospects, they volunteered to start their own farms. They were very poor and illiterate, these settlers. Right after the Six Days' War they established Neve Pasha. They have been on the front lines, so to speak, for many years. They are hard people, used to suffering. They have no illusions. They don't trust anyone, not even us. They know that in the name of some agreement with the Palestinians, even the very murderers of their children, we'd sell them out in a minute. I'm afraid they haven't got much use for us."

"And also we have to go protect them," said Avi sarcastically.

"Yes," said Yitzak. "The area commander is worried that because of the operations tonight there will be retaliation on their moshav. To be truthful, they don't want our help. But we are still responsible to put in an appearance. So, you three will go. This will not be a provocation. They know you, Brandt, and you, Avi. And they are big soccer fans. They will like that Brandt is there because Hapoel plays tonight and they'll be glued to their TVs and they've seen Brandt on television. You're the most famous soccer referee in Israel, Brandt."

"They never once recognize me," said Brandt. "Years now I'm going to this moshav for these 'emergencies' and they never recognize me. They don't know me. To them, I am just another Frank."

"A Frank?" I said.

"An Ashkenazi Jew. From Europe. They don't like us. They don't like the way we treated them when they came here."

"How was that?"

"Like shit," said Avi. And since he was himself a Sephardi, like the moshavniks, a Jew of Middle Eastern origin, we did not comment further or dispute his summary. We all knew, even I, that it was indisputably true.

So, this was our "special" mission. We jumped into our Noon Noon, Avi gunned the big patrol truck's engine, and we went roaring down the road. For miles, we saw nothing. Vague shapes gleamed in darkness. Then, off to the north, flickering yellow and white parachute flares trickled down the black sky. Mosques and high buildings and tall villas pulsed into view. "Look how many villas there are!" shouted Avi over his shoulder, slowing down to admire them close up. "They claim to the whole world that Israel keeps them in poverty! So, look at the poverty!" We sped up. We heard cackling gunfire. We saw red tracers stitching seams into nearby pockets of darkness. Searchlights swept over a column of APCs and tanks. We were in the thick of the operation. But at a fork in the road we veered away west, down a pitch black stretch of Arab homes, farms, and fields, these much poorer, anonymous smudges of tin and cement on a muddy void, the operation fading behind us as the silence of Gaza under curfew closed around us. There were no patrols visible now, though they were present, implanted deep within orchards, waiting, camouflaged by rows of snaking trees or else crawling with motors at low hum and lights switched off down alleys and back streets, faces smudged black, guns poised to fire, or they were, we knew, down there in the occasional wadi we passed, stealthing on foot through gashes in the earth. Only once, a Noon Noon bearing six soldiers tore past in the opposite direction at high speed and with its headlights dimmed, the soldiers' parkas billowing like torn ragged sails in a gale.

We were in the deepest recesses of Gaza, alone, our only link the shortwave radio, our only protection our snub-barreled short CAR-15s and the handguns from home that some of us wore jammed into belt holsters at the small of our backs, ugly, blunt little Spanish-make Taurus automatics or Smith & Wesson five-shot .38 Detective Specials and the like, which you weren't meant to have with you but did. And always one bullet in the clip or chamber for yourself — an outcome infinitely preferable to falling into the hands of some of the crews, gangs and militias we pursued. In the ear or mouth and *Shalom!* as the keffiyeh-masked butchers close in.

Avi stepped hard on the gas and now we broke into countryside even more desolate than the lonely lane of hamlets and groves. The close, hot air smelled like a dog's breath. Stars riddled the sky like bullet holes. The vibrating armored truck blurred vision and made my sand- and wind-stung eyes tear. I tugged down my goggles and bandit-masked my face in the plain black kaffiyeh I wore around my neck. I had bought it in the *shuk* in East Jerusalem in the Old City, years ago, from a vendor who claimed it was from Reddiah, Saudi Arabia, and was of a type worn by Bedouin marauders of that region, though none of the Bedouin trackers in our unit had remarked on it. Still, I like to think that it was true. And then, suddenly, unprepared for the spectacular squalor of the place, I saw Neve Parsha hugging the ground, almost invisible; no high towers or other disturbing architectural landmarks — just the long one-story cottages, row on row, and those ugly sheet iron corrugated sheds and workshops, poultry houses and storage warehouses.

There were fogged-up bubble-wrapped crop tents, and the stench of skeletal goats and bony nag horses hung over the place, but I couldn't make out corrals or pens where the pathetic beasts, which I glimpsed off to the side, bathed in ghostly moonlight, might be kept. There was not a single light on in the place that I could see. But then I saw at the gates the silhouettes of five men heavily armed with Kalatchnikovs and short Galils. They lifted hands in a wave as we slowed through the gate, and Avi gently gunned us up a dusty road that ended before a shed with plastic garbage bags stretched over the windows. The door was shut but a thin seam of light bled through the spaces between the frame and door. Brandt pushed the door gently forward, stepped inside. We followed.

There, nursed by a little lantern, sat a man alone on an upended wooden milk crate, a Kalatchnikov automatic rifle between his knees. His gun, I noted, was not just any Kalatchnikov but a Chinese Kalatchnikov. These are very prized in Israel and distinguished from their more common Russian counterpart by certain parts that are coated in a rubberized material burnt umber in color. It is also sleeker and more elegant and uses the very same ammo as the Russian model, or for that matter the Galil, Israel's own assault rifle, or the American M-16 from Colt. You could not legally carry one in or out of the service unless you belonged to a certain kind of military commando unit and had taken it off a dead enemy in combat. Then it was yours to keep, your trophy. Most donated theirs back to the IDF, to be put in the Army Museum of Terrorism. But some kept them. This man had. He had taken it from the corpse of one he killed. There were certain elite units you would never learn anything about so you didn't bother to ask. Clearly, he had served in one.

His face was the hickory color of cured tobacco. When he

moved, hints of bronze light ripped over the fierce angles of his face. His eyes were sunken hollows carved of stained mahogany. When his lips moved, as they did when we entered, they parted not to smile but to prepare for speech, exposing the tips of his white teeth like bone fragments in a fatal wound.

He seemed to recognize Brandt, whose face looked, frankly, unhappy. He didn't pretend to like us either. The flashing of teeth from out of his dark face was the extent of his hospitality. He wore a yarmulke that capped a head of steel gray curls. He wore payos, the earlocks of the ultraorthodox. But in all other respects, he looked in dress, build, and manner like any moshavnik or kibbutznik. The red, blue, and yellow plaid shirt had been laundered and pressed hundreds of times and was faded, threadbare. So were his blue jeans. His shoes were desert boots, the kind worn by commandos and terrorists alike. There was nothing to distinguish him from the majority of Israelis but for the look in his eyes. They were beautiful black velvety eyes but contained at their center something much harder than flesh or spirit, a flint spearhead of unshakable conviction. Clearly he disdained me for my failure to blindly embrace and embody something, as though I would know exactly what it was without our ever having spoken, and in fact he was right: I knew precisely what it was. It was his belief that the Israel granted us Jews in the Torah, stretching from Lebanon to the Euphrates, and all the way to Amman and Damascus, was the Israel that we should have today. It was his belief that attainment of it justified the use of any and all means, including population transfer and any kind of violence.

"So, Brandt," he said, "what do we hear?"

Brandt grunted and scratched under his chin. "Nothing, Elchanon. You don't want us to be here and we didn't want to come, but others there in the great headquarters in Tel Aviv put us together. So: do you offer us some coffee or what?"

Elchanon laughed with more warmth than I would have thought him capable. "I have nothing against you, Brandt." He looked at all of us. "Sit!" he commanded. We found seats.

He rose slowly and began to fuss at a workbench on which stood a small tripod, a blowtorch, and a small blue tin beaker with a handle and a base scorched black. There was a big brown bag of Turkish coffee. Elchanon scooped out three handfuls and tossed them into the pot. He then poured in water from a plastic pitcher that he lifted off the floor from under the workbench. Last, he removed a box of wooden matches from the pocket of his work shirt, took one match out, and struck it to life on his blunt, hard fingernail. It flared brightly in the dark shed. With his right hand he turned the gas release lever on the torch, held it up, put the match to the nozzle, and a blue-white spearhead of pure fire hissed out. With his left hand he casually removed a cigarette from his shirt pocket, placed it between his lips, and lit it with the blowtorch. Not a word transpired between any of us during all this.

Now I could see his eyes very clearly. They were large, brown, hard — not a trace of warmth in them. Underscored by brown hollows of blackened skin, his sleepless eyes were determined never to rest, as if he, Elchanon, had been seated in this metal hut not even guarding but waiting . . . not for one night but entire days, weeks, even months — blowtorching cigarettes to life, smoking incessantly, not eating, living on mud coffee, tobacco, fire. He drew deeply, with obvious pleasure, on the cigarette, then rested the torch on the table so that the flame burned directly on the pot's scorched bottom. Then he turned down the flame to a feeble bud of blue light, propped a block of wood against the cylinder to prevent it from rolling, and removed four cups from a shelf above the worktable. He took down a tin of sugar as well, and a spoon, which he examined, wiped on the corner of his shirt, then examined again. Finding it satisfactory, he laid it beside the sugar tin.

"So, there's your coffee," he said begrudgingly. "You are also hungry?" Clearly he expected us to say no.

We did as he wished.

"Suit yourself."

We all pulled our chairs and milk crates from the various corners of the shed and arranged them in a circle around Elchanon's crate, where he sat perched again, as we had found him, with his elbows on his knees, hands hung loose and head tilted slightly forward, just waiting, though for what we couldn't say and maybe he couldn't either. We listened to the water bubbles fight to rise through the mud coffee's thick brown sludge. We watched Elchanon's face, waiting for him to speak. He didn't. I looked around me. Tools hung from the walls, all well used but relatively new, with bright red or blue or green plastic handles: shovels, rakes, hoes, axes, sickles, and shears. There was a buzz saw in the corner. A calendar on the wall was the only decor. Rust streaked the metal walls.

"It must be hot as shit in here during the day," said Brandt. "How do you stand it? Why don't you build this thing of wood? It's cooler."

"Wood burns," said Elchanon. "One Molotov and poof!"

Brandt nodded. "Has it been quiet?"

Elchanon shrugged. "What is quiet? They shoot at us every chance they get."

"They don't want you here," I said.

Elchanon looked at me. "And you? They want you here?"

"No," I said.

"Maybe yes," said Elchanon. "You have an accent. American, yes? Maybe you are their friend."

"Look at the uniform he's wearing. How can you say such a thing?" said Avi.

"What do I care about that uniform?" said Elchanon with an angry grin. "When the time comes that uniform will come to throw me from my home."

"Your home is in Israel," I said.

"This *is* Israel," said Elchanon.

"I don't see many Jews around here. Mostly Arabs."

"And you. You are not Israeli or Arab. You are American."

"I'm a Jew from New York. But I have Israeli citizenship. I serve in the IDF. That makes me as Israeli as you."

Elchanon nodded with a sarcastic smile. "So easy to be an Israeli," he said. "It was harder when my parents came from Yemen. They were made citizens and had to serve in the IDF as soon as they stepped from the plane but they still couldn't get a job or even a decent place to live. So the government put them in tent camps. That's where I grew up — in a tent camp. Now they give you someplace nicer to live?"

I shrugged. "Right now I live in a barrack in an old British fort in Khan Yunis. You should come live there with us. Better than a tent." I looked around. "But by the looks of the houses you have here, you don't live in a tent now."

Brandt glared at me. I pressed my lips tight to signal half-hearted regret for my insolence, nodded, and shut up.

More time passed in silence. Now the coffee was ready. Elchanon rose without a noise, moved to the table, and poured out three cups. "Sugar?" We all nodded yes. He added sugar to our cups. Then he handed them around and although he knew that like all Israeli soldiers we had drunk hundreds upon hundreds of cups of mud coffee and knew exactly what we must do now, he said, as all Israelis say when handing you your cup of mud coffee: "Don't drink that yet. Let it settle."

And we returned the customary nods to signal that we understood and would let the sediment drift to the bottom of the cup.

The first sip was like a shot of methamphetamine. It loosened our tongues, even Elchanon's.

"So," he said with a perverse grin, "what made you leave New York? I hear it is like Sodom and Gomorrah in America."

I laughed. "It really is, in its way. Too much of everything."

"The women: they are loose."

"No more than Israel."

"Not true," said Avi. "I had an American girl. She fucked all the time, no big deal, anytime I wanted. My Israeli girlfriend makes me promise a ring each time she takes her panties off."

"But who would you want to be waiting for you when you come home from war?" said Brandt.

"The Israeli girl. Of course. You can't talk to American women. Too selfish. And their heads are full of noise." He made a motion by his head to signify a dizzying amount of noise filling up one's head. "They don't really hear you. All they seem to think about is themselves. Isn't that true, Nathan? You would know."

I shrugged. "I felt this weird loneliness in America that I never quite shook — over there no one meets your eyes in the street — and no matter what I did, who I had for a lover, what we called love left us both angry and hurt and feeling more alone than when we were single." I shook my head. "Maybe Americans have too much of everything — food, cars, clothes, sex — and we're all ruined over there, men and women both."

"So, American, where do you stand with your politics? Are you a Laborite? Or a Likudnik? Or are you a Communist? There are Communists in our government. Maybe you are one? You want to give these Arabs a state of their own?"

I looked at Brandt. He offered a little smile, as if to say, *Answer at your own risk.*

"I don't want to give anybody anything. I don't think about these people at all, except when the army sends me down here. You like it here? Good luck. To me, Gaza is a shithole."

Elchanon's bottom lip depressed with mock awe. "You have strong feelings about this, I see."

I nodded. "Sure."

He clapped his dark leather hands together in fake applause; flashed an unamused smile of snarled yellow teeth. He looked at Brandt and Avi with raised eyebrows. "Very nice what you bring here. What is this, a kibbutznik?" He looked at me. "You are kibbutznik?"

"No," I said. "But I have many friends who are. And I understand what they are saying."

"They are socialist Communists," he snarled. "They are against God. They . . . they love the Arabs. Their great-grandfathers used to dress like Arabs. Did you know this?"

"Not all of them. And anyway, so what? It was poetry to them," I said.

He said. "You are against Israel. You are an enemy."

I gaped at him in disbelief. "What are you talking about?" I said in a shaky voice. "I'm an Israeli soldier."

"You are a traitor," he said.

"Hey," said Brandt, "take it easy on him. Don't you see: he's a new immigrant. He came all the way from New York City to protect your ass."

I glanced at Brandt, who crossed his eyes good-humoredly as a signal not to take any of this seriously. But I couldn't help myself. Elchanon's words struck deep and hurt.

"And so, I'm a traitor. I'm the enemy. That means what? That you put me in a league with Arafat?"

Elchanon waved his hand dismissively. "You are the enemy of Israel. Either you are with God and with Israel or you are not. And if you are not then you're just another Arab. Just the same."

"And Brandt?" I asked with cold fury. "And Avi? These are also enemies."

Elchanon looked at Brandt and laughed. "Of course."

Brandt nodded. "Avi and I are enemies from way back."

"And you, Avi? You're the enemy?"

Avi tilted his head back with heavy-lidded eyes and lips pursed wistfully. He nodded with theatrical gravity. "It seems so."

I should have taken their cues, stopped there, let it go. But I couldn't. I felt my rage mounting unchecked.

"But there's three of us and one of you. There's more of us than you. So, maybe *you're* the enemy."

Brandt shook his head and tisked disapprovingly. "Don't need to do that, Nathan. That's not a good way to go."

"And — and this?" I stammered, looking at our accuser. "I'm here to guard his fucking ass, and he calls *me* a traitor?" I looked at Elchanon. "You motherfucker. You stinking motherfucker."

Elchanon's smile drew tighter, colder. He nodded slowly, absorbing my words. He did not use such words himself, I could tell, was a religious man who watched his language, though not his opinions. Having openly stated his point, he now regarded my face of "treachery" with a calm, even casual eye, as a kind of emissary of all the enemies of God and Israel amassing beyond the gates of Neve Parsha. I wanted to strangle him. At the same time, he frightened me — terrified me much more than any Arab. I could not understand him. Not even a little. I have always prided myself on an ability to fathom outlooks remote from my own. But with him, who should have stood beside me, not against, I drew a blank. A Jew with earlocks and a yarmulke. A Jew who wore a tallith. Who said kaddish for his dead and motzi for his bread and wine. A Jew and yet, somehow, not a Jew.

"My mother," I said, voice trembling, "was in the Holocaust in Europe. Do you understand that? They tried to kill her. They murdered her family and her friends. I came here on my own because I am a Jew and want to defend Israel, the Jewish people. How dare you . . ."

"I dare," he said, "and I don't care that you wear this uniform or that you are here. I didn't ask you to come. I don't live in Tel Aviv or Petaq Tikva. I am here, on the edge of what they call Egypt but that belonged to us not long ago: the Sinai. Now it is Egypt. Before we gave it away, all was quiet. Now, we have trouble. We are giving away our country, bit by bit. In Sinai I fought in 'sixty-seven and then in 'seventy-three. I saw friends die at Chinese Farm in the Sinai. Now we gave back what they died for. And now this government or the next will try to give back this, my home. Land that God gave to me, to the Jewish people. And you want to return it to the Arabs, the Amalekites. They kill us and we give them our land. This is the arrangement. So, they are enemies of God and of me. And so are you. But the day is coming. Soon it will come. And we will take care of you and your kind."

"How?"

"As it is written in Tanach: 'After the war against the goyim will come the war between the Jews.'"

"You *will kill* us? Kill *me*? You, a Jew, will kill *me*, a Jew! My mother was hunted by Nazis, her family and friends were put into ovens, and you will point your gun at me and fire?"

Elchanon looked right at me: "Sure."

Brandt stood. So did Avi. I remained seated, transfixed by the inscrutable expression in Elchanon's eyes. He wore a calm, murderous smile. I saw that he could kill me as easy as that. But I could never bring myself to kill a Jew. Not even one with a gun pointed at me. I did not come into this world to kill Jews but to protect them and myself as well — of course, myself as well. Would he shoot my mother too, if he could? With her French accent, in her flower-patterned, quilted housedress and the scarf tied around her neglected hair like drooping bunny rabbit ears, and her blue and pink house slippers? Would he shoot, this Elchanon, my father, a Bronx-born American Jew, in his leather jacket and Florsheim loafers, with his iron-hard potbelly and a Smith Corona cigar poking from his face? Shoot them dead as sinners and traitors and bad Jews? They *were* "bad" Jews, as was I. We hardly ever prayed or went to shul. In civilian life I drank too hard and slept with my best friend's wife. I smoked cigarettes like a chimney. I read novels with dirty passages. During sex, I liked for the partner to take my member into her mouth and when I felt like it I pulled out and penetrated her from behind. Sometimes we tied each other up. And what would he think of the tattoo of a black panther on my shoulder? Or the earring I wore in my left ear in civilian life? Or my passion for the Rolling Stones, who sang songs like "Sympathy for the Devil" and "Street Fighting Man"?

But what if he made a play for his weapon to shoot me? Right now?

"Come, Nathan. *Y'Allah*. Right now."

But I sat there. What if he lifted that Chinese Kalatchnikov right now? Would I waste him? Hoist my CAR-15 and put one, one single shot, into his gut? That would give him something to pray about. Then I'd pray too. Each morning and at night. Better to pray get-well prayers for him then please-save-me-God prayers for myself, like please stop the agony, O God, please more morphine O let the nurse come now come now or an angel of the Lord to stay his hand . . . but no hands are ever stayed in this world . . .

"Asshole," said Avi when we were outside.

"They are up to something," said Brandt.

Avi nodded. "I saw it in his face. What about you, Falk?"

"I don't know," I said. "You think . . . he means it? He would kill Jews?"

"Of course," said Brandt. "So would you. I promise."

"Never," I said fiercely.

Avi regarded me with mild disdain. "Look, Falk, God bless you for coming to Israel. But don't be better than us, OK? Don't be better than him. And don't be better than me. If someone points a gun at your head, what the fuck does it matter if he's Jewish or not? Shoot him before he shoots you. This is the rule."

"What rule?"

"The rule that is."

"But I . . ."

"Did you hear me, you mother's cunt? Don't be better than us. Understand? Or not?" He glared at me as if his anger were my fault, and spread his boots wide in a combat stance. I saw the back-alley street fighter he must have been as a Fez gutter boy, ready to bleed for the sake of being right at any cost, his dark, lean face dour with crossed pride.

But this was about my dignity, not his.

"Shit on that," I said.

"Mother's cunt," muttered Avi, his anger fired. "He shoots, you shoot. Understand?"

He was now pacing back and forth before the Noon Noon.

"Jump in," said Brandt casually. "Let's get out of here." A true referee, he chose no side in the dispute. "Besides, Avi," he said, "since when do you give a shit? Remember? Nothing you do changes when your number's up, right? How many times have we seen that? So why the hell quibble? Live well, make money, screw like a champ. If you die in bed, you've won the game."

"Brandt, you'd make a good American." I laughed.

"Someday, God willing," he joked back, playing along —
trying to defuse tensions.

"Motherfucker," Avi swore, his temper mounting. "He
shoots, you shoot. Got it?"

"OK," said Brandt, winking at me, "he gets it."

"And you too, Brandt. Do you get it? You also?"

"OK," said Brandt with that ironic smile. "He shoots, I
shoot."

"To kill," said Avi.

"Definitely," said Brandt. "Definitely."

"But even a Jew?" I asked, still sickened by the thought.

And Avi looked at me with the eyes of Elchanon, and all of a
sudden I understood. I understood completely. I understood in my
bones.

WHAT DO YOU KNOW?

A week later, during the Ramadan, the holiest Islamic holiday, we were placed on high alert. This was in Rafiah, a squalid little Gazan town along the Egyptian border. Half the town lay in Egypt, the other half in Israel. Between them ran barbed wire and checkpoints and between those ran our patrols.

The patrol snaked through the city and then burst out into open desert so vast you ducked your helmet in despair. Sandy grit chafed your delicate white eyeballs despite the goggles. And you fingered the trigger of your CAR-15 or Galil or whatever you carried with an almost sensual, stroking pressure, since at once you were under the strictest orders not to shoot under any circumstances, barring outright hostile gunfire (and even then, in most cases, not to respond until ordered to by a superior), and yet also, at any moment, some gunmen might quick-trot alongside your vehicle, blow your brains out, and melt back into the crazy zigzag of hovels, alleys, and streets. This kind of delicious tension possessed for me the kick that a horny boarding school student must feel when under rigorous mandate to refrain at all costs from onanism. Of course, I was also bored to death, and had no wish to actually kill. It was only the idea that titillated, the restrictive administrative taboo that I ached to violate. To let off one jubilant round into the sickly yellowish sky of a terrorist's leg, like a barbiturate injected against psychotic instability.

But then, how the inhabitants hated us! One felt it in their black, chronically mistrustful looks that either glared or quickly averted . . . never a soft gaze. No pity. Yes, one wanted to be pitied by the hater for this very hatred. Why should it be so, I wanted to ask, that you hate me? But then, there *I* was, armed to the teeth and riding through *their* streets . . . yes: theirs. I didn't want to know them or rule over them. Didn't even speak their language . . . nor they mine. And last week, a second lieutenant had been shot riding shotgun in a jeep, just this way, maybe seeking pity from their eyes when a handgun appeared from the crowd, darting forward in a disembodied hand, and the pulled trigger sent pieces of his head into the driver's lap. "So keep your eyes peeled," said Asaaf, my driver, a thick-set, ruddy sergeant in his late thirties, with thinning orange hair and a hardened face spattered with freckles that looked like dirt flung by a tractor wheel. Up near one pale blue sun-bleached eye festered this raspberry-colored patch of skin cancer, high on his left cheek, the eye there set in a doubtful squint. In civilian life he was a kibbutznik cotton farmer and had lost a brother, Eli, in the Yom Kippur War. The boy was burned alive in his tank.

The Ramadan was now in its second day, the streets almost completely deserted and possessing that desolate air of ceremoniously arrested and sanctified time that lends religious holidays a melancholy tinge.

Our wheels' thick, toothy treads mowed through the dust. The mounted machine gun in back squeaked on its swivel as we crawled along. The noise drove Asaaf nuts.

"Cos emach," he muttered, "mother's cunt": one of a handful of Arabic phrases we all knew. Another: *abu zakan,* "Father of the Beard," assigned to those with serious facial hair, and then there was *cos sortach,* "your sister's cunt"; *cos abach,* "your father's cunt"; *jib aweeya,* "Give me your ID card"; and lastly *maas salaam,* "peace be unto you."

We came upon two figures against a wall. A squatting man in a kaffiyeh, his long pale turquoise and white robes hoisted over his knees, defecated on the street in full view of his little daughter, who stood off to the side waiting patiently; she a little barefoot waif in rags, and he with his dust-smudged face quite solemn and betraying no hint of shame. The long black stool hung between his legs like a tail until his sphincter snipped it and he wiped himself off with his left hand, rubbed his fingers in the dust, and, standing, let his robes fall to their full regal length. In the faded purplish sash that bound them was a long scabbard sheathing a jewel-handled knife.

"Arabs," said Asaaf, disgust and respect mingling in his voice. He shook his head. "Can you imagine taking a shit in front of your own daughter? To him, she is not even worthy to feed. On the other hand, if she fucks someone before she's married and loses her virginity he'll order his son to cut her throat in order to regain his lost honor . . . What a fucking people these Arabs are! And with this we must make our peace!"

"They're not all like that," I said.

He glared at me, pulled over the jeep, and switched off the ignition. "How do you know? What do you know about them?"

"Nothing," I said.

"So how do you know?"

I shrugged. "I don't," I said. "I just imagine it must be so. Besides, how a man wipes his ass is none of my affair. Just as long as he doesn't shoot at me."

"What's to stop him, my naive friend? He is our business. Our jails are filled with Arabs who defend their father's honor by murdering their sister. Good sons! Who wipe their ass with one hand and murder with the other. Except in jail, they make them use toilet paper. And there they will wipe their ass with paper for the rest of their fucking life. Do you know what they do in war to their prisoners? Huh? Do you know?" He fairly shook.

"I didn't know," I said, "that we're at war with all the Arabs."

"I'm talking about all those fucking Arabs who hate us! The Syrians! The Libyans! The Iraqis! Even the Egyptians! What do you know? You're from New York. You weren't here in 'seventy-three. You didn't see what they did, the Syrians, how they tortured our POWs. Or the Egyptians, what they did, the torture. What do you know? I was eighteen years old in that war. I have friends . . . I have one I went to high school with: he can't walk to this day because of what they did to his feet. Do you know that some of us carry a little handgun in our boot? To put one in the brain in case we face capture, OK? Do you know this? What do you know? Nothing you know, nothing." He stared at me. Nodded. Then shook his head. Then nodded again, because I didn't reply. I was thinking about the brother he'd lost, the one who roasted in his chariot. But he thought that my silence signaled my concession. And a faint smile, lightly seasoned with bitter satisfaction, crept over Asaaf's dry, spittle-caked lips. "Finally, I have met a fucking American Jew who admits that maybe he doesn't know everything. This is a miracle."

I chuckled and slapped his shoulder and grabbed his thick, hairy, sunburned neck. "*Nu,* Asaaf. You see?! There is a God, you stinking atheist!" But at the time neither of us really believed it.

The jeep growled to life. We continued our crawl through the streets. Asaaf worked the wheel slowly, slowly, made a left at the rubble pile, a gentle right down an alley greased with blood red light. Street after deserted street passed. In the distance figures hurried away, shadows and skulking dogs with fish-bone ribs. "Keep your eye on that one," Asaaf said, nodding at a "cousin" in robes. But he melted away through doors; almost, it seemed, through the very walls.

"We're coming to the place where the officer was assassinated," he said, his voice tense, grim. We turned into a broad marketplace of closed and gated stalls. An agitated breeze disturbed the ragged scalloped edges of faded awnings inscribed with Arabic. Asaaf stopped the jeep. We gaped before us in disbelief. Asaaf plucked a shell casing from the jeep floor and threw it at the animals' corpses. A black cloud of disturbed flies rose buzzing in a high-pitched shriek from a row of dead horses. One of the horses, honestly: I hadn't known a tongue could be that long, how it dangled from the frozen jaws, the horse's broad breast matted with black poured blood from a cut throat. It was a bay. The others were gray, black, one white. Their staring eyes were like black glass.

The camels, though, had the peaceful look of executed hapless professional intellectuals who had offered up their necks with solemn dignity to the slaughterer's knife. One of the goats was not completely toppled on its side, like the other twenty or so animals that littered the dusty street; had, in death, only fallen to its knees and remained there, horned head dropped to the ground, slashed throat agape with something red and yellow dangling from it. He seemed almost alive.

"Cover your face," said Asaaf, "if you don't want to breathe flies or smell this crap."

We removed the kaffiyehs that we wore about our necks and wrapped them over our heads and faces, the way the terrorists do. Then we drove slowly, winding through the maze of animal corpses.

"Sacrificial offerings for the Ramadan," said Asaaf, voice muffled by the scarf.

A congealed muck of blood, mud, and dust sucked at our tires, a red river of life spilled out of their butchered necks and some disgorged bluish entrails crawling with flies in such volume as I had never seen or imagined. Where had they all come from? It was as if every fly in Israel and Egypt had convened on this single Gazan street in the middle of desert, and also feeding on the dead, tearing at hinds, stomachs, genitals, were wild pariah dogs with bared teeth chomping nervously at the strange-tasting flesh.

RISK

The last thing I need is this," shouts Yitzak, finger stabbing the map of the West Bank spread over the folding table in the communications room of Hebron jail headquarters. It is an operations map, all flowing lines. Until now the table has supported a Risk game board map of the world, where a dedicated group of us was recently locked in a fierce contest over North America. For hours we had sat together with heads bowed over the board. There was Yitzak, with razor-kissed cheeks reeking of aftershave and his lounge singer lips sucking on his bling chain; frowning, bearish Dedi, conjuring subtle tactics to life with his dark laser stare; Binny, a notorious yet unindicted hoodlum in civilian life, grinning with clueless bafflement and thoughtfully tapping a stubby forefinger — one that he'd no doubt used to pull triggers on many unmarked guns — on a single solid eighteen-karat gold front tooth. There was also Pagi, a black-mustached Polish immigrant garage mechanic with obsessive-compulsive disorder and who spends so much time in the guts of military engines that his skin has turned machine-oil black; and there was Avi, smugly neat in a fresh change of uniform and gazing with gloomy dejection at Pagi's oily proximity and with sour disdain at the whole undertaking of our play.

In fact, we were all sort of stumped, because for reasons that no one could quite fathom, most of our forces in this protracted game had gathered in Asia, a unique and — as anyone who knows anything about the game of Risk will attest — ultimately futile strategy. Slowly, though, while egos raged around me, I had been attempting to establish a foothold in Australia, where Dedi had a large number of forces concentrated. With a bit of luck, I could root him out. But then came the intelligence officer with the goddamned flow map. He also brought in a manila envelope containing three black-and-white photographs, and a police colonel.

The colonel explained that the three men in the photos were terrorists wanted in connection with the bombing of a bus in the Tel Aviv Central Bus Station, an incident in which seven Israelis were killed, a real massacre . . . and that was the end of our Risk game (at least for the time being). Down it went on the floor, carefully set beneath the radio table. Udi, the radio operator, a gawky and bespectacled blond kid who sits there with a headset on, had been advised that if just one game piece went missing from anywhere on the board he would end his days in a front-line latrine, cleaning bungholes with his notoriously disrespectful tongue.

"Don't worry, Yitzala, I won't touch the pieces, and also, by the way, this *is* the front line" says Udi with a grin.

Udi has a big yin-yang symbol tattooed on his forearm, an object of some curiosity, as tattoos are still not all that common in Israel.

"Front line, my ass!" snaps Yitzak. "Hebron is the dick. I'm talking about the asshole itself. Do you understand what I mean by that?" But no one does. He can be talking about Lebanon. But Hebron is bad enough for anyone. As in Lebanon or Khan Yunis or Gaza City, the windows of our barracks have screens around them because here too the locals like to toss in grenades as a way to wake us up. No eggs and coffee on a tray for us. But just to drive home Yitzak's point, Binny claps Udi hard on the back of his head and we all laugh to watch the boy's frail skull roll around on that skinny neck, his blond hair flying pell-mell.

"Move *their* pieces," says Binny. "This, I don't care. But my pieces, the blue pieces, beware of the blue ones. Do you see them? Those . . . if I see one missing! Then, I will kill you, do you get me? I will personally rub you out."

"Gangster," mumbles Pagi appreciatively, impressed that Binny is a well-known associate of the Russian Mafia. He is also a completely useless member of our unit, which is why everyone loves him so. In the Israeli army, not everyone loves the best soldier but everyone loves the worst. That would be Binny.

Though Binny's served time in Russia, he's never been arrested in Israel and so is forced to serve in reserves just like any average citizen. Sure, he can shoot better than anybody, probably. But why bother to play with guns? Reserves is his little getaway from all those back-alley turf wars of Tel Aviv. No, for Binny, better to stay behind in the communications room, playing Risk while the stupidly heroic patrols come and go. But though Binny plays obsessively, he still soldiers now and then. Yitzak, however, gets so caught up in the games that he doesn't even listen to the patrol leaders who arrive to deliver their periodic debriefings from the field.

Instead, he sits there with the red plastic dice clenched in one fist, furrowed brow bent over the board, scanning the countries, the placement of the various forces: yellow, red, green, white, blue, and, of course, his own black. Yitzak always claims black for his armies. It gives him a piratical feel of Machiavellian power. A nice escape from having to be the goody-good Israeli soldier who doesn't shoot civilians but who gets shot at. In Risk he can conquer like a brute, play as ferociously as he likes. He does. He is good. Not as good as Brandt, who is of course ahead in the game, his red troops spreading like a cancer over the board. Patrol leaders come and go, and Yitzak waves them out the door with grimacing impatience.

Even when seven Islamic fundamentalists were murdered, we thought, by Fatah — it later turned out that settlers did it — Yitzak snapped at the corporal who came rushing in to announce the emergency: "Not now, not now! Wait! Wait!" and, glaring at Dedi, hissed: "Let me into South America without attacking my flank and I'll leave you alone in China."

Dedi smiled and, looking around the table, said, "But I don't care about China. You can kiss my ass in China for all I care." And this with frantic troops rushing from here to there and boarding Zaklams, tall clunky armored cars with machine gun turrets, and scrambling into Noon Noons and jeeps for the convoy forming to get out to the Islamic college where the bodies were discovered. Already we could hear low-flying helicopters overhead, airlifting paratroopers out there. But Yitzak sat with elbows dug into the table, forefinger pressed to his furrowed brow as if trying to burrow through his skull for a way out of his fix. Eventually, though, we arrived as well. It was night. We stood there over the seven blanket-covered corpses on the ground. The spotlight from a jeep shone brashly down on the figures and a soft breeze stirred the blankets, as if one of them was flipping us off and rising to go to the bathroom. Beside them body bags lay stacked. But all Yitzak could think about was Dedi in Brazil. "Just let me get into Venezuela" he pleaded softly, "and all of Asia is yours." We had foot patrols rushing out in every direction and a small team of Noon Noons and jeeps forming up to raid a suspected Fatah stronghold, with a possible firefight in the offing, and a paratrooper captain tried to explain to Yitzak what he wanted and Yitzak nodded, distracted, but then he turned to Dedi and said brusquely: "Then, Mexico. Just let me sit there for five moves without attacking me."

"I'll consider it," said Dedi.

It isn't really kosher, making these deals, but it's how we play, our own little Israeli spin on things, to spice it up. We make a hundred treaties and countertreaties. Alliances form and dissolve in a single round of moves. The current game has been going on nonstop for a week, with breaks only to eat and nap. And, oh yeah: patrols and operations . . . the minimum for us players, though. Even I, the lowest in rank, a mere private, is exempted for play. Besides, it is my game board. Yitzak wouldn't dare to exclude me. I can just smile, yawn, announce that I'm folding shop, and shut down the whole shebang, as I did once. Yitzak learned well from that. I play: of course I do. I am a player who owns the game.

But now, this stupid intelligence officer arrives to us with his silver-haired, preposterously grave police colonel in tow, bearing black-and-white photographs and worse, much worse, a damned map with pushpins and little colored flags — almost, unforgivably, a mocking double of our Risk game board, which waits on the floor like a disowned cur for a little attention from its distracted, newly adopted master.

Yitzak fumes. He leans against the back of the radio with a coffee cup in one hand, cigarette in the other, his unbuttoned tunic revealing his rather flabby stomach and on his face a dark scowl of obvious resentment. The ramrod police colonel occupies the very center of the communications room, talking in a low but very audible voice to the slender, bespectacled intelligence officer. The colonel wears a police dress uniform, pale blue with dark blue borders. The intelligence officer wears pressed and starched fatigues. His epaulets bear the type of rank insignia known in the IDF as "falafels" — brown maple leaves, each connoting high rank and that from a distance do look remarkably like the falafel balls you eat in pita pocket bread stuffed with French fries and vegetables and sweet and sour condiments and over it all a thick white goo of Tehina sauce, which you buy at one of many falafel stands first thing when you arrive at the Tel Aviv bus station en route to your girlfriend or mistress or wife on a twenty-four-hour leave — the stands three deep with soldiers and where the terrorists explode bombs in shopping bags left under a bus seat or bench, and that is, by the way, why we come to your home in the middle of the night in the Arab towns and villages and drag you out in your pajamas and blow up your house or else have a tractor from the Engineering Corps rip it to pieces wall by wall and then we take you in for interrogation by the Security Service boys, who make you give up what you know and what you didn't even know you knew.

The Risk game is by Udi's boot, sometimes only inches from it, but by the look of things is intact, awaiting Yitzak's entry into North America. But there will be no entry today. The colonel stands at the center table with chin balanced thoughtfully on fist, gazing down at the pushpin board map — it is mounted on a Styrofoam board to receive and hold the pins and, again, it very much resembles a Risk game board.

The colonel's map has all sorts of geographic contour information and flowing lines to indicate God only knows what — none of us can really read it — and he points down at the lines, his eyes lost in deep reflection, and says something to the intelligence officer, who grunts, and then they both look at Yitzak, and the colonel, in a very low, very deferent voice, asks a question.

"I don't know," says Yitzak in a surly tone.

"Approximately," says the colonel softly.

"I don't know. They're experienced men. They don't need much. Just tell them where and when. They'll do the rest. One day is enough."

"So. Tomorrow, then."

Yitzak holds up his cup in a sarcastic salute. "Of course. And to your health," he says. "And to the health of the police."

The colonel regards Yitzak with unamused disinterest. Then he motions to the intelligence officer to join him outside and they leave together.

Dedi says, "There's no point in insulting them just because I pissed all over your North American ambitions."

"So, that's it? You've made up your mind? You won't even leave me in peace if I just go to Mexico?"

"Olé." Dedi smiles.

"Motherfucker," spits Yitzak. He slams down his coffee cup, spilling black liquid all over the top of the radio.

Udi protests, "Hey, you're going to short me out!"

And Yitzak: "Go fuck yourself, Udi! Fuck you and fuck this colonel with his photographs." Yitzak glances at me with a begging look that is really quite touching to see.

"Falk," he says, "team up with me in Canada. We'll wipe out these shits and then move together on Dedi in North America."

"I don't think I can make that kind of decision right now, Yitzak," I say deferentially. Risk partner or not, he is still my commanding officer.

"And if I sweeten your coffee with a two-day leave, you'll consider it?"

"You can't do that," says Dedi. "That's bribery. You can't bribe."

"Like hell I can't. Two-day pass and then, a week later, a twenty-four-hour furlough. Good, Falk? I get Mexico and Venezuela; you take the rest."

"And Australia? You don't touch me in Australia."

He hesitates. Then: "Agreed."

"Bullshit," says Dedi. He begins to shuffle around the room, more agitated than I've ever seen him. "Bullshit!" he says again. Then: "Bullshit! Bullshit! Bullshit! Bullshit!"

Yitzak nods, happy for the first time in I don't know how long. "No," he says. "No. Now, you kiss *my* tokus, Dedi. With lipstick on, baby. With red lipstick on."

Dedi looks fiercely at me, for an instant, gripped by a feeling of betrayal. But this does not remain. How can he blame me for accepting such a deal? No one in their right mind would decline it — except him, of course.

Then the colonel reenters with the intelligence officer and they stand over their precious but indecipherable map and once or twice bend to it, whispering and with only the greatest deliberation (punctuated by many false starts and stops and underscored by looks of obvious complex, hesitant thought), the colonel, with awkward, trembling fingers, actually relocating two pins to different coordinates. Then both men stand there staring down at their handiwork and nodding gravely while Yitzak squats next to Udi's leg, peering at the Risk map of the world, which he now feels poised upon the brink of conquering and Dedi with a look of shocked disgust stares at the board from afar and I sit on the floor in a corner of the room, my back up against a stack of quite comfortable sandbags, smoking a cigarette, tapping my ash on the cement floor and thinking of a meal of steak and chips with a Goldstar beer.

And then another and then several more Goldstars at this steakia on Agrippa Street that I am recalling, with its awning rolled up and grill smoke billowing out onto the greasy drizzled Jerusalem night street, and beside me is the shape of a woman who should be my girlfriend but is not — only a dark silhouette whose form I cannot ascertain and do not wish to. Some woman, not my girlfriend, it would be then. OK. That is settled. And I know who that faceless form is but can't admit it to myself just now. But there is her silhouette nevertheless, and I climb her bedroom stairs with a half-downed bottle of brandy in my fist and my free hand riding her naked ass, and I hold that image in my mind, trying not to put to it the face of Maya, my best friend's wife, until Dedi calls out for me and Brandt, who has entered the room, to step outside, please, for a moment — he would like to have a chat, if that's OK, and Brandt nods that of course it is OK and I too come to my feet but now struggling to hold the faceless image in my head, for the image is moving now, it is undulating as Maya might and has a face with parted lips and closed eyes and her hands are entwined about my neck. Our boots scrape on the cement floor. The colonel and the intelligence officer follow us out with their eyes and then bend their heads together, whispering. Dedi is on the porch with one boot up on the rail and a cigarette going in his hand. He brings it to his lips, takes a drag; the sky, low, gray, omnivorous, eats the light. Gradually, things grow dark. Around the armored car, or Zaklam, a crew is putting their full combined weight on a big steel pole jimmied between the Zaklam's tread. On the rail, near Dedi's cigarette hand, lies the manila envelope.

"What's up?" say Brandt.

Dedi glances at the envelope — then nods toward the armored car. "When that's ready, we go out. You, me, Falk . . . we'll take Rami to translate. I want you to drive the Zaklam. Falk, you'll be the weapons man."

"So," says Brandt in that wry voice of his, "are you going to show us what's in the envelope?"

"You know damned well what's in there."

"I know what, yes. But not who."

He shows us. There are three of them. They don't look like much, but then no one ever does. I wonder how such candid and uniform shots of the terrorists can have been obtained. At some point they must have been detained, then released in some fucked-up exchange deal, free to murder again. Two sport mustaches, look very Arabic, but the clean-shaven third can easily have passed for an Israeli of Middle Eastern origin. Probably he has, as part of his cell.

"They all escaped," says Dedi. "They operated a murder gang between here and Beersheva and Beersheva and Tel Aviv. This one" — Dedi taps the clean-shaven one — "might also have conducted operations as far north as Haifa. He's the bomber."

I wish Dedi would spare us the case histories and just allow us to mount up and move out. I don't see how it helps to know any of this, or even what specifically they've done, which atrocity they're responsible for. Let's just take them as painlessly and quickly as we can. Let's assume the worst, that they're armed, know we're coming, are desperate enough to fight rather than be taken. Let's go now.

Instead we must endure long, droning lectures, first from the colonel, then from the intelligence officer, both of whom will be going out with us. At the last minute it is decided that we won't take the Zaklam. Much too slow. The Noon Noon will do for a mobile light infantry operation. One jeep to lead, the Noon Noon following in a convoy. Six of us. Three of them. And then, our potential reinforcements will stand by on alert but continue with their routine operations. No point in pulling men from the field if we aren't 100 percent sure of finding the suspects. We aren't even 25 percent sure. Our intelligence on this operation is so-so.

Yitzak listens to all of this with his eyes trained through the open door of the communications room on Udi's boot as it shakes nervously under the table supporting the shortwave radio, the wrinkled leather boot bobbing up and down, just inches at times, from the as yet undisturbed Risk board.

"That's all fine," he snaps, "but I want my men and equipment back" — his wristwatch snaps up before his face — "by no later then ten p.m. tonight. It's your operation. Good luck."

As we file off the porch, Yitzak calls me over: "Falk!"

"You don't have to go," he says. "You have no family here. You're a loner. You can sit this one out."

"That's very sweet, Yitzak. Now can you please remove your hand from my balls? I know you like me, but that's more than I want."

He smiles. "You're a good boy, Falk."

"No, I'm not. I'm a good Risk player and the sooner we catch these assholes the sooner we play."

"I don't deserve you, Falk. You're too good a soldier for the Israeli army."

Now I grin too. "Will you miss me if I die?"

Yitzak laughs. "You are a sick New Yorker. Don't forget: we have a deal. Tell Dedi if he doesn't let me into North America I'll wipe him out. Tell him I swear this."

"I'll let him know," I say.

We follow the colonel and the intelligence officer in their jeep. The chance of finding anything is slim. Still, we feel the tension as we drive behind them. There are gray-green haggard-looking orchards to each side of us, and garbage dumps filled with bad-smelling refuse and then strings of half-finished villas and then the refugee camps, with their look of sprawling flea markets of human misery. There are rows of badly deteriorated sand-colored one-story huts with sheets of transparent plastic stretched over paneless window frames held affixed by rusted nails and criss-crossed strips of old duct tape and then rocky fields through which the road runs, and we climb through hills sprinkled with grazing livestock: goats and sheep and even camel herds, and everywhere along the route are the hulks of abandoned and stripped automobiles gone to rust and men in white kaffiyeh headdresses but otherwise dressed in regular slacks and shirts and sandals or else shoes or old boots, and children with flies crawling on their faces and shrunken T-shirts hiked over their puffed little bellies, and women in their robes and jallabiyahs and head cloths, and whoever we pass ceases, with an undisguised look of hatred, whatever he or she is doing to watch us rumble by, and the sun is a grayish pea-fog color and somewhat faded, but as it begins to fall, to sink below the horizon, it becomes a huge bright red disk in a very short time, and when we reach our destination it peers over the lip of the hill like a blood-soaked head gaping incuriously at our small but determined band.

The cluster of houses sits at the foot of the hill. Only one road leads to it and we block it with our vehicles. Some women and children emerge from the houses. This always happens when we come. We do not see any men around. We remain by the jeep and Noon Noon until the colonel, who is directing the operation, gives out instructions. I am to go with him.

He wears an antique Webly five-shot revolver on his hip, in an old cracked leather holster. He has no other weapon that I can see. A sentimentalist. The intelligence officer, who speaks Arabic, goes with Brandt and Dedi goes with Rami, our unit's best translator. I ask the colonel if he speaks Arabic. He says that he does not. I do not ask why we do not need translation, though the others do. I have learned not to ask too much or too often. In the final analysis, the fewer questions the better. It is not true that the more understanding one possesses of an operation and situations, the better the chance to survive. Knowing much does not improve one's chances even by half of 1 percent, in my experience. In the end, information seems to make no difference at all.

We split up, and each takes a house to search. The colonel waves me forward, falls in behind me. I pound on the door of the house, a big spread with clay-colored walls adorned with glazed hand-painted tiles. Each tile repeats the same flower motif in red, green, orange, and black. I note this as my fist strikes wood. I have never seen such tiles before in the walls of homes I previously have raided during operations. I bang hard on the door and, with a deep sense of futility and also shame, tilt my head and shout in Hebrew up at the empty windows: *"Tiftach et ha deled!"* (Open the door!) No one answers and again I pound. The colonel steps away from the house, peers up three stories at small terraces covered with flowerpots in which nothing grows. Laundry hangs from some of the terraces on makeshift clotheslines.

I'm listening at the door. It's dead quiet in there. "They're not answering," I say with a feeling of relief. "Maybe they're not home."

He frowns, passes his hand lightly over his gray hair. "Or maybe they don't understand Hebrew."

I nod. "It's possible."

"But not likely."

I admit that it is unlikely. Already the other teams have gained admission to their sites. It seems ridiculous that we should not gain entrance to ours. I am about to suggest that one of us circles around to the back when, suddenly, the door opens. A woman stands there. She looks about forty. She wears a jalabiyah and a traditional ornamented full-length dress. She has very undependable-looking eyes. She can barely look at me. Her eyes seem to be lying. This can be fear, I tell myself. Fear can make your eyes do that. When I was a boy certain harsh teachers or policemen or bullies had made my eyes that way, I'm sure. *All right, maybe it's just fear,* I tell myself. Yet I don't believe that, never do, for I dread too much their great trust in violence, which exceeds even our own.

"We need to come in," I say in Hebrew.

She looks at the colonel. He steps forward. His demeanor is very nonthreatening — relaxed, even gentle.

"May we come in?" he asks.

"What for?" she say boldly in good Hebrew. Now her eyes glare hotly at us. Now there is no duplicity, only defiance.

"We are looking for these men." He produces three small photos from his shirt pocket, shows them to her. The skin of her jaw grows drum tight as she studies the photos. She barely looks at them. She is thinking. "No, no," she says impatiently after the third photo. "No one like that is here."

The colonel looks at me and his eyes make a motion that we should step away from the door, to confer. We do. The woman stands there regarding us distrustfully. From behind her comes not a sound, which I find quite suspicious. Surely a place so large houses others. The colonel's hand rests on his revolver, which he has not yet removed.

"I don't understand," I say. "If these are terrorists we're after, shouldn't we bring out more troops, take more precautions? This is a strange raid. A knock on the door and a chat. I feel like we're visiting neighbors. What kind of operation is this?"

"A poorly planned one," the colonel says, smiling. "I grant you that. But take my word for it. This is the best way. For what we're doing, this is the best. So, we tried politeness and now we're going in. Do you have a flashlight?"

"Yes," I say.

"Good. I'll go first. You back me up. OK? We move one behind the other. Just stay right behind me. Watch my back."

"Fine."

"OK."

He turns to the woman, unbuttons the flap of his revolver, and draws out the weapon. The old, outdated pistol is very large and ugly to look at. It is a vicious gun in its way, even though somewhat antiquated. It cannot stand up to automatic fire, though in very close quarters, in the hands of a skilled shot, it can be quite effective. My sense of the colonel is that he is a better-than-good marksman. He steps up to her. "We must come in." She fills the doorway, to block our path. He shoves her aside, walks in. I follow, head ducked apologetically at her outraged figure lying on the floor on her side and now shrieking at the top of her lungs. And from behind her now materialize other women, all wailing as well, some with shrieking babies in their arms that they must have smothered with their hands, and little, loudly bawling kids clinging to their dresses with tight little fists. It is a familiar scenario. Usually by the time we arrive the men are gone and the women put on this show in order to demoralize us, make us feel the shamefulness of our actions, as if to say: *See? Look at what you have here. Fully armed soldiers against defenseless women and children!* But they placed themselves there intentionally. It is all theater. And they are not always defenseless. In the caves around Beth El, during a hunt for terrorists, one of our boys, a lieutenant, came across a woman clutching an infant. He asked if she had seen the fugitive he sought. No, she said. As he turned to exit from the cave, she shot him in the back.

You harden yourself. Shut your ears. Don't meet their eyes, though you certainly can. But it is better not to.

The colonel forces his way past a partially closed door, behind which stands a man with a pencil-thin mustache and dressed in a nightshirt. He pulls the man outside, smacks him repeatedly across the face while hissing questions in Hebrew that the man can't possibly answer, and then brusquely throws him aside and waves for me to follow. It is all a show, so much performance. The drama of coercion. We enter a bedroom. Nothing there. Exit past the man seated on the floor with a hand covering his struck cheek, a scowl of angry dismay on his face. Perhaps that too is an act in this war of armed amateur thespians.

We march right past him into a corridor leading to a narrow stairwell that we take two floors up to the roof. The colonel stops at the roof exit. "If he's not out there, we'll abandon this shithole."

I nod, wondering why he refers to the place that way. Actually, it is quite clean and doesn't smell as badly as some of the places I have searched. By those standards, it is palatable.

A small, narrow door painted black. The paint peeling. The door frame orange with rust. A hook holds it closed. But the hook is off. The colonel stares at the hook, as do I. "Look," I say, nodding at the hook.

"Maybe," the colonel says skeptically, "but you know, they always come up here to hang their sheets."

"Still . . ." I say.

"Still, it doesn't necessarily mean anything. In your building . . . where are you from?"

"Jerusalem."

He gazes at me, impressed. "Jerusalem. A Jerusalamite, huh? Good! So, the door to the roof there. It's closed or open?"

"Mine is latched," I say.

Taken aback, he says: "How do you know this?"

"Because if it's left off my neighbor, an old Kurdistani woman, makes a big noise about it. Gets very upset."

He stares at me as if I am just a stubborn, crazy, incomprehensible American and waves me forward with his Webly.

"Go," he says. "I will cover you. You've seen the photo. You know who we're looking for."

"Who *you're* looking for. I'm not looking for anyone."

"Never mind. You're army. It's your job to go in first. Army always goes first."

"Why isn't there more army with us? I'm a one-man army right now. In the army, we don't operate alone."

"You're not alone. I'm here."

"Whose idea is this operation?"

"My idea. You see? There's no one else around, just women. We don't need a lot of troops. I want to show what we can accomplish with a handful of good men. You're a good man. Yitzak told me you're good at house-to-house fighting. You go out there."

"You don't know what I'm good at. You don't know anything about me."

"But will you go out there?"

"Yes." I nodded wearily. "Of course."

"See how good you are?"

"Fuck you," I say.

He grins. "Go. I've got you covered. Probably, there's no one out there."

Someone is out there. I spot him immediately. The roof is an expanse of shabby, cracked tar circumscribed by a low, crenulated wall. The overcast sky is flooding over it like a river in which other white houses float like detritus, and behind the leftmost air duct movement occurs the instant I hit the roof running. I slide behind a sheltering air shaft and drop to one knee, the stock of my gun up to my shoulder, and look back at the colonel, who crouches recessed in the dark stairwell, framed by the rusted door. He is hard to make out there in the dark, his gray-haired head floating from the rumpled collar of his pale blue uniform. I motion toward the leftmost air shaft to indicate the presence of someone but am unsure he understands. My spittle tastes metallic. I shiver, cold, on the windswept roof, look about hopelessly at the vast gray billowing clouds: I have left my parka in the Noon Noon and feel underdressed. I wonder who crouches behind the air duct, after all. Just a snippet of white shirt I see, the top of a head of black hair. My heart pounds but I don't feel afraid at all or excited: just keen to get whatever this is over with. So I shout in Hebrew, in my most alarming voice: "Stand on your legs, hands in the air! Hurry! Hurry!"

The white shifts and the top of the head ducks down into the gray metal of the tarnished air duct. He doesn't run. The CAR-15 in my hands feels heavy now, though it is lighter then most assault rifles and far more compact. I feel its metal and plastic. It does not seem like much. I wonder what he has. I think: *Hand grenade.* Icy, pure fear sears my chest. I duck my face for just an instant, eyes squeezed shut, breathe, listening to it, heart hammering in my ribs' hollow drum. Then I open them and look again. The top of his head appears and disappears, appears and disappears. What is he doing? He cannot sit still. Well, why should he? He knows that I know where he is. If he has nothing he'd give himself up, right? So he must have something. But I am unprepared to assume that he is definitely armed. To think that would paralyze me now. I feel absolute dread lodged just around my abdomen, from which, if I allow it, fear will spread to every nerve ending, the tips of my toes and fingers, the very roots of my hair, and then, as I have seen with others, I will be nailed to the very sky, unable to move, to free myself: crucified in oxygen and time with the police colonel waiting and the hidden man not more then twenty yards away and perhaps able to kill me if he likes. I tell that to myself, which keeps me focused on the weight of my weapon, which I keep aloft, and it seems to weigh a ton. And then, I know: I will have to stand. Out in the open. There are no other options. I will have to walk right up to him. My gut tells me this. It will have to be a stroll right up. I can call to the colonel to radio on his walkie-talkie for reinforcements. Reluctant though he'd be to do so, he'd have to, would have no choice. They would come then, in force, a couple truckloads, and secure the area and set up a killing zone. But I don't want that. The thought of all that oppresses me. The easiest thing seems to be to stand. I do. The colonel waves me down. "No, no," he shouts. The half-hidden head bobs, then is still, as though listening.

"Stand on your feet," I shout. "Hands in the air."

"Get down," hisses the colonel.

The head rises enough to become a dark, narrow brow and then a pair of dark eyes that peek and duck.

"Stand up, hands raised," I shout in a calm, declarative voice without a trace of doubt in it; my stare meant to convey a sense that to do so is obvious, to do otherwise, perverse. And then, from the window of an adjoining building that overlooks the roof, a loud wail erupts, followed by a second wailing voice and I glance over. There stands a woman with hands clapped to her covered head, her mouth a wide oval of unremitting grief. And behind her stand the other wailing women. All wailing like Edvard Munch's man on the bridge. Then, from behind the police officer break out more wails of grief and from down in the street, faintly, more wails and also the cries of infants and the thin, unconvinced voices of young children attempting to sound angry but with no idea of what real anger is, and the suspect stands up, a man in a shrunken white shirt.

"Hands in the air!" I shout stupidly, though his hands are already up. I had noted as he raised his arms that his unbuttoned sleeves reach only to his forearms. His hands are now raised high but they cannot be high enough for my tastes, and if I knew how to say it in Arabic I would have him kneel but in Arabic I know how to say only "What is your name?" and "Give me your ID card." So I speak with my posture and my gun, its raised barrel aimed squarely at his chest and my right eye squinted and right cheek leaned into the stock so that my left eye is a wide open, unblinking portal to extinction if he moves even an inch. He does not move. Stands there. I say nothing. Distant wails the only sound. The colonel is out on the roof now; I hear his shoes behind me on the tar.

The suspect wears not lace-up civilian shoes but tan desert boots, and as I approach my suspect, who has wonderfully dark mahogany-colored skin stretched tight over a thin, very densely boned face, his eyes hold mine. They are fierce-looking, unafraid. He has bony wrists. He is thin, lanky. His white shirt a size too small over a green soccer T-shirt. His unbuttoned cuffs slipped down his densely boned sinewy forearm. His long, spidery fingers, large and limp in the air, curl toward me from dun-colored palms. His pants are brown suit slacks, baggy and stained in places with a fine silt of white powdered dust, from crawling. His lace-up desert boots are of a type I have not seen in Israeli or Arab stores, and I wonder where he has gotten them. Not typical urban wear for here. They are a certain type of boot for crossing long distances on foot over rugged terrain, and I have seen the print left by such boots on the desert floor of the Negev, pointed out to me by a Bedouin tracker or "gashash" as such Bedouin soldiers in the Israeli army are called. One gashash named Ahmed had shown me, by the light of a jeep-mounted floodlight, in the midst of a desolate wadi in the Gaza Strip, the exact sort of imprint made by such apparel as the suspect before me now wears, and though the erupted wails sink my heart a bit, the children's cries tormenting still, the boots on his feet make me feel very glad at this moment to be alive, for now I know what I have caught.

And then I am right upon him, the thin white cotton of his shirt bunched in my fist so hard that I can see not only his slender brown shoulder but the long ridges of his spine right down to the waistband of his white elastic briefs, and I press my knuckles into his shoulder, urging him down, down, first on his knees, then on his face with hands and feet outstretched, and if I had a revolver to hold on him that would be best but I don't and I lay my rifle down since the colonel with his drawn, ugly Webly is almost upon us, and I want to shout, "Point that thing away!" but think to myself that just now even taking an accidental bullet mustn't distract from the perfect moment at hand, this capture, and so I draw a length of gun rag from my battle vest. I lay it on my knee and gently take first one hand, then the other and pull them behind my captive's back. His face in partial profile is very patient and dignified. His brown, dark eyes do not look up or try to see me but stare off a little sideways past my knee, waiting. His trim black mustache cuts a neat, straight line above his upper lip. His chin looks quite strong. He is a fine specimen of a captive, and I feel very much like the big game hunter who has bagged himself a trophy catch. I even want to speak to him gently, soothingly; tell him everything is going to be all right, the way you address a fallen horse panting on its side with sideways eyeballs of terror bulging from its head, but his eyeballs do not protrude — he is not visibly afraid, only patiently waiting — and everything for him is not going to be all right, not by a long shot. No, when he passes through my hands into those of the police and then of the territorial security services, things will be about as far from all right as they can possibly get. So I do not make that promise and I say nothing whatsoever. I only tie the knot securely and firmly, knowing that by the time his wrists swell the rag will come off, replaced by handcuffs.

"Oh, it's one of them," says my police colonel.

I look up. "Yes, I know."

"That's very good," he says, a little too eagerly, not to give away his clear intention to claim credit for the catch.

"That's very good," he repeats.

I say nothing, and come slowly, lazily, to my feet. He reaches down and I say: "That's all right."

I reach, take the captive's arm, and pull. He comes to his knees and I hoist him up, his full weight on my hands until he finds his feet.

"Y'Allah," I say and we begin to walk. He says nothing and does not look at me but merely walks without resistance, very dignified. But the colonel very stupidly takes the captive's other elbow. He grips it tightly and the captive looks over at him with disdain, as if to say, *What is the matter with you?* And we all descend together from the roof in relative silence but for the distant wailing on the first landing, where the women wait, and from all sides the wailing presses in. Heavy-breathing, agitated bodies jostle us at every step, a crush of women and children that line all the landings from the roof to the ground floor, and as we squeeze past they pull on the captive's shirt and weep and scream and he says to them in Arabic things I cannot understand in a low, calm, dignified voice, and the colonel behaves, I feel, somewhat like an ass, slapping away their hands, getting flush-faced, angry with them and once or twice receives for his trouble a wad of phlegm in the face, which infuriates him. I do not want to make him out here to be some sort of ignoble villain — he is not: to the contrary, he is a hero in his own right, here in this shithole of a place, hunting those who would try to infiltrate his country and murder his people, man, woman, and child. He is no villain but only performing rotten duty, as am I, as is the whole unit. But I must wonder too how it is that someone so obviously with right on his side — after all, the man in his grips is responsible for the slaughter of innocent men, women, and children on a public bus — still can emerge looking like such an idiot while the slaughterer, the cold-blooded killer, can seem so dignified, and I realize that we live in a world that respects and even admires murderers, killers, barbarians, and that has no use whatsoever for plain, bumbling, commonplace men like the colonel — who is only trying to perform an exceedingly thankless job — and that even I do not admire his unthanked commonplaceness but secretly applaud the posturing of the political fanatic with innocent blood on his dignified hands. And of course I am moved by the women, the children, who treat the fanatic like some sort of folk hero. Who are not faced with the aftermath of the captive's actions, who do not visit the corridors of Beilleson Hospital to see the legless and armless infants, the eyeless grandmother punctured by shrapnel and nails, the weeping wives and fathers, sisters and boyfriends, crowding the halls to receive updates on their mortally wounded loved ones from the over-worked staff or waiting to hear if their missing loved one is among the as yet unidentified body parts. They pluck at his shirt and wail and kiss their fingers to his face and scream and they do not see this hero's handiwork spattered over the sides of the bus, the blood and dismemberment, the truncated schoolboy, the disemboweled hairdresser, the headless rabbi, and he looks very dignified, this exploder of nail bombs, even a little haughty, as we descend, and I clutch his arm tighter, in a rather rough and commonplace way, and jerk him down the stairs with obvious violence so that he looks at me, surprised, and I snap, *"Y'Allah!"* and the colonel shoves him from behind and we drag him, we classless and unglamorous Israelis, into the burning sunlight, where the other units apatheti-cally wait, and they all look a little surprised when we hand over our catch.

"You didn't radio this in," I say to the colonel, amazed.

Rather stupidly, stubbornly, he says: "What for? We handled it."

"I don't agree with that," I say. "It's a bad risk. It's bad procedure."

He shrugs. "We did fine."

"Yes, but I don't agree."

"We did fine," he repeats.

Hands are clapping my back, cheerful voices all around: "Falk caught himself a terrorist . . ."

"Nath-an! A man among men. A real cannon!"

"Hey, Falk. You better tell your mother what a good soldier you are!"

"Falk! A good boy!"

"All honor to you. Really!"

And so forth.

But I am focused on the colonel's face.

"It doesn't matter," he says.

The captive turns his face to me. Now they are putting on handcuffs, and because he is passing into other hands he has experienced an instant of doubt, at which he turns to me for a flicker of reassurance or even just acknowledgment, and he says something in Hebrew that his accent prevents me from understanding and I say, "Seal your mouth!" and with the others shove this killer into the back of the truck.

And now, there is no map in the communications room anymore. There is no colonel. The intelligence officer gone too. There is only the world of our Risk board, restored to its central and proper place. On the first night of resumed play, Yitzak scrutinizes the board for a long time, referring to a sheet of paper in his hand on which he has drawn the exact position of each player on the board, including the number and distribution of our armies, and will not permit play to resume until he feels positive that all is as it had been. It is. Play commences. Once more the words "Kamchatka!" and "Venezuela!" and "Quebec!" sound over the constant chattering from the shortwave. Dedi slaughters Yitzak in Mexico. He keeps Yitzak's troops bottlenecked in there and hammers him from two sides. He wipes us all out, each one, one after another, until only Yitzak is left and Yitzak shouts, "I'm a terrorist! Fuck you, imperialist Zionist dog!" and throws his last spare handful of troops into a futile and senseless assault on Dedi's invincible forces, and, one by one, Dedi wipes them out, and no sooner has Dedi captured Yitzak's last piece and Risk card than Yitzak demands the rematch — this now his third — and Dedi laughs and rolls his eyes and the rest of us, we sit there chuckling, shaking our heads that after all, it's just a fucking game, and what are we down here for, to play fucking games? But Yitzak grows furious with us and shouts — no, practically orders us — to a rematch and no one takes him seriously until we see Dedi standing with him in the corner after Yitzak has thrown an insane fit, is almost in tears, and then very mirthlessly we take our seats and receive in hand the same color of armies with which we have played now for months — Yitzak would not so much as hear of a single deviation in the arrangements — and soon all our pieces are on the board, strategically placed, and Yitzak, gaping maniacally at the board, blows into his clenched fist, throws the dice, and, shouting, "Brazil!" leans past our sour expressions to see which way the dice have fallen.

G-BEAT

Then we were sent back to civilian life, and four months later our unit was called up again. Since, theoretically, you're only supposed to serve one month a year, maybe two at the outside, some of the men voiced a piddly objection that we couldn't be summoned again since we were already pulling three times more reserves then any other unit in our command. The reply that channeled back from staff headquarters was delivered to us by Lieutenant Yitzak at our base camp in Rafiah. While slowly, lovingly he scratched away at his exposed armpits, in the bright white wife-beater T-shirt blazing between the unbuttoned halves of his uniform, Yitzak told us that with the war in Lebanon raging up north and more of our troops bogged down in that quagmire, there wasn't enough rotation to give other units the depth of experience that we had.

He also told us that intelligence had reported that after the beating they took in Beirut, Arafat's terrorists had once more shifted their focus to Israel's administered territories, even while the Islamic fundamentalists, via Egypt, were pushing up from Saudi Arabia and down from Iran and Lebanon, trying to spread the fires of holy war in Gaza. Hezbollah was also involved, and Hamas was on the move. Apparently even crazy old Saddam Hussein in Iraq was pitching money at the fray.

It was therefore up to us, as the most experienced reserve unit in counterterrorism, to stagger this assault. Which, translated, meant that the army didn't have a clue about how to handle any of this and therefore, in the meantime, we sorry-ass reservists would have to do. They would pull us from our mortgaged homes and inflationary civilian jobs anytime they damn well pleased, and if we didn't like it, tough shit. And the more they called us up, the better at this kind of soldiering we got, the greater the need to call us up all over again. Our misery increased exponentially with our prowess.

We were learning new things all the time. On our second night in the Rafiah encampment, one man from each of the three platoons in our company was "volunteered" to pull a new type of experimental duty called "G-Beat."

One of the lucky chosen few, I found myself stationed in an armored truck outfitted with a gigantic bulletproof, Hollywood-style floodlight mounted in back. It moved like an antiaircraft gun, by means of a bucket seat that swiveled, while the operator's feet danced a kind of shuffle step from side to side. The great white beam pierced miles of bare wilderness. While I sat behind the light, Sayla, another from our lucky trio, a short, well-groomed, irritatingly cheerful telephone repairman in civilian life, stretched flat on the ground on his belly, hugging close to one of the truck's front tires, removing his helmet now and then to run a smoothing hand over his neatly combed pompadour. He manned a Belgium MAG machine gun. The third lucky star, Rami, the vehicle's driver, a rock bassist from Haifa with granny glasses and a bushy headful of thick brown hair, hid fifty meters away in "ambush," concealed in a shallow ditch that ran parallel to the border fence. Armed with a Galil assault rifle propped on foldout tripod legs, he was our crossfire. He also had beside him a satchel packed with grenades.

This, then, was G-Beat.

Of course, the Egyptian troops across the border fence shot at us. Yes, we had a peace treaty with Mr. Mubarak, but every night there were so-called infractions committed by his troops, though violations of any scale, large or small, even those just short of total war, were still and always considered by our side merely "infractions." Because of the so-called peace treaty, nothing short of full peace was admissible by either side.

Still, every bullet fired by Egypt, every mortar round, RPG, and grenade rocket that they launched against our troops was dutifully recorded and processed by our intelligence staff. Then, on the morning after, a peace-loving Israeli liaison officer armed with a complete and detailed log of the night's violent infractions crossed the border gate at Rafiah and handed the data over to a waiting and quite mystified Egyptian liaison officer, who in turn passed it up his puzzled chain of command. Certain swift actions were then taken against the offending Egyptian soldiers. The problem was, there seemed to be a number of our "peace partner's" troops who appeared to dislike the state of nonbelligerence. Like the entire Egyptian army.

So, say that the three hungry, unsheltered Egyptian infantrymen just over the fence from us and outfitted with little more than Kalatchnikovs — Russian-made assault rifles with eight clips of twenty-nine rounds each, plus all sorts of portable antitank and antipersonnel ordinance — began their shift in typical fashion: building a fire not only to ward off jackals, whose humpbacked shapes lurk at the edge of their encampment, but also in a pathetic effort to warm up against the frigid desert night, a cold so raw it froze your canteen to your lips. They hugged themselves in those tattered brown field coats with flapping Chaplinesque sleeves. Their faces, lit by flames, looked devilishly peeved. They hopped from foot to foot in unlaced boots with soles bound together by tape. Bored, they sang Egyptian rock tunes.

Heaving a big sigh for the trouble I was about to cause, I flipped on the searchlight's toggle switch; the generator hummed to life. Sayla tore the canvas coverlet away. He lay down again, his squinting eye sighting his weapon. "OK," he shouted.

I hit On. An immense tubular beam shot like a muzzle flash from a tank round, deep into their territory, probing. Moving my boots along the round metal grid underfoot, I swept the beam from left to right, and back again, illuminating trees and bushes frozen in fearsome silhouettes suggestive of everything from Arab djinn spirits to Goya's countrymen impaled by Napoleon's dragoons. The beam alerted every Egyptian infantryman, aircraft, artillery battery, tank unit, wild beast, and poison insect for a hundred miles to my existence.

And what is the purpose of this?

I asked myself that question as my boots did their seated desert dance. I had no answer. I did my senseless little suicidal tango with a mounting sense of impending doom while Sayla, looking up, called out, "Why are we doing this?" and shrieked with glee for the absence of a sensible reply, and sighted his MAG again.

No one ever really explained to us the purpose of G-Beat.

We vaguely understood that we sought squads of terrorists traveling on foot, or gold and hash smugglers, or Egyptians seeking a quick way to visit their relations on the other side of the

randomly drawn border slicing right through the center of the city
of Rafiah. No Arab could cross to our side who did not have a
return ticket to fly home. There was also some sort of exit tax
imposed by the Egyptians that most of the "cousins" could not
afford to pay and, in addition, we Israelis had our own reentry tax
waiting for them once they crossed back over to our side.

Apparently, avoidance of this reentry tax through fence jumping or wire cutting or else underground tunneling was well worth
to the local Palestinians the very real risk of getting shot.

But our chief objective were the terrorists. It was mainly for
them that we lay in wait.

However, after a while, Rami, our ambushing crossfire man, stood
up from his hiding place and trudged up to the truck with a dis-
gusted look on his face. With his thick shag of hair tumbling out of
his helmet, he looked like John Lennon in an antiwar film. After
hours spent watching the Egyptian soldiers on the other side of the
fence dance around their pathetic fire to keep warm, he finally
couldn't take their silent misery anymore, declared "Fuck this
shit!" and, reaching into a toolbox, removed a boom box, which he
plugged into the truck's portable generator. He inserted a tape that
he retrieved from a pouch in his battle vest. Suddenly, "Sergeant
Pepper's Lonely Hearts Club Band" boomed through the night
and the excited Egyptians broke into a kind of psycho disco war-
path step around the flames, the Kalatchnikovs slung from their
shoulders swinging back and forth. Rami stood a few feet from
the truck with a look of grim satisfaction, clapping his hands and
occasionally screaming out snippets of the lyrics in poor English:
"Is twenty years a dog to gay . . . Sergeant Pepper make he go
away . . . Get it down brothers!" and so forth.

Then they began shouting, *"Yacobi! Yacobi! Ochel! Ochel!"*
Hebrew for "Jacob! Jacob! Food! Food!" This posed another

riddle that I could not successfully answer: why they would use as euphemism for us Jews the name of a biblical figure who wrestled with an angel and, laying his head on a rock for a pillow, dreamed of seraphim climbing and descending ladders between heaven and earth?

At this point we broke out our food supply, which was considerable. Israeli soldiers eat well. Chicken cutlets. Mashed potatoes. Salad. Bread with butter and jam. Fruit. We made a stack of jam sandwiches, put them in a bread sack, and, swinging it over our heads as David and his slingshot, tossed it over the fence.

With no thank-you, they fell to it, sat cross-legged on the ground and stuffed the sandwiches into their mouths; their cheeks puffed like squirrels'. They ate so fast that like snakes they had to stay perfectly still to swallow the big lumps I feared they'd choke on. Then they jumped to their feet and, shouting "Beatles! Sergeant Pepper!" danced for as long as Rami cared to keep the music turned up. At one point we were all gyrating in place, Jew and Arab, with dreamy, moonlit expressions. "G-Beat," said Sayla softly, undulating next to me. "Huh, cutey? How you explain this?" I didn't know then. I still don't know. There are things I don't quite know how to communicate: how, for instance, as the music faded, the scale of desolation that its absence unveiled revealed the pitted blue face of the watching moon, like some forlorn desert god; the sense of deep loneliness we all felt I'm sure, Israeli and Egyptian both, as the cold night drove into hiding most of those things that make the desert day a hell, but at least a living one — the flies, scavenger birds, soldier ants, scarab beetles, scorpions. We were but for ourselves utterly alone in a void. It was like sleeping awake. The desert night, impossibly, frigidly pure, was a temporary form of living death. Nothing moved. Only the scrub brush writhed like witches risen from the dust and the leering demonic snouts of the jackals ringed the campfire of the Egyptian soldiers, who pelted them with rocks.

We didn't sleep: just sat and stared or dozed half-awake, surfacing in and out of an aching dry fatigue that completely defeated the will to live and made rest impossible. Out there, all one could do was be miserable. It made me realize just how awful conditions must have been for the Egyptians, to inspire what came next. Or maybe they just acted under orders. Who knew? I think that they were simply too different from us for me or Sayla or Rami to ever comprehend, and besides, who cared anyway? Why must we understand anything? We were soldiers; what our officers called "matches." That is, one-strike flames that burned up and died. Is it an insult to term a foe that disguises himself as a peace partner and shoots at us an imperishable mystery? They shot at us, plain and simple.

First came automatic single fire, one round at a time; then short staccato bursts that played the bulletproof searchlight like a deadly xylophone and raked the ground around our truck.

Rami ran cursing to his ditch, thick hair flapping from under his helmet and one hand fumbling to keep his granny glasses on while Sayla, helmetless, not a hair out of place on his pompadour, hid behind me and over the radio called in the infractions as they occurred. All I could do, all I was permitted to do, was train the light on them in the hope of blinding their aim. It didn't work. Is there any easier thing to do in the whole world then take potshots at a moon-size spotlight on the black target range of a Middle Eastern desert?

The celebration was full on. They fired off everything in their arsenal: flares, RPG, mortars — exploding at distances but on our side of the fence and once or twice right in our midst, which sent us diving. And Sayla, shimmying up to my ear, said in a voice parched with terror: "G-Beat, huh? What are you going to tell your American Jewish friends about this? What are you going to say? Go ahead, my cutey, explain G-Beat," and my baffled look sent him into silent convulsions of cheerless mirth.

Eventually, the stress wore me out and I nodded off to the sight of red tracer rounds lobbing through the night air as Sayla's voice counted, "One hundred and twenty-one, one hundred twenty-two, one hundred twenty-three . . ." like sheep jumping mined electronic border fences.

In the desert, a fly walks on your face with the same proprietary air that you stroll on the earth. Its tiny legs take your cheek for granted. Your shut eyelid seems like a good place to idle away the time. In fact, it is this sense of a fly's impunity that stirs the rage that awakens you into parchedness and your own perspiring stench and lets you know that desert morning has come.

As I sat up, I saw Sayla bustling about, preparing for our exit. He shut down the generator and stored away the food and reloaded munitions. He tightened nuts on our rims with a ratchet and kicked the stops out from our tires. Rami hadn't slept the whole night and came stumbling back through the white heat, his skin a sickly yellow in which several pimples stood out prominently; his red eyes stared out at us, bruised with fatigue. He curled up next to the searchlight and passed out. I slid into the passenger seat. The Egyptians were slumped brown piles around their cold campfire.

"Look!" shouted Sayla. "It's time to pay the piper for last night's Disneyland."

An Egyptian jeep dragging behind it a half-mile-long yellow dust cloud roared into their camp and before braking to a full stop discharged a steam-pressed officer with a cane-length iron mine probe, who laid into the nearest man on the ground with a whack that I could feel all the way back to my side of the border. The howling Egyptian trooper jumped to his feet and received seven — I counted them — bone-breaking blows before the officer turned on the other two culprits. They were both big men, one with a thick black handlebar mustache, and it was oppressive to see them cringing and gibbering frantically as they took their punishment with hands raised piteously in self-defense. Beside me, Sayla watched with more compassion than I knew was in him. For once, it wasn't funny and he wasn't laughing. "Shit," he muttered. "Shit."

Next, a truck filled with Egyptian soldiers collected from outposts along the frontier pulled up and the three penitents were driven aboard at the point of the probe, like sheep. The officer looked at us, grinned, and waved. We didn't respond. His face went cold and, spinning, he jumped into the jeep and pulled out in a cloud of dust fifty yards tall and rising. As the truck fell in behind, the three soldiers yelled out: "Hey, *Yacobi! Yacobi!* Beatles! Sergeant Pepper!" and the others also yelled. Then, suddenly, their pants were down, a bunch of them, bare, hairy asses hanging out, mooning us with scorn, and they yelled: "Fuck Pepper!" and "Beatle Jew shit!" as the truck vanished into the jeep's dusty wake.

For a long time we just sat, flies probing our flesh for vital signs.

"G-Beat," Sayla said matter-of-factly, without a trace of laughter. "How the fuck will you explain it to your American Jewish friends? To your mother? To your girlfriend? To your best friend? To yourself?"

I shrugged. I shrug.

GOOD-BYE HOUSE

Quickly, the weather's mood changes, grows sullen and begins to storm and argue with our truck. Rain spits in our faces. We make no stops. The ride is hard. The bumping vehicle's hard metal floors beat up our asses. Our heads shake, cigarettes dangling from our lips. Sparks fly off occasionally. We roll. Are jolted and tossed. Thunder beats on far mountains, like brickbats on garbage cans. We pull closed the canvas fly, huddle and shiver.

I draw on a hooded poncho. It gets cold, dark. We stare at each other in lightless space, at what we can make out of each other's faces. And slowly as the sky darkens we fade away into smells, touches, coughs, curses. We are silhouettes there in back of the truck, reeking of perspiration, the sweet stench of unwashed skin. Only big dark hollows show where our eyes should be. We stare at each other's darknesses from out of our own. We pull on our battle jackets. I put on mine. Minutes pass. I add another pair of socks to the ones I have on. It takes me twenty minutes to lace up the boots again with my vibrating hands. I tremble like a virgin, like an old woman with cerebral palsy. And then, the trucks slow. We draw back the canvas fly. We are on city streets. Faces flash by, angry, hunched heads in kaffiyehs, black peering eyes, despising us. We pass dirty, depressing buildings. Ratty trees. Khan Yunis, someone says. I will come to know this place well.

Khan Yunis, of kisoks and sulfurous wind, of ragged boys with shorn heads, in torn jeans, T-shirts, and sneakers, who follow our trucks with rocks in their hands as we nod to the numbing rhythm of the tires, and skip and fire their stones; some bounce on the metal floor harmlessly and one or two glance up against a leg or a chest but the soldier it was meant for looks down at it with proud disdain.

Here in Khan Yunis, asshole of the world, we meet a cold, fierce downpour that stabs our bones with homicidal fury. We stop off in the garrison, yet another converted British fortress with a big brown muddy square. Under iron gray skies, on a sheltered, crumbling concrete porch through which rain bleeds, and from which yellow naked lightbulbs dangle like pus-filled teeth, the sallow-skinned troops lounge a foot away from the hemorrhaging leaks, the splashing flood blackens their boots and forms nightwaters and bad dreams on which reflected naked lightbulbs float like evil spells.

The troops smoke or chat or play cards, seated on wet milk crates or lounging shirtless, pretending not to feel the cold, as if dressing for a drought will restore the summer sun. But by the time we arrive the sun has slammed the door and left, replaced by a white floating-disk moon thinly veiled behind roiling, rain-swollen clouds. Later, when the skies clear, we will see the moon peering through our windows like a remorseful drunk.

"What are we here for?" asks Asaaf, standing next to me. Brandt, Binny, and Uri join us.

"What did he say?" asks Uri, looking Asaaf over with an

appraising eye, as though to see whether or not he has any use for the man's opinions.

"He asked why we're pulling in here," I say.

Asaaf looks at us all. "I thought we're going to Rafiah. What are we doing here?"

Brandt says: "You sound like a basic trainee. What does it matter? Here? There? It's all shit anyhow."

"Because here," says Asaaf with lips pursed in wistful irony, "two days ago, this is where — not too far from here — they shot up the settler's car. And they killed that baby with the parents." You can always count on Asaaf to know such awful things.

"Fuck!" says Brandt. And adds: "Shit!" And looks away at his bad luck.

"So what does that mean? There will be a reprisal?" I look around. "They will do something?"

"Yes," says Brandt. "You bet. And we're going to do it. You watch. How many times have we been through this, Asaaf?"

"There's some fucked-up job to do: we're called. We get it. We always get it."

"Watch," says Brandt. "Watch how we get it."

Uri and Binny move off to talk. There is a cauldron of hot coffee set on a table in the barracks; beside it a stack of blue plastic cups. I help myself to the brew. There'll be no sleep tonight. It isn't too bad, the coffee, is already sweetened just so. So, we are in for it. I should have known. They tell you it's nothing, a "chupah," a treat. Translated: "shafted." There is sediment in the mud coffee. I like to chew it. I wonder what Maya is doing now. Pulling an all-nighter on just a cup of the coffee, I'd think of Maya all night. Her reddish blond hair bobbing between my thighs. And flares drifting down reflected in her long-lashed, laughing eyes. Would she smile up at me as she blew death? Or shiver? I'd swaddle her in a parka, after she was done — oh, my lovely girl, I'd hold her close.

Look, over there: see that wilting stream of red fire? Those are .05s, I'd say, strings of long-range machine gun volleys. Aim for my soul, Maya. Kill me. Oh, kill me, my love, kill me. Right in my bull's-eye groin. The dogs here cut through our headlights with reflecting marbles in the sockets of their eyes. They are blind with fear, starved and skeletally ribbed. It is a canine famine-feast, a slaughtering ground of horses and camels, men and insects. I sip the coffee. I'd serve her some too, this coffee that keeps all the patrols awake until morning. This is what we drink, I'd say. We call it "mud coffee." And in my uniform, an erection grows. The wet damp muddy cold stimulates my cock. This is the taste in our mouth that wipes out the memory of your cunt, the taste that escorts us back onto the road, out of the garrison, as we travel once more en route to our head-fuck mission. This is my semen in your mouth, and then a sharp right onto a signless turnoff that winds up a wet, narrow road past ramshackle houses interspersed among half-finished ugly gray cement villas.

We're hunched in the rear of the Noon Noons, riding with sick stomachs, farting, our CAR-15s between our knees and with manic, enervated grins and stuporous expressions: buzzed to the gills, stoned on the porno of imminent destruction, and yet she is still kneeled before me, my thighs hugging her shoulders, my left hand cupped behind her neck and her face thrown back — as my right hand smoothes her dangling wet hair and gives it a sharp tug, she winces and smiles and says, "Ooof!" and "That hurt," and I say, "You're too beautiful for your own good" and, leaning down to kiss her softly, taste myself in her mouth. But the trucks stop abruptly. We have arrived. And anyway, she is married to another man, Dotan, who has become my so-called best friend over the past year. And in all that time, I have never even touched her. Not even to shake her hand. My heart imagines that it too has erections that burst from my chest and grow across vast areas of space to her door in Jerusalem, to her bed, to her cunt, and penetrate and hoist her aloft and she cries with terrified joy, the only kind real lovers know.

We've arrived. Sergeant Dedi shouts: *"Y'Allah!"* We groan to a stand, stiffly jump down. It's stopped raining. From the telephone lines overhead dangles a PLO flag, tied to a pair of sneakers and flung over the wires. We're in Fatah country, in one of the "cousins'" neighborhoods. That's what we call Arabs: cousins. A group of women stand around with hands at their faces, swaying and moaning. Mute, terrified children cling to their long skirts, sucking thumbs, their wide, distrustful eyes frowning at us. I wink back at one, a little girl with dirty blond hair: cross, she looks away.

Soldiers of the Engineering Corps busy themselves unloading gear from the back of the second Noon Noon. No one tells us how to deploy. We just stand around. Out come cigarettes. Candy bars.

"Is that the house?" I ask Brandt.

"Sure, where else?"

It's a big place, made of cinder blocks and shale. Why is it their houses never seem quite finished? Lack paint or a wing or sometimes windows or even a roof. But they live in it as though its always been that way. Maybe it has.

"What'd they do?" Asaaf asks Dedi as he walks past. Dedi says: "The house belongs to the parents of a guy who threw a hand grenade in Tel Aviv Central Bus Station. Good-bye house."

We nod, dragging on our smokes. What a pleasure a smoke is in a place that stinks this bad. Where does the stench come from? Something big and dead somewhere. Probably a donkey has pitched over and just rots where its heart stopped, or a horse. They just leave them there for a million flies, ants, beetles, grubworms, and, of course, the dogs. When only the bones remain the kids kick them apart until they're dismantled and carried off by animals and rain. But the smell will linger for long after. It permeates the very walls of the homes. Nothing more to say to that. I only wonder if we'll use explosives to blow the place.

But no, it's a wrecking job. Up pulls a truck with an armored tractor on a flatbed. Some of the troops curse. This will take five times as long, which is the intention: to protract suffering, set an example for others to see.

A soldier climbs into the cab, carefully adjusts the seat, dons goggles and headphones, and guns the engine. The tractor crawls off the flatbed like a giant space insect and rumbles toward the house, the big hungry shovel pointed at the low wall surrounding the residence. The women begin to wail and scream. Their men are not about. They are in hiding. Now soldiers run in all directions to deploy and Dedi orders us to form a cordon around the target's southern wing. We trot over.

"Take up positions every thirty meters," he commands.

We do as he asks. I notice high pale green ratty-looking eucalyptus trees thrashing in a moil of rain clouds and draw my parka closed. I'm standing with Asaaf to my left and Brandt to my right. Already we've formed a "hulia," as they call it in the army. A threesome. From now on, we'll do things in threes. It just happens that way: three men partner on the spot, and afterward it sticks. Hard to say what conjoins us. A certain ironic attitude, I guess. A grinning kind of unrelenting disbelief about how fucked we really are.

It's best not to look at the women now. So, we don't. Or at least I don't. Their screams, though, mount in our ears, shrill beyond belief and inflected with a kind of stylized wailing that makes it seem spurious, but that's true of all the cousins. There's always a dash of theater in their trouble. It's their way. Still, their voices are harrowing. And the younger women, maybe too young, I most can't bear to listen to, with their soft, breathless gasps of real, raw emotion.

I try to focus on the tractor. Already, it's smashed through the yard wall, which crumbles into big chunks, and crunches over them, leaves a gaping hole. Now it comes up to the house, as in a battle, and rears and smashes through. The shovel jaw rips out the cinder blocks, again and again and again, eating, tearing, and the tractor backs away and charges and a wing of the house goes down and that portion of roof collapses pathetically and I look away.

Houses at their wrecking acquire a human quality that they do not have during their lifetime. Their limbs look broken. Their entrails hang out in wiring. Their windows become eyes in a disfigured, tortured face. And the women's voices rise into crescendos of naked sorrow that are torn from them without a trace of motive, and against this I raise my hands to stop my ears. So does Brandt.

But Asaaf shouts at the women: "Why the fuck did you send him to do that? What the FUCK — FUCK YOU! DO YOU HEAR? FUCK YOU WITH YOUR SHOUTS! Who told you to send him to blow up our buses? Who told you? What did you think?"

But no other soldiers are speaking; they just stand around with their hands over ears or at rest on their weapons and cigarettes smoking in their mouths, faces deadpan, or they eat chocolate waffle candy bars and watch the tractor do its work.

It labors relentlessly. Its appetite is inexhaustible. The house is candy to it. Smashed pillars crumple in its jaws, shattered window frames flap like broken kites. One clownish, still-standing door glares with smoldering accusation, like a condemned prisoner, before the order is given to fire. Then, finally, the whole roof slams to the ground with the thudding crash of a slain elephant and raises a yellow dust cloud that drifts over everyone, soldiers and women and children alike, and we wave our hands before our faces almost festively, for a moment indistinguishable from each other — our grimaces can even be mistaken for smiles — Jew and Arab, drained of our forms, reduced to pale impressions, rubbing our eyes at the stinging, strange dream we are in.

WHY NOT?

So, finally, there is no reason for bad nerves anymore. And anyway, it's too late for that: the green fatigues are on us like a lock. We're bolted tight into our boots and battle vests. Does everyone have eight full spring clips containing twenty-nine rounds each? Who knows? One hopes so. We're off to work. Our work is war.

But we do not eat mud with our food. No, our cook Rami is pristine. Plates heaped with hot chicken cutlets, we eat, perfect little golden French fries, fiercely diced salad. For dessert: pudding. Rami doesn't kid around. When he appears hands dart into backpacks, emerge with cartons of Marlboro cigarettes. Only the best for our cook. Short and thin, dressed in a uniform tailored so tightly to his contours, it could have been painted on, he drives his own civilian car to deliver the food, right to the outposts and even to some of the ambush positions. Out there in the middle of brown, rain-swollen misery, hunched behind the wheel of his blue Citroën, traversing terrain on civilian tires that only tanks, jeeps, and APCs should cross.

The taste of his wonderful breaded cutlets mingles with the stench of gunpowder and death. No one quite cooks his way, *shishlik* seasoned with funerals, steak smeared with camouflage paint ... and we are in Khan Yunis, where our Noon Noons roar through the center of town, our bellies full. Once upon a time they sent us here to look into a little something that needed our special attention and we haven't left since, except for months-long leaves home, during which we pretend to live civilian lives before they call us up again. And as we pass now through the gray decrepit streets in a blue downpour, bystanders stop, soaked, to chart our progress with eyes full of hate.

No one needs to ask why we're ordered to take this particular highly visible route on public thoroughfares — we know: we're here to make the point that you may think of killing us but we're ten steps ahead of you, a small but no-nonsense column of seasoned reservists, easing slowly through your streets.

And yet the bombings continue. A hand grenade is tossed under a bus in Tel Aviv's Central Bus Station; an explosive left by a swimming pool in an attaché case in Netanya; shooters are sent on a massacring free-for-all in downtown Jerusalem at the height of the shopping hours; three teenage hikers are found slain in the Jordan Valley. It all starts out of here, or else up in the West Bank. And our eyes narrow as we absorb the looks of hate, icily measuring their expressions for a sense of which among them will commit desperate acts. According to their eyes, most are ready to kill or die. Yet such data is not hard enough for the Ministry of Defense to beef up the military response. And we can't stay this mounting tide.

So that, as I observe Brandt, hunched bleary and unshaven in his store-bought rain poncho, and despite his surfer good looks seeming just now more like a hobo than a soldier, and see Dedi, big and bearish, with furrowed intelligent brow and large hands curled disconsolately over his assault rifle, and witness all the others with their helmets lowered over eyes masked in shadow, I see that we are so tired and we are not enough, for there are far too many of them, too few of us, and none of us wants to be here.

A hand rubbed over an unwashed, grizzled cheek. A yawn. An angry head toss at a bystander with an impudent smile: *Better move it or else!* But he doesn't move: you do. The stench of human shit in the streets mingled with warm blasts of cooking smells makes you retch.

Now and then someone balances with a hand pressed to an oozing wall and heaves and gags. Today in the *shuk* where we've dismounted, it is Binny with hands on knees, keeled over, a long string of drool dangling from his lips.

No, not just the smells but our very presence here is sickening to us. The stomach-churning unease of these heavily postered, paint-spattered walls infects us. Pausing at bullet holes, we finger and sniff: *fresh*. Both sides of the line, Jewish and Arab, bear damage from the constant gunfire.

And Binny stands up, face white as whey and eyes forlorn, and draws a clenched fist across his slack mouth, then looks out at the whole of Khan Yunis and says to it, "Why don't you just come shit in my mouth instead of rubbing my nose in this?" and we all laugh.

"Fall into line," says Dedi wearily. "Amir, Falk, take the rear. Binny, up front with me. Brandt and Pagi at center."

He steps over to Amir and me. "I want you two especially to watch those roofs over there, to each side." He points out the gated top windows boarded up with shutters. "From there a few weeks ago was shooting. We think we got the ones who did it. But, who knows? OK?"

"Sure," I say.

But he continues to gaze up there, not finished. "Now it's quiet. But curfew ends at fourteen hundred hours." His wristwatch snaps up before his eyes. "That's twenty-eight minutes from now. Then it's going to be chaos around here. You don't know this *shuk* well. It's not Hebron. Hebron, compared to this, is Fifth Avenue in New York. This is a real circus, OK? The police told staff they identified sixteen different terror gangs operating out of this market alone. Not just for terrorism but bank robbery, arms smuggling, drugs, and a better hot car ring than the one we shut down in Gaza City. Brandt, you remember that one?"

He nods lazily: "I do."

"You should. You almost got your head blown off. Those were terrorists and professional criminals operating together. A bad scene."

"It was bad," Brandt agrees.

"So, if that is bad, this...this is fucking horrible. OK? Hamas and Fatah and PFLP and Fatah Hawks and Islamic Jihad, and they say they think also Hezbolah has operatives down here working out of this butthole *shuk*. You remember the soldiers in Rafiah they shot in the back? From paratroopers? Let's not end up like that."

We all nod. Who hasn't heard of that? In Israel, when the news broke people tsked and shook their heads sadly for the "poor boys, only in their twenties." But those of us who were then on leave, in our respective homes, heard the word "Rafiah" and broke into sweats, and our wife or girlfriend, leaning over us, said: "Honey, what's the matter? Is that where you are? Honey? You look so pale."

So we set out, weapons pointed at the roofs, except for Dedi and me — we keep our muzzles trained on the doorways and street. Here and there men straggle out of buildings with arms raised: we wave them back inside, shaking our heads *NO!* They plead. *NO!* we bark and point our guns. Back *inside!* In they go. But one man steps from a doorway and rushes off.

"What the hell is that!" shouts Amir. Dedi orders, "HALT!" The man hurries on, disappears within an open door, which slams shut. Dedi runs to it. We trot behind. His fist hammers on blue weathered wood painted with an eye to ward off djinns, evil spirits. He pounds. Then steps back and launches his boot at the door. The frame cracks. From within voices shout in Arabic. Locks tumble open. A man — not the one we saw — peers out fearfully. Dedi shoves open the door. We drag the guy out. Brandt and Rami aim their guns at the roofs. Dedi guards the suspect. Amir and I stick our heads and hands inside, grab hold of another one, drag him out. They are both on their knees now, hands behind head. Amir squats before them, translates Dedi's questions: Why did that man break curfew? Where is he? Why did he come to your house? Why didn't he stop? The men stare at him sullenly. Dedi strikes the first man hard across the face. The blow snaps his head to the left. He returns face front, tears in his eyes.

This I have seen before. Prideful sneers evaporate under the blows from Dedi's hand. Playing at this kind of warfare is fun until we catch you. Then we are not so much fun. We remember the white donkey that we watched you kick to death before the eyes of our patrol, just to rouse our helpless anger, since we are under strict orders not to respond to provocation, which somehow you knew. You had your little fun tormenting the creature for hours: a young white donkey with pink inner ear chambers and a gimp leg. You smashed in its head with pipes and broke rocks and bricks on its neck and gouged out its eyes and smashed its knees and teeth with a rubber mallet and sliced open its belly and pulled out its entrails while it was yet alive, all for our amusement; a whole mob of you gathered in the square outside the central mosque, right there in Gaza City, at three o'clock in the morning. We remember the eyes you took from its poor head and how you tossed them at us, laughing and jeering. Not very friendly of you, so forgive us if Dedi's hand seems to contain a little more iron than you think is justified. That last blow echoes through the streets.

And now, they yield. They call out a name in rapid, anguished singsong, and the man who broke curfew steps out with hands raised and drops quietly to his knees alongside his two comrades and waits. Amir drags him to his sandals and stands him up against the wall and Dedi looks him over and in a low-key, quiet voice says for Amir to translate: "I called for you to stop. Why did you ignore me?" And his hand, Dedi's, looks like a hammer.

The man meets Dedi's question calmly. Their eyes lock. Each dares the other to look away.

"I am in a hurry," Rami translates.

"But curfew ends in twenty minutes. Why can't you wait twenty minutes?"

"I can't wait."

"Why not?"

The man's eyes fall. Dedi's haven't moved. The other men study Dedi's face anxiously. One of them looks at us. We glance up at the roofs and at both ends of the street. In a few windows faces peer out but otherwise we seem safe.

"Why not?" Dedi says again.

No answer.

The slap explodes.

"Why not?"

Again the loud, harsh thunderclap of bone against cheek. "Keep your hands raised," says Dedi.

The man's eyes fill with tears. His hands barely stay aloft. If he talks he will be butchered by his own side. Fatah Hawks will come in the night, wearing masks and bearing axes. His death will be slow.

"Don't drop your arms," Dedi says.

"I can't . . ." the man begins, and Dedi's hand attacks his face. His cheek is a dark, swollen purplish lump.

"Why not?" Dedi's voice rings out. "Why didn't you stop when I called your name? What are you up to? How do I know you're not up to something? What are you planning?"

. . . Or, are you trying to prove something, to make a point? Why aren't you home at your wives' tables, surrounded by your children, your doors locked, and spooning a nice mash of black beans and hummus with olive oil into your mouths, until the curfew ends and we blow our whistle and your mosque calls you out of your homes to riot, but most of you won't — no, not today; you'll just return to unlock your doors and roll up the gates from your shops. In only, say, five minutes you could have been in your stalls, making sales, but instead here you are now with us and our memories, and we are recalling some not-so-nice things that your fellow countrymen and possibly even you have done, including to our soldiers, who are only good boys serving their homeland, after all, working down here in this shithole to defend their families and protect their homes from your vicious little plots to send shooters up King George Street with submachine guns and grenades — remember that one? Your friends — are they your friends? — they say the shooters were from right here in Khan Yunis — smuggled their concealed guns into the dressing room of a sporting goods shop and came out shooting and tossing hand grenades on King George Street at the height of the shopping. Shot an old woman. A girl soldier. A father of three children. Blew his skull right off. Some of us who were at home then saw it on the news: the talking head came on grim-faced, reporting what your friends had done, and for a week after I, we, everyone, felt a leaden knot of tense despair each time we shopped downtown; the sort that soon enters the bloodstream — you know, oh yes — and affects white cell count, the whole immune system, you name it. More of this for you. Good work. The bullets cutting into their vitals left the shooters' victims sprawled out on the sunny Jerusalem pavement on a warm afternoon that the weatherman the night previous had accurately reported, and each of the now dead or wounded had, when still alive, made decisions before mirrors, rummaged in drawers and closets, tried on different outfits until they felt pleased with what they saw, and they stepped out that morning appropriately dressed and with no clue that within hours they'd lie bleeding out their lives or outright dead on beds of hot Jerusalem asphalt. In their sports shirts and slacks, in their festive spring dresses, surrounded by spilled shopping bags, capsized briefcases, abandoned backpacks: drowning in their own blood. That's often how one dies, gagging on blood. It wells in your mouth and the throat closes to prevent it entering your lungs, where, of course, it already is. But the throat doesn't know. Throats can't differentiate.

A cockroach crawls over a jihad slogan in a slow, halting, ultimately futile ascent, higher, higher, until a gust lifts him off and sends him hurtling with spread wings down down to the rancid excremental gutter with its endless festering detritus of rotting vegetables and discarded animal entrails.

"Why not?" Dedi asks, and Binny jumps on the radio, requesting that curfew be extended until we get some answers to our questions. Now the announcement is heard throughout the *shuk* from mounted loudspeakers of mobile Border Police patrols, caged jeeps crawling through the streets and alleys with a loud metallic voice in Arabic advising residents to remain indoors until further notice. In the far distance a gunshot rings out. We all lift our heads, even the man who broke curfew. Dedi's raised hand darts out. The blow reminds us all of why we're here. "Why not?"

But he doesn't say. Claims not to know. Can't explain why he chose to defy a military edict, charge out in front of a patrol, and ignore our request that he halt in order to answer our inquiry.

"Why not?"

Again, he doesn't know. Neither do we. Or the other two men on their knees. They too don't know. Their hands are raised. Their knees hurt, I can tell. And our man's cheek is burning with the impression of Dedi's hand. And Dedi's hand by now must sting. But he is not weakening. Soon, though, if no answer comes — and by now we doubt it will — we'll turn all three over to Security Services and they will find out. They have their ways. Always, they seem to learn what they need to know, even if sometimes too late. They're very good.

"Why not?"

No answer. He doesn't even bother to reply. He doesn't know. *Just one of those things, you know,* his eyes seem to say. But we don't know. Once we thought we did but no longer. We don't know anything anymore. Once upon a time it seemed that we did know something, but then they came up on that kibbutz in the dead of night with Kalatchnikovs and kicked down the door of the children's house and massacred the babies in their cribs and one by one held them up at the windows, in full view of the surrounding troops, for the soldiers to see and then shot them in the temple and tossed the sometimes headless corpses out the window . . . and that was a long time ago when most of us were kids.

"Why not?"

He doesn't answer.

And we don't know.

It is hot in the street, though the afternoon shadows lengthen. The flies swarm over our faces, Jew and Arab alike. To them, we're all the same tasty meat. And we're waiting for an answer that we know will never come, despite the force of Dedi's hand.

PART 2

THE BEDOUIN

I

There was a long, lean, gray feral thing tucked inside the unbuttoned combat tunic of Bachshi, the unit's top Bedouin tracker, and he was showing it off to Ali and Bismela, the other two trackers who served under his immediate command. When Bachshi spotted me, his taut, muscular dark face flashed a yellow gash of rotten teeth.

"Yacobi," he said with a laugh, calling me by the slightly derisive Arab nickname for Jews.

I frowned, and when we were face-to-face, put my fingertips to his chest, shoved him back a step. His eyes set in cold hostility. Again, I shoved him hard, and his eyes were now completely murderous.

"My name's not Yacobi," I said.

Bachshi peered down at the captive hare, which had frozen to his touch. "No," he said, his tone grown formal. "Your name is Yacobi and this, this little coward thing, is also Yacobi. I have named it after a great falseness of a man who thinks he goes by another name but, you see, he and the Jew are the same and so both their names will always be Yacobi."

"No," I said, "it is your Bedouin mother who is nameless. Your mother, who is a whore and less than a dog."

The blue-black irises of his homicidal eyes glinted like gun barrels aimed straight for me. Then, suddenly, our hands shot out across each other's shoulders. We embraced, laughing. Bachshi lifted the hare by the scruff of its neck, dangled its limp, petrified body before my face. I brushed it away.

"Where the hell did you get that from?"

"Your mother birthed it an hour ago, over there" — he peered past my shoulder — "where the locals have their shitty little fig orchard and you Jews go out in the mornings to piss in front of the Arab women working in the field."

"Enough of that," I said.

"All right, then, my brother. Enough. Enough. So, what do you think? Ready to make and move some cash?"

"That hare looks half dead to me. Bet serious money on that? Man, I don't know. Why don't we stick to the video watch game idea we had? Remember how Yitzak got hooked on it? The other day I had that watch in my hand, showing some of the guys how the tank shoots jets out of the sky by using the buttons for setting the date and time, and he tried to snatch it from my hand, with this stupid look on his face, like some kind of addict. He's still convinced that he can now beat out any man in the unit. People for sure will bet just to see Yitzak lose. We'll make a killing. I'll play him myself. Take the sucker to school. Best out of three. Invite the whole division."

"But, my brother, that's bullshit," said Bachshi. "Remember the Risk game that you brought two years ago to Hebron? Another one of your crazy ideas. Remember? No one bet. Not a single *grush!* Sure, Yitzak played it day and night. And that crazy fuck lost in the end anyway. He's nuts. But no one else really gave a shit. There was no money in that, nothing."

"So, say we go with the hare: after the betting, what will you do with Bugs here?"

Bachshi held the hare up by the nape of its neck, showed it around to the group of men, shrugged. "Eat it," said Bachshi. "What else?"

With a wry smile, I nodded. "Some life. Why don't you give it a fucking break? Let it go. Win or lose, he's screwed. You'll eat him in a fucking stew. That's nice. Real nice. Say, no offense intended — OK, Bachshi? — but before I lay down a single cent on this mightily fucked rabbit, can I get some kind of proof? Know what I mean? Let me see it work its stuff, and then, well, maybe we'll talk serious."

At this Bachshi's face became an affectless mask and his tone grew formal again. "Do you doubt, my brother, that I will do what I say I will do?"

"No, nothing like that," I said. "I don't doubt that you can do every single unbelievable, miraculous, marvelous fucking thing that you say you will. But Bugs Bunny here, what if it just sits there, shitting on your shoes? Then I'm left holding my dick. And all that money down the drain."

"Don't be a fool," he said. "This is a desert rodent, brother to the rat and cousin to the motherfucking cat. It's even now conniving how to escape. All I have to do is put it down and it's gone."

"So," I said, "do it. Show me what I'm betting on."

Sternly, perhaps a little stung by my obdurate skepticism, he stepped forward, laid down the hare, stepped away. It stood perfectly still, twitching its whiskery black nose. A faint breeze stroked its fur. Beady black eyes watched from the sides of its head. Then it sprang and he lunged, their bodies merging and Bachshi's hands snatching it from the ground. Where the rest of

Bachshi went at that moment, I don't know. I saw only his hands. Then he rematerialized with the long, limp, trembling hare helpless in his lean brown fist.

"And you can do that every time?"

His eyes searched mine with cool disdain.

"OK," I said.

And that's how it happened that not only half of Third Brigade but units from Paratrooper Recon, Engineering Corps, Military Police, and even civilian-clad operatives from Sheen Bet Security Services all turned up in the big gymnasium in Gaza City to see a host of uniformed contenders try, pathetically, to grab the hare as it careened back and forth within a shouting, clapping circle of soldiers before Bachshi stepped into the ring and caught it easily. Some fights broke out, shoulders got shoved. Real hurt feelings showed. A lot of wallets were raided. But from that, the two of us made a serious bundle.

We became, Bachshi and I, temporarily notorious among the units. I became known as a good guy to place a bet with. And, true to their word, Ali and Bismela ate the poor fucking hare.

Later, I would think about it often, wondering whether Bachshi's expression in any way resembled the look on the face of the dead man or the terrified hare when he crossed the line of no return. Hard to say. I never imagined that things would turn out the way they did. That he would do what he did. We were pretty close, as much as it is possible for a Bedouin and a Jew to be. Each day we went to the desert and roamed out there all night, and there was no time for subtleties, ambiguities, shades of gray. Everything was as clear cut as the Negev moonscape. We operated around the clock on high alert, living mostly on the move, positioning ourselves in wadis, my exhausted eye glued to the whirring incubus of my night vision sniper scope, or "killer," as we called it, scanning, searching the border fence, beside which an occasional gnarled dead tree twisted in the corpse-white desolation.

One night, my heart slammed against my chest wall. There were three tiny figures moving slowly in the greenish X-ray incandescence. I lowered the scope, wiped my eyes, looked again. Men.

I put down the killer and held up three fingers to Bachshi and Micah, our unsmiling driver, a somewhat withdrawn young man with whipcord muscles and cold gray-blue eyes, a tree trimmer in civilian life whose handshake felt like bark. "Maybe a kilometer off. Passing through the fence. They've cut the wire. Let's go."

We jumped into the jeep and took off at high speed down the blacktop patrol road, our headlights off, a nightmarish slalom through the dark. Micah, as always, had little to say as his Ferrari reflexes guided him one-handed through hairpin turns, while Bachshi on the radio called in the sighting's coordinates. I picked up the killer and tried to spot the intruders but it was just too heavy and jumped in my hand as the jeep's wheels bounced over deep ruts and the cabin fishtailed. Seldom ruffled, even under such conditions, Micah hummed as he drove, but I could barely see three feet ahead and sat with my lips clamped.

Then Bachshi shouted, "Stop!" Micah braked. Bachshi jumped out, walked off, was swallowed up in an instant by the desert night from which his voice returned: "My brother, bring light over here."

Micah switched on the small spotlight mounted on the side of the jeep and trained it in the direction of Bachshi, who squatted with his hand held up before his eyes and said: "More to the left." Micah moved the beam. Bachshi said, "Come look."

I dismounted and walked to where Bachshi's finger pointed: saw three pairs of perfectly articulated ripple-soled boot prints in the brown sand.

"Three, like I say."

"Yes," said Bachshi.

"What are they carrying?"

"RPG, I think. Kalatchnikov. A shitload of ammunition."

"Headed where?"

"Northwest."

"To us?"

"Yes, to you."

It meant that he thought they intended, because of the location, to penetrate an Israeli civilian settlement rather than launch an attack against soldiers stationed over the Green Line.

"We'd better call Yitzak," I said. "Tell him to talk to the major. Also, report this to Gaza City. Request a five-kilometer cordon thrown up around the area."

Micah called it in.

We climbed aboard the jeep and swung off the road, following the spoor, the searchlight beam trained on the boot prints, the jeep crawling along. I fished in the gearbox under the Belgium MAG machine gun, removed a fat flare gun, loaded a big round into the chamber, snapped it shut, pointed it above my head, and fired it at a slight angle away from us so the terrorists should clearly see and know that the rear was closed to them; they must continue forward; there was no avoiding us.

From up ahead, to the northwest, rising flares burst with brilliant, spidery drift over enormous umbrellas of radiance. One, two, three, four, shot up in a row, wistfully exploding, floating drunkenly down. Then we heard machine-gun fire open up, mischievous, probing. Then molten red tracer rounds looped through the dark. Then ceased. Now straight white darting rounds of rapid-fire gun bursts stitched the sky. These were not exchanges but directed fire, to articulate strategic quadrants through which the units moved, tightening the net.

I had no doubt that we would catch them. We continued to follow the ripple-soled tracks. An hour later, though, there was still no sign of the intruders. In the far distance the silhouettes of tanks and jeeps roared through the night. When the tracks branched into three directions, I felt, for the first time, that we had lost the scent. I asked Micah to switch off his engines, got right on the radio, called in this new development to the major directly. Bachshi was too professional to take offense. He knew that I had no choice.

"*Nu?*" said the major. "I don't see them. Where are they?"

"We don't know yet. But it looks like they split into three directions."

"Shit," said the major. "What does Bachshi think?"

I asked. Bachshi replied crisply, carefully. Our eyes didn't meet.

I got back on the headset.

"Bachshi thinks they have buried their arsenal, are hiding themselves in the landscape. He'll need two days, he says, and a unit of three men to find them. He asks for me and Micah and another tracker."

There was a pause.

"What do you think?"

"I don't know. I'm no expert. Bachshi is. It's your call."

Another pause. Then: "I don't like this." Then: "You can have Ali."

"He says we can have Ali," I told Bachshi, covering the handset's mouthpiece.

"Good," said Bachshi, meeting my eyes now. "Tell him we'll pick up Ali at Outpost Nine. We'll prepare for the ambush there."

Begrudgingly, the major approved the arrangement. "Catch them!" he snapped and signed off.

"Look," said Bachshi as we drove to Outpost Nine. We cruised at low speed in complete darkness, our headlights and searchlights switched off. He pointed to the northwestern sky, where three flares, first red, then green, then blue, floated over the deployment of three platoons. The units were spread roughly half a kilometer apart, advancing south to draw the cordon tighter.

"I don't think he trusts your plan," I said to Bachshi, whose face grew hard.

"No, my brother" is all he said. Then: "Too bad we can't lay bets on this one with the major and make a killing off that bastard."

The major, whose name was Aron but whom we called simply "the major" had bright orange hair and green-blue eyes and was covered head to foot with a rash of freckles. He was the tallest Israeli I had ever seen. The major was not polite or particularly loved but was very trusted by his men. He brought into a room a dark sense of uneasiness, a dramatic sense of peril. He would have made a great movie director. We were in one of his films now. But he had just given me the feeling that we were only a small scene, an odd take that might or might not make it into the final cut. I could tell: he didn't believe for a single second that we would catch the infiltrators. He believed in Bachshi's tracking skill but not in his strategic ability.

When we pulled into Outpost Seven, no one emerged to greet us. We ducked through the flaps of the mess tent. A sergeant was there, seated alone at a table with his weapon beside him on the bench, a cup of steaming coffee cupped between his gloved hands. His uniform looked rumpled and his uncombed hair jutted at weird angles. He was unshaved and had clearly just woken up.

"It's hot," he said, without meeting our eyes.

"We came for gear."

"I know," he said. "What do you think I'm doing up? They called from the major's jeep."

"Where are the others?"

"Rafiah. They went to buy a TV from Fatima. The game's on tonight and our set blew a fuse."

"So who's watching the border while you're sleeping and they're buying TVs?"

Now he glanced quickly at us, then turned away and said, looking straight ahead: "Take what you need to make your little party. I promise to mind my own business if you promise to mind yours."

We poured ourselves coffee, hot, black, and sweet, good mud, from a huge vat of it kept at low simmer on the portable gas range and partially covered with a big round, shieldlike iron lid.

"What is that? Cinnamon cloves?" asked Micah respectfully.

"Anise," said the sergeant. "A whole bottle."

"In there?"

"I said so, didn't I?"

"Gear still where it usually is?" I asked.

"Where any fucking jackal that wants to can still slip in and steal it," said the sergeant, tapping the table's surface with the heel of his palm. He looked hungover, maybe from anise, or coming down from pot.

"No one talked to the major about that?"

"Allon talked to him. Remember the last time in this shithole? That was six months ago. Allon talked to him again last week."

"So, what did the major say?"

"He told him to mind his own fucking business."

"Bullshit," snapped Micah angrily. "You just don't want to take responsibility! What are you, stoned? Son of a bitch! You, what are you even doing here, you fucking jobnik! What, did you forget to load the general's stapler so they shipped you down here to practice buying TV sets on the black market from an Arab whore?"

"Fatima's not a prostitute. She's a recreational facility and also a reputable member of the business community. She's the wife of Achmed, the grocer, who's an entrepreneur, a far-seeing business-man, the new Middle East, the future. We're the real future, not you assholes running around with pots on your head, playing cow-boys and Indians. So get your gear and fly from here. I've got a giant headache and you're making it worse."

"That was dumb," I told Micah as we headed for the gear tent. It was at least a hundred meters to the rear and anyone could have just walked in and stolen enough ammunition to keep a ten-man squad supplied and on the move for a whole month. "We've got to keep good relations with those folks."

"I don't care," said Micah. "I'm through with cynical assholes like that turning everything into a sickness."

"It's not a sickness," I said. "They're being practical. Look where the hell we are. You want to live on jam sandwiches and a transistor radio? Those boys'll get you anything you need, if you're nice to them. And by the way: you don't care about money? It's all you talk about. Stock market. Car prices. Real estate. You're obsessed with it."

We arrived at the tent and ducked our way in. Bachshi was already there, sorting through supplies. He squatted on his haunches and had gear neatly arranged on a gray wool blanket.

We observed his work with respect. I gave him a deferent, querying look: "Good?"

He nodded.

Then we took black greasepaint and helmet camouflage and went outdoors to smudge one another's faces and slip the nets over our helmets, held fast with thick bands of black elastic, and went in again to unpack the TOW launchers and rifle rockets and wipe them clean of oil with strips of flannel.

Micah took an M202 and filled a shoulder bag with grenades. I took a medic's kit and we each loaded up with extra ammo clips and cans of rations. We took rope and wire cutters and lastly a field radio and stashed it all in the jeep and without a good-bye to the sergeant drove off slowly with our lights blacked out and flares, now only white ones, flickering and floating overhead in the northern sky.

We reached Outpost Nine in minutes: it was only a kilometer away. Ali waited for us with his face already black-smudged and his helmet in webbing. A Belgium MAG on its stock leaned against his leg. His big backpack was loaded down, I knew, with a box containing 250 rounds of ammunition belts, neatly folded.

For three hours we crept along the dried streambed of a deep, canyonlike wadi. There seemed to be more light down here then on the desert surface, as though moonlight can be canalized and collected in a bowl. Above us, an inky darkness swallowed any object close by, but down here, where there was light, the rocks cast shadows and we saw escaping lizards, snakes, and mice slither and dart and bound away. We saw a fox bathed in light. Once we looked up to see a passel of fierce-looking, hideous black snouts and glowing dolls' eyes peering down over the wadi's rim, and for a time they trailed us along the wadi's ridge but Bachshi lifted his hand, Micah braked, and after gathering rocks Bachshi silently aimed and struck several of the pariah dogs. They vanished soundlessly. Then we continued on, rising and falling along the irregular, jagged track and could still see occasional flares to the northwest.

We came to a point directly southeast of the flares, where the wadi's right bank dipped and widened enough for a jeep or even a truck to navigate through, and we took it up to a dense cluster of rock formations to our left, the desert yawning open to our right. Now we traveled overland, Bachshi keeping our course flush with the rocks, so that we could move and blend undetected. We sustained a slow, methodical pace, our engine a barely perceptible growl. Above us the blue-black sky held planet-size stars glimmering diamondlike and cold.

Then we were out upon the plain, exposed, the last rock formation overshot and the flares falling far off in the distance to our right and in the north a faint amber-colored glow that we all knew to be the Israeli town of Kadima, shockingly close, within easy striking range of the marauders. This heightened my sense of urgency, and I too began to wonder if the major wasn't right. Maybe on this one, Bachshi didn't know what he was doing.

He held up his hand. He slipped from the jeep, leaned close to the ground, shone a pocket flashlight on something. He switched off the flashlight, moved farther along, shone it again. This he repeated until he was more than two hundred meters off. Then he returned at a trot and got in the jeep and said: "They are here, on the plain, not far. I am sure of it."

"Together?"

"No. They have buried their gear somewhere close. And then they divided up. They are lying on the ground, maybe covered over with scrub brush. Or a lightweight camouflage tarp: that too is possible. But they will not hide for long. In the early morning they will find their way to their gear, collect it, and they will make an assault. I do not know the area north. Where is the nearest settlement?"

"Yad Kadosh," said Micah. "I have a cousin, Yaron, who once lived there, but now he's in Kadima. It's about four kilometers over that ridge, there. Due east."

"Then that is where they will make the attack. You should call the settlement to advise them of this."

Micah did so.

"What do they say?" I asked.

"They are skeptical. They said they've got three platoons of troops there. How would anyone try to attack?"

"We should advise the major." Micah held the handset up to me. "You talk to him."

The major received my update in terse silence.

"And this is what Bachshi says?"

"Yes."

"And you?"

"I told you: his guess is better than mine. I don't have a clue."

"You are nine kilometers northwest of our operational grid. You're completely outside it, in fact. Are you still part of our operation, or are you three exploring each other's assholes?"

"Bachshi thinks we should move due west. I agree. We've sent an advisory to Yad Kadosh. In fact, we're heading there."

The major said nothing. Then: "What are we doing northeast of you if the infiltration is moving due west?"

"It looks like you've contained it."

"Contained it?" His voice uncharacteristically rose: "What am I, Bachshi's fucking decoy?" A pause. Then: "I'm sorry. My nerves are . . . I haven't slept in days. Problems in the house. My kid is sick. The little girl. *Nurit*."

"I'm sorry to hear that." I hesitated. Then: "Something serious?"

"I don't know. They found something. Something with a medical name. Remember that shaking in her hands I told you about? And now I can't get back. Headquarters wants me here."

We shared a silence. Then the major said, "Does he want a platoon sent over to assist and meet you at Yad Kadosh? They can come double-time and throw up a cordon due south of where you see Kadima . . . "

"Do we want help?" I asked Bachshi, not covering the mouth-piece.

"No," said Bachshi. "No help." I relayed the answer to the major, though I knew he had heard.

"I don't know," he said. "The odds that you'll find them are poor. But if you do, the odds that they'll kill you are great. They are three and you are three. But they have the element of surprise. I don't know who's stationed at Yad Kadosh. I'll ask. Wait there." After a minute, he returned to the line. "It's Be'eri. So he's got a full company of APCs. If I tell him to go fishing, he'll put half his machines in the field. You'll find yourself caught in a crossfire between them and the terrorists or them and us and the terrorists and probably the fucking security guards at the gates too and also everybody's mother-in-law thrown in for good measure. This is a shit situation you are in. Can you think of one good reason why I shouldn't pull you back?"

"Bachshi seems to understand the situation. He feels he has it in hand. I have a lot of faith in him."

"Faith," said the major, tired. Then: "OK. But promise to report to me if you find something. Repeat: do not act until first reporting in to me. Promise me."

"Right."

I communicated all this to Bachshi, who absorbed it with the same disdainful look that he had worn when handling the hare. And something else. I had noticed it all through the mission but did not know what it was. The shadows under his eyes. They hadn't been there before. And his look of not just guarded pride but a kind of despairing insolence. Something was wrong, I felt, but there was no time to ask.

It was not long after our contact with the major that we saw two of them through the killer scope's green field: shapeless lumps in the turf, set fifty meters apart. There were many boulders and they blended in easily. They lay hidden under the hard-edged creases and folds of tarps, which had somewhat molded to their forms. One lay asleep, curled on his side, and the other had formed a kind of cocoon around himself, from which the barrel of his Kalatchnikov poked out. His face, hooded, was a small bearded, yellowish triangle. A sequence of boulders formed a partial screen and redoubt. But in all respects it was poor camouflage. They could easily duck from one boulder to the next in a firefight, but only if they weren't first surprised. In fact, their position was surprisingly amateur.

Still, the elements of speed and surprise were critical if we were to succeed in their capture or elimination. Ali set up his MAG with Micah alongside to feed ammo. Bachshi and I set up the crossfire from a slight incline due west of their position. We advanced very slowly to our posts, crouched low; arranged ourselves with noiseless, slow-motion movements.

We lined them up in our sights. I focused on the sentry. And then, all at once, we opened up with long bursts. And even when their tarps were in pieces, fiery fragments drifting in the wind or flapping off of what remained of their corpses, Ali was firing still, and through his white hot barrel I saw the pulse of red rounds pump sluggishly into the two decimated carcasses. And even when the firing stopped, we stormed the position by assault, firing at each corpse, followed by Micah's 202 grenade launcher. We took no chances. And we lit up the night, counting on it that the third terrorist would see the whole gruesome show and know, seized by panic, how completely alone he now was, for both his comrades were certainly dead. The idea was to take him prisoner with no shot fired and find out who had sent them.

He was discovered, though, we later learned, three kilometers from Yad Kadosh. The spotlight of a helicopter gunship fixed him, and they broadcast over loudspeakers an offer of safe conduct if he laid down his arms on the desert floor and dropped to his knees with hands clasped behind his head. His barking gun disrespectfully declined. The gunship replied. Kill time: ten seconds.

For failure to consult the major before launching our attack, we were each given a long-winded verbal reprimand but then sent on forty-eight hours' leave — Bachshi to his tribe's encampment and I to Jerusalem, which I rode to, appropriately enough, I thought, in the caged rear of a jeep from the Border Patrol's canine corp., for I felt somewhat like a dog, as I was on my way to fuck another man's wife.

II

I knew that Dotan was up north with his unit in a communications truck on the Beirut-Damascus Road, getting the shit shelled out of him, so I went directly to their second-floor Rehavia flat in Jerusalem. I had first met him three years ago at a party in this very home, when I was freshly mustered out of regular army service. I had not yet been assigned to a unit in the reserves and there had been time to kick around the Jerusalem arts scene, meet folks, make connections, figure things out. One night I found myself getting tanked at a raging all-night party and after everyone else left I sat at Dotan's kitchen table, drinking with him until daybreak. Together we had knocked back Arak, smoked up packs of Time cigarettes, and exchanged slurred anecdotes about the abstract expressionists, whom we both revered.

We liked each other. He was slender and refined, with warm black eyes and close-cropped hair, and he dressed all in punk-rock black with black and white sneakers. He looked like a Tibetan monk hooked on Iggy Pop. That night I also noticed how hard I found it not to stare at his wife, Maya, who would dissapear into the bedroom for long stretches and then suddenly reappear at Dotan's shoulder, nursing a tumbler, leaning close to his stud-pierced ear, looking sinfully pretty and smiling at everything I said.

She was tall and stood a little wobbily on these crazy, endearing, old-school white high heels, which seemed a touch desperate — it was heartbreaking, really: they tried so hard and were badly scuffed, as though relics passed down to her by generations of disappointed women.

She wore this flimsy green halter that showed off her braless, high breasts and creamy, flat belly, and her long, slender legs were draped in mauve-colored pants. Her reddish blond henna-stained hair fell around her cheekbones like a stage curtain from which two sparkling, mischievous eyes peeked out at me, the charmed audience. She had a wide, red, kissable mouth. And she had rather strange hands, I thought. When she spoke they spelled out pretty gestures and signs in kinetic arabesque that I longed to decode; a language all her own, and more fascinating to me than bloody legends of famous fallen painters. In her way, she made me feel that Dotan and I were just a couple of boring drunks who could use a lesson or two in joy.

That night, she showed us. She was so lovely, and Dotan and I laughed at her antics. She got very ripped. She went stumbling around the room on those high heels, spinning her arms and giggling like a young girl gone mad on her first glass of champagne. "You have a nice wife," I told Dotan, and he smiled. "I have a crazy wife," he said wistfully as she ran to their bedroom and emerged with a sample of what she called "Really Very Real Anti-social Social Realism." This was a five foot by two foot canvas stenciled with hundreds of red lips. "A visual memoir," she explained, swaying a bit and staring, red-eyed, past my shoulder at Dotan, "a private history of withheld kisses," and the mood quickly soured,

Dotan shutting down and sitting there, dragging on a cigarette. "You'd better go" is all he said.

I had exited hurriedly, leaving behind my contact info, and the very next day, all contrite, he phoned to apologize and our friendship commenced. But now it had come down to this: he up there and Maya stroking my hair with both hands and I kneeling in his bedroom to store my gear and weapon under their marriage bed. And she was all that I cared for, and I tried real hard not to think of him up there, catching hell. Their home was done up in African tribal kitsch. I had never before noticed its ugliness. I took off my clothes and then her clothes and fucked his wife, my lover.

Maya and I were at it all night. With her hair wrapped in my fist, I kissed the back of her neck, softly, for an hour, while penetrating her from behind. Then I lay beside her, her hair still wrapped in one fist, stroking her thighs with my free hand, taking her nipples in my mouth. I only had to softly graze her vaginal lips with my cock to bring her to climax. I then entered her and rammed her as hard as I could until she came a second time. Then she pushed me back on the pillows and took me in her mouth and caused me to explode. It was better than talking about ourselves or what we were doing. We had nothing to say to each other about that. They were unpleasant subjects, and we wished to keep things pleasant. It was pleasant to fuck while around us war raged and our personal lives went to pieces. Nonetheless, there was unpleasantness. Her marriage was unraveling. All our friends hated us. The phone rang in the flat. Dotan calling. She let it ring. Her revenge for ten years of sexless marriage. The phone rang twenty, thirty times. This was not pleasant to listen to. I lay in the bed, the rings echoing in the flat while she heated up a pot of leftover beef noodles, and we ate out of it with big spoons, sitting naked and cross-legged on the bed, facing each other, the phone ringing over and over, us reaching out to touch each other's faces, to smile, but inside feeling sick, anxious, depleted.

"Tell me what you did down there this time," she said.

"You don't want to know," I said.

"You bastard," she said.

So I told her everything.

When I was done, she looked rather shocked. "And when they were lying there," she said softly, "you also squeezed the trigger of your gun?"

"They were waiting to attack Israel. So, yes, I did."

"But it sounds like it was Ali who did most of the shooting. With the . . . what's it called . . . the big gun?"

"MAG."

"Yes, the MAG."

"Ali fired a lot. But we fired too."

"How do you know if you hit?"

"Something is hit, you know."

"But maybe when they are hit by your bullets they are already dead."

"Yes," I said quickly. "That's very probable."

"Do you really think so?" she asked me carefully.

What I said would be very important to what she chose to believe about me from then on.

"I can't be completely sure," I said, to leave some margin of doubt and so support the "probability" in her mind that not a single round fired by me had ever entered living human flesh. Because I now understood that she couldn't imagine me capable of both killing someone and making love to her.

She nodded and curled up, holding herself. "I don't think you actually kill anyone."

"It is over pretty fast."

"Do you go to look afterward?"

"No," I lied.

"So, you don't actually see them up close?"

"Not really, no. Ali, Bachshi, and Micah, they laid them out. I just stayed behind to monitor the perimeter. There was still a third man out there and we weren't sure, you see, where he was. So I stood guard."

"Yes, I do see," she said.

I told those lies very well.

She wore only a pale green halter; her soft, reddish blond triangle of pubic hair peeked out trustingly from its hem. Her normally mischievous eyes were fawnlike with trust, the way they got when I was inside her, leaning on my elbows, navel to navel, cradled by her thighs; when I peered down directly and possessively into her wide-eyed gaze, which made her get very wet and dilate to the maximum width of her sex, open herself completely to me, the intimacy of our rocking embrace, my full possession of her.

But looking into that gaze I had never before lied as I now lied. Because there had been no perimeter. We had discharged all our weapons at them and then run stumbling and still shooting in a drunk-feeling state of elation up to the bodies. They were on fire, large shreds of flaming tarp aglow and flapping in the wind, like burning flags. Countless rounds had scored direct hits on what remained of their decimated trunks, which were barely recognizable as human, all blasted apart and one, its legs on fire, black-scorched from the waist up, smoke pouring from its caved-in face. The ground nearby was littered with body parts, soaked in their blood. It felt sick and vicious to lie to her wide-eyed gaze while recalling the stench of their burning flesh, and in order to cope my insides sneered at her, at us, at life itself, with a kind of bitter satisfaction, and her pretty face struck me as hopelessly stupid for believing the rubbish coming from my mouth.

"And that is the first time you ever shot at someone?"

"Yes."

Then we passed a cigarette back and forth in silence. Again the phone rang. It rang and rang. Maya stared at it. Then she looked at me, the phone still ringing. "I can't believe that you are a soldier," she said. "I can imagine Dotan as a soldier, but not you."

"I'm not a soldier now," I said, taking her nipple in my mouth to try to stay the sickness inside.

"Hmm. Not one now, no," she said. "But then you'll go back and be one again, and I can't imagine it. I bet you're really one very kind soldier."

"You seem to know all about it," I said.

"I do, darling, I know all about you," she said proudly.

I didn't say anything. Removed my lips. Moved away. Far away, in my head, back to the burning plain, the smoldering lumps of death. Reached for the cigarette, drew on it with a frown.

"Tell me you love me, sweet one," she said.

I kept silent.

"Please," she said.

I ground the half-smoked butt into the ashtray. Rolled over onto my shoulder, facing the room.

She placed her fingertips on the small of my back, and it made me want to scream. Her pleading voice came over my shoulder. I felt her breasts press into my back, her chin rest on my shoulder. Then her arm encircled me. "Why does it have to be like this? I don't understand. It's only one little thing to say. It will make me feel better."

"Somehow I don't think so," I said nicely.

"But I want you to tell me. I need to hear it from you."

"Nonsense," I said pleasantly. The expression on my face was not pleasant, though.

"But sweet one . . ." she said.

I rolled over. "Let's not talk it all to death, Maya. Here I am. Here you are. And he's up there. Isn't it all as it should be?"

"Are you sure?"

"Yes," I said. "Absolutely."

"I've taken such a big risk, doing this with you. It's so little to ask in return."

"Is that all you get from me? Some sentimental words? Don't I give you something more than just fucking words?"

So, feeling my anger, as I intended her to, she relented. I had gotten very good down there in Gaza at making my anger immediately felt. We drank and fucked and talked all night of other things than ourselves, and it was as it had been before, as I had dreamed about things being when I was down there in Gaza, waiting to come here, and she didn't ask me again to tell her about what I couldn't articulate, which was, for me, a great relief. I couldn't imagine ever uttering the word "love" to anyone. I was very glad to go to bed with her but didn't want all that other stuff, not the verbal part of it, anyway, and really, not any of it. It was just a lot of shit, I felt, all the talk, of forever, of "Us," and I wanted things to remain nice and clear and simple. Of course, they weren't very nice and certainly not so clear, but dusk was falling in the window, the room growing dark, and I drew the covers up and dozed off, pressed against her warm thigh, satisfied with the cold free fall in my head.

When I awoke I saw that her eyes couldn't seem to make me out. It was as if a switch had been thrown in her brain. She cradled a nearly empty bottle. She gazed at me with eyes glazed by a film of whimsically brutal intention, an alien, murderous light. Reaching past me for her cigarettes, which lay on the night table, she bumped me hard with her shoulder. Sneered. Lit up. Dragged. Exhaled. Stood up, and as though she weighed three hundred pounds and not one hundred and fifteen, drew on a kimono over her nudity and padded heavily in her bare feet on a wobbly course across the bedroom's hardwood floor.

She disappeared around the bend into the kitchen, where I heard her rummaging furiously, opening and slamming cupboard doors. And this was followed by a loud crash. Then another. Dishes smashed, one after the next, hurtling at the ground, swept off shelves by her dainty manicured hand, plates destructing on the floor in a rage of shattered porcelain.

I couldn't move. Lay there frozen, the sound somehow more jarring than gunfire.

In the kitchen the carnage continued: glasses, bowls, cups, platters, casserole dishes, vases, childhoods, nights of pleasure, adulthoods, futures, pasts, sanities, dreams, by the dozens, suiciding to the ground.

Calmly, I rose and went to stand in the doorway. She was crawling like a nightmare commando on hands and knees among hundreds of sharp-edged shards, bloodying herself. Gathering some fragments into a pile, she began to hammer her wrists against the slicing edges, drawing blood. As I stood there watching, I felt dead inside.

At that moment came a knock on the door, which I presumed to be neighbors. I was wrong: police. Two, just standing there.

"We've had complaints," said the shorter one, with a trim black mustache, swarthy, pockmarked skin, and curious, almost gentle liquid black eyes that radiated a certain empathy. The other was tall, slender, and blond, with a deadpan, unreadable face.

"What is going on?" the nice one asked.

"Going on?" I said, hearing my own voice, its casual air of nonchalance, as from a great remove.

Nice nodded to Not-Nice and cautiously they edged past me toward the kitchen, slowly, glancing to the left, the right, as they moved, hands hovering near their holsters. The light emitted a brownish gold radiance that cast Maya in a bronze, shadowy aura as she hammered her wrists against the glass, the black-looking blood streaking everything and cheeks, arms, legs, crosshatched with jagged scratches, and gleaming, powdery glass splinters embedded in the pores of her pale white skin.

They stood there. Not-Nice, whose face now showed a lot of emotion, said: "What are you going to do?"

"Do?" I said.

Nice said, a little coolly: "I suggest that you get her to a hospital."

"Sure. You help me get her there?"

"No," said Nice, all business suddenly. "We can't do this." That's all. And they just turned and left without any further talk, though, to his credit, Not-Nice looked back once at Maya with a crushed expression on his face.

I didn't take her to a hospital, though. When she was done with her wrists, I lifted her from the floor. She didn't resist. She sagged, though, and God, was so heavy as I dragged her across the floor to the bedroom, trailing blood and broken glass behind us like the viscous, glistening spoor left in the wake of a snail sliming along the ground.

I rolled her into bed, tilted back her head, pried open her lips and poured down more whiskey and then some brandy, and she sucked on it greedily, blindly, until she was blacked out, completely unconscious. Then, I undressed her and, inch by inch, examined her cuts.

There were no deep ones, despite the plentiful blood. Though quite ugly, they would not require stitches. All in all, she hadn't lost more than a pint of blood, I estimated, the amount normally donated to blood banks.

With tweezers, I plucked out the embedded glass, and there was a lot. With a wet cloth soaked in warm, soapy water I washed her down and then rinsed her and found more vicious splinters, and put Mercurochrome on the worst cuts, and, little by little — a Band-Aid here, a swipe there — I reduced the seeming horror to a manageable scale.

That night I set myself up to sleep in the living room. I stacked her very best books next to the sofa, for reassurance; brought over a fresh bottle of Courvoisier VSOP, a snifter, a pack of English Silks, and stayed up until three or four in the morning, hunched over J. M. Coetzee's masterpiece *Waiting for the Barbarians,* sipping my drink, smoking reflectively, trying not to cry, searching for some kind of meaning in the lamplit curling arabesques of smoke until I couldn't keep my eyes open any longer and passed out.

Over the next day I "nursed her back to health," as they say in the Brit novels she so loved. She was fragile; her hands shook. She sat in her nightie on the bathroom floor with her shoulder leaned against the toilet bowl, throwing up. She tried to light a cigarette but couldn't strike a blessed match. I helped her back into bed, fed her aspirins, drew the blinds. She slept. On her instructions, I called her best friend, Ora, who came right over to assist. Moshe, Ora's husband, was with his tank division in the Golan and wasn't having much of a war, really, beyond sitting up there next to Syria, maneuvering his tank around, popping off a round now and then, roasting mud coffee and complaining about the boredom. So Ora had some emotional reserves to spare for Maya.

She spent that entire day at Maya's bedside. That night, she slept on a cot in the "study," the nearly empty room in which Maya kept an IBM Selectric typewriter and piles of unused clothes that lay in heaps on the floor. I remained at my post on the sofa. While

Maya slept Ora and I shared a joint and a bottle of wine. We threw on a Joni Mitchell album and sat slumped side by side on the big enfolding sofa, passing the joint back and forth, reminiscing about our childhoods and laughing gently. We fell asleep slumped against each other's shoulders.

It is possible that Maya awoke in the middle of the night, saw us there, and got the wrong idea, for some time before morning she took down a bottle of Irish whiskey from the liquor cabinet and polished it off. This she violently brought up in the foyer, on her hands and knees, by which time Ora and I were stationed over her, trying to coax her into the bathroom. She ignored us. She made it to her feet and stood there swaying, eyes varnished with violence. She staggered into the living room and over to a big round blue lamp painted with orange and yellow African tribal motifs and with a swing of her clenched fist toppled it over, the lightbulb popping with a ghoulish white flash, like a demon's smile in a cave.

"Maya, no, don't, darling," Ora pleaded.

"Darling," snarled Maya. She looked at me and slurred, "What are you really doing down there to those Arabs, you motherfucking pig! You're not a soldier! You're a fucking policeman! Go-wan, policeman, say loveme darling, you fucking pig!" These last words she screamed, and as she turned to the glass bookcase she lifted the giant obsidian ashtray from off the coffee table and hurled it crashing through the glass cabinet doors. Books spilled out. A row of knickknacks crashed to the ground.

Ora looked at me, terrified. "Oh my God."

I shrugged. "Absolutely nothing to do."

For the next half hour we just stood there, Ora weeping, watching Maya repeat her routine of the night before. This time, though, there were no police.

When she was done, we picked her up and washed off blood and swept glass and at the end of it all, with Maya rolled into blankets, fast asleep (we thought of tying her hands to the bedposts but decided against it), Ora and I found ourselves clinging to each other, crying, and then on the sofa making furious, tearful love. The telephone rang and rang, perhaps Dotan, under bombardment, calling from Lebanon, or Moshe, bored with popping off rounds at the scenery. Ora climaxed with a cry and the telephone ringing. After, she pleaded, with the telephone still jingling crazily: "Don't go away, don't move — oh, God, please, stay here in me." That night, she slept on her cot and I sat naked in the living room, chain-smoking, reading Coetzee. Eventually, the telephone stopped.

The next day, Maya, Ora, and I all sat around the kitchen table together, picking at our breakfasts. The phone rang: Dotan or Moshe. Maya's eyes shifted from Ora to me and back to Ora, and for an instant I feared that she knew what had transpired. Perhaps she did, but it was, I could tell, inadmissible for her. Her suspicions dived deep and disappeared. I was in uniform, my gun on the floor beside me, and I was going back to Gaza.

"I need to speak to her," I said. Ora, with a close-faced shrug, rose, took her cigarette from the ashtray, and went into the living room. I glanced angrily at the telephone. It was ringing and must already have rung fifty times. This was Dotan, for sure, somewhere phoning out of his communications truck, unable to reach his wife. I wanted to rip the cord from the wall. "Why don't you disconnect the phone?" I said. "Unplug it from the wall."

"No," she said. "I like it." The cigarette trembling in her fingers went to her lips. She drew, leaned her head back, exhaled. "It's reassuring," she said, her hair stumbling around her shoulders. Small, jittery silver fish earrings hung from her ears.

"What kind of reassurance do you need?"

"Nothing you can give, sweet one. Please don't try to be reassuring. You're not the reassuring type. It doesn't suit you, not even a little. I can see that now. It's all right. I love you even more."

It made my stomach twist to hear those words. I kissed her on the forehead. "I'll try to call you from down there."

"No, don't bother, sweet one. You know you won't. You don't ever unless you're coming, and even then it's only because you just want to fuck. And he might be back this time, you know. Then what? If you come, call Ora. She'll tell you if it's OK. And she'll contact me. All right?"

"All right," I said. And added: "That's a fucking hell of a thing to say about us."

But we both knew that it was true.

Ora and Moshe were our only real friends at the time — and actually, they were Maya's more than mine — before her drinking took the turn it did. We usually spent good times together, eating steak, shooting beers, and, as the nights wore on, pulling on whiskey and brandy, blowing dope, and then dancing till dawn in this greasy little café we knew of along Agrippa Street, moving to music that played from a scratchy radio. It was called Chez Uri's, a nice little dump, with clusters of furtive types hunched in the corners, a few whores backlit by cheap lightbulbs and blue grill smoke rolling through the counter window. Occasionally, a taxi pulled up and killed its lights and the driver ordered food in a loud voice. Inside, the cigarette smoke lingered over a battlefield of slow-dancing couples. The owner, a fat, balding, mustached Moroccan with velvety brown heavy-lidded eyes clapped hands and nodded approvingly. It felt good to hold Maya, to be held by her. "My sorcerer," she whispered. No wonder. Her husband hadn't fucked her in ten years. Ora and Moshe didn't dance. They sat smoking and staring intently at the wooden floor. Moshe, a big, broad, swarthy man with a large mole on his right cheek, would occasionally glance up at us with a grim smile.

Only months before that, when Maya and I were just contemplating adultery, Moshe had seemed to think our getting together was a good idea. Her now estranged husband, Dotan, had been my best friend and close to Moshe. We had all been such good friends, the very best of friends, and we had been together all the time in Maya and Dotan's kitchen, smoking, drinking, talking, planning our futures. We had all worked together producing a multimedia cultural program at the Israel Museum, and it had been great fun and we had staked our futures on the collaboration. Often the newspapers wrote of us, portrayed us as the bohemian cultural elite of Jerusalem. We were the stuff of gossip columns and cultural pages, with photos of us all standing together, shoulder to shoulder, slouched and aloof-looking, the bad boys and girls of Israeli culture, though really we weren't very bad at all or even that exciting. For excitement, the women, Maya and Ora and Laura and Shirley and Sylvie, went to the Turkish steam baths to do each other's nails and put henna in their hair. The guys — I, Dotan and Moshe and the human rights lawyer we called Australian Bill, and sometimes the sculptor Danny Ben-Ami and the playwright Roy Isacowitz and the journalist Robert Rosenberg (husband of the lovely artist Sylvie) — sat around with booze and cigarettes, talking a lot of heady shit. We were happy. Ed Codish, the poet, hung around with us at times, getting drunk and looking like John Berryman. And the composer Steve Horenstein hung with us. And the famous American poet David Rosenberg and his companion, the Israeli novelist Michal Govrin, were also around. We wore jeans and checked shirts and T-shirts and looked like abstract expressionist painters. Sometimes the high-powered kibbutznik, editor, and politician David Twersky went slumming with us between stints of reserves in the artillery stationed around

Beirut. And sometimes Israel's greatest painter, Ivan Schwebel, joined our clique and challenged us to one-armed push-up contests. Dotan was a big Jackson Pollack fan, though not much of a painter. But when Maya got on his nerves, he was silent and morose in the way of Pollack, and he kept a cigarette burning down in his clamped up lips. Maya, though, was no homely Lee Krasner, and she was a wonderful artist. She was a Canadian-born blondish redhead, tall and slender, pale and viciously intelligent and too beautiful for her own good. She liked to drink; she was the big drinker of our group. She led the way. While we talked, she drank. Her drunken talk was often sweet and silly but also sometimes wry and self-indulgently cynical. And when we awoke from our blackouts and we could not remember a single word uttered the night before, Maya was still at it. We had to babysit her in the kitchen, as she had the worst hangovers of all — pathetic affairs, really. She hunched all pale and doughy with her hair hanging in sweat-damp strings and shaking so badly she couldn't light her cigarettes. And really, that wasn't even the worst of it. The worst was when Maya drank alone. Only Dotan knew about that then. It was his secret, and then it became mine . . .

By the time I met them all I had already gone through the regular army and had enjoyed it. After basic, there had been combat duty up north and though certainly that entailed some grave risks they had not been of the sort that would deeply affect one. Rather, they were of the kind that are, in their fashion, fun. All-night ambushes in blackface at remote border spots. Machine-gunning jeep patrols along the terrorist-infiltrated south Lebanese frontier. Foot chases after suspects through the snaking alleys of fly-choked kasbahs and watching Katyusha rockets trail black smoke through the thin pale blue sky. Sometimes the rockets fell close by, slamming to earth with a spray of fire and dirt. That scared you, but that too was all right. It was a sobering kind of scare when the mists parted for an instant to reveal the truth about soldiering. Then you felt sick inside, for you saw that soldiering is a murderous business. But soon the mists returned, quick and obscuring, and it all become again a kind of game you played, and I like games. For in a game one believes that things like injury and death don't really occur — except perhaps to others. It's great fun though to live in the shadow of their threat.

This is what I told myself in those days after the army, when I got together with Maya and Dotan and we all went to work together at the museum, doing the shows. This is what I told myself, sitting drunk at their table, head ducked slightly to the left in a fake boxing bob-and-weave pose, a scar under my left eye, a cigarette dangling from my lips, and a sneer — yes, a sneer — on my face. It's just a game. A game played against a video demon.

I was sneering at the demon in my skull, shadowboxing it. It was a demon with its face obscured by the sort of keffiyeh head wrap worn by the terrorists, the space for eyes a dark triangle with the bottomless blackness of a well, and from which cold pupils peered out. But whose eyes were those? In Maya and Dotan's kitchen, still their friend and guest, I was like a feral cat that a steam shovel had plowed under and gutted and left crushed with a sneer on its whiskered muzzle. Crushed but sneering. And quite drunk.

And we drank all the time, for this was in a time of the static, never-ending Lebanon war, of soldiers routinely dying daily in those fields and streets, of terrorist bomb and shooter attacks on our city boulevards and buses and of massive Katyusha rocket bombardments against our towns in the north and Israeli-Syrian artillery duels and between F-16s and MiGs in the cold white skies over the Bekaa Valley and us in Jerusalem drinking. In southern Lebanon were constant ambush bombings and in the Gaza Strip Israeli soldiers were shot dead in towns and markets and refugee camps and in Jerusalem, we drank. Our so-called peace partner Egypt nightly discharged small-arms fire and even an occasional shoulder-held rocket at our troops and in Jerusalem we smoked hash. All this was what we thought of as "peace." Such times are a blessing, we told ourselves. We could handle it all. And even if a neighboring rogue state nakedly decided to develop a nuclear reactor with the declared intention of dropping an A-bomb on our heads, we just sent over the boys in the F-16s to knock it out, which is what we did in Iraq, and that was that. Life was easy. And we drank and got stoned through it all.

Thus, we in Jerusalem lived not as if in a state of constant war — which it was by anyone's definition — but rather in some sort of between-the-wars, bohemian Paris mind-set of art, literature, and happy drunkenness at the edge of impending but as yet indecipherable doom. Disaster had already come, but we didn't yet know it. We had a big happy circle of artists and writers and so forth and we lived it up with heroic desperation. Then the Lebanon war, impossible to win, escalated — more troops were needed, and predictably it all fell apart. We men were called away to reserves constantly and back and forth we went, from army to home, home to army, ping-ponging from "normal" to insane.

Yet I had not yet stolen Dotan's wife from him; I had only gone to reserves and been assigned to duties in Gaza. Micah, our driver, took a snapshot back then of the four of us: me, Uri, Brandt, and Bachshi, posed alongside an armored car in Gaza City, during a pause in our "police" duties. But I don't have that photo. It's just imprinted on my brain. And by that time, the sneer was glazed on my face. It could not then be effaced, except, perhaps, by scorch marks. And I was so desperate to remove it. More desperate than I had ever been in my entire life. And I felt, strongly, that Maya was the key.

III

It was good to see Bachshi, Ali, and Micah. I had missed them more than I knew. I had been with Maya for only three days but the contrast between the lives I lived in Gaza and Jerusalem was so jarring that it left me feeling shaken about who I really was. Only constant action could erase this.

Bachshi and I immediately set to launching a lottery among the platoons, and then, amazingly, as though his own manhood had been challenged, Ali challenged Bachshi to a contest of speed and reflexes, claiming loudly and publicly that he could snatch a hare from an even greater distance than Bachshi, and in only half the time. I did not see how this was possible but did not challenge Ali's claim. If anything, I encouraged him to increase his boasting as the pool shot up to positively astronomical sums.

A kind of fever gripped the division. Two more hares were caught by local Bedouin, who had heard about the lottery and sold them to us, so we now had a stable. Pagi, the mechanic, set up an indoor arena in a dining tent, which he ringed with tarpaulins to prevent escape. He lovingly raked every single stone from the ground and covered the floor with a layer of fine white sand that had been shipped up to him from the coastal outposts in the sandbags that we used to reinforce machine gun nests in the cliffs above the beaches.

We were given light assignments, both because of our recent firefight and to permit Bachshi and Ali to train in whatever fashion they deemed necessary. They behaved strangely for competitors and were together virtually all the time.

For instance, when we were all four ordered to visit the battalion psychiatrists in Beersheva, to be checked for any residual negative psychological aftereffects of the firefight near Yad Kadosh,

Bachshi and Ali demanded to be interviewed together. Micah and I could overhear them in the psychiatrist's cubicle, each praising the other's combat performance. "No! No! I am sure both kills belong to Ali!" we heard Bachshi say. "He had the MAG! My weapon is a slingshot compared to his. He deserves a decoration."

"Have you been recommended for a decoration?" asked the woman psychiatrist, a major in rank.

After a pause, Ali said: "Of course there will be decorations. Do you see these ribbons? This is from the Green Patrol. And this is from action in the Litani. And here, do you see this? I earned this in combat along the Jordanian border. I helped to kill four infiltrators. We chased them a whole day and night in the caves around Beit Shemesh. It was the most dangerous thing I had ever done."

"Do you ever feel any remorse or guilt, Ali, any shame, for what you have done?"

"I don't want to take credit for my brother Bachshi's great heroism," we heard him reply, sidestepping the question. He added: "Your leadership got us there, Bachshi." Ali then turned to the psychiatrist: "It is Bachshi's instincts that got us there. He has a nose like a hare. Can smell anything."

"Bachshi," she said, "are you proud of what you do?"

There was angry silence.

"You seem angry," the major said to Bachshi.

More silence. Micah and I rose, sidled over to a spot in the maze of cubicles where we could spy Ali and Bachshi in profile. Bachshi's face was hard-set, his eyes narrowed in distaste. Ali, on the other hand, was grinning broadly in evident mockery of his friend's sudden bad mood.

"It is nothing." Ali laughed convivially. "He is upset because I have compared him to a hare and because someday soon I will win a contest of skills involving much money, including his own."

"You will win nothing," spit Bachshi. "When the hare sees you, it will lift its leg like a dog to piss and still have plenty of time to run."

Ali laughed loudly and the psychiatrist tried without success to return the discussion to the matter of the terrorists' deaths. But they were quite proud of the killings and didn't want to talk about nonsense like remorse and guilt.

Micah and I were not as proud and did not have much to say. We did not speak about it with each other at all, and we each in turn shrugged and stared at the floor and smiled emptily at her questions and looked baffled. It was a relief to get out of there.

Back at the base, others wanted to talk about the kills. Ephraim, tall, lean, muscular and dark, entered our ten-man tent dripping wet from a cold shower out back near the latrines and stood there carefully toweling his naked privates with all the solemnity of an artist putting the finishing touch on a great masterpiece. Then he stood there slapping talc onto his balls and cheeks with relish and then snapped a bold gold chain bearing a mezuzah around his neck. The whole time he kept his eyes fixed first on me, then Micah. Then he said to Micah, his voice husky with awe: "It's a good thing, what you did. We're all proud of you."

"Thanks," said Micah noncommittally.

"It must be hard. You must think about it. But there's nothing to think about, huh? This is what we are here to do, huh?"

"Yes," said Micah, "whatever you say."

It was clear that Ephraim wished to somehow partake of what we had done by asserting his membership with us in the same unit, imply that it could just have easily been him as us. But this was not so. It could never have been him, though neither of us would ever say as much to him. We would not tell him that it could not have happened to him because of his poor relations with the Bedouin trackers, the gashashim, as they are called.

Because Ephraim often belittled the Bedouin trackers behind their backs. He mocked their uniforms, which were, admittedly, a hodgepodge of elements from different corps: tunics from the paratroopers, berets from the Golani Brigade, desert boots from reconnaissance, fatigue pants from infantry. And they carried mine probes like British parade ground swagger sticks. Half the battle ribbons on their chests were traded for or purchased. They wore jump wings, though few of them had so much as hopped off a helicopter. They were, in fact, afraid, on the whole, of airborne missions. "Yes, they'll lead you to the action," I had heard Ephraim loudly jeer within earshot of the trackers, "but once the battle starts they run for their lives. You can't depend on Bedouin to fight."

And there was that time during a break in coastline shore patrol when we had left our jeep to huddle with Ephraim in a flimsy shack, to get out of the gale-force wind and sip a cup of hot black mud coffee, which Ephraim prepared with a craft and a devotion to detail worthy of an artisan, as though he were a mendicant in some Droog guild of caffeine imbibers.

When he poured it out into our hard blue plastic mugs he searched our eyes intently for hints of ingratitude. We were all very grateful, though. Except for Bachshi, whose people believed that gratitude is something to be felt not by the guest but by the host — that serving visitors is a great privilege. And truly, there is no hospitality to rival that of the Bedouin, who will share with you everything under his tent. So Bachshi's hard-etched, narrow nut brown face yielded nothing to Ephraim, his unreadable eyes fixed coolly on the floor. At which Ephraim flinched, his feelings stung. He placed the empty saucepan back on the tripod and sat down to sip his coffee and study Bachshi with an economy of interest. The Bedouin easily ignored him. He wore his distancing mask, and the degree to which Ephraim vanished from his view was palpable — a solid wall of utter dismissal. Ephraim's yellowish, sleepless eyes roamed over the Bedouin's face, tracing the rigid, shelflike bones of his cheeks, the hawkish beak of his nose, the fierce calm of his implacable brown eyes.

"Hey, Bedu."

Bachshi looked up at Ephraim without any trace of discernible feeling. You could not tell what he thought of him or anyone or anything for that matter.

"Tell us, Bedu, who make the best soldiers in the world?"

The way Ephraim said it, it was hard not to smile; we all struggled to suppress our grins.

Bachshi said simply, stiltedly, in that icy formal way: "The Bedu makes the best soldier."

"But the world says it's the Israeli soldier. And you're in the Israeli army. So, what does that make you?"

"It makes me a Bedu in the Israeli army."

"But are you the best soldier? And if so, as what? Bedu or Israeli?"

"Both," he said without hesitation.

"But what about your uniform? Aren't you loyal only to the uniform of the army you serve? Even if, as you claim, you are the 'best soldier,' still, you're an Israeli soldier. So, that makes all of us Israelis the best soldiers in the world!" Then he looked around at us, pleased by what clearly he considered a triumph of logic. To me, his reasoning seemed quite flawed.

"There are more Bedu who are not Israeli soldiers than those who are. And they too are the best. It doesn't matter the uniform he wears or what country he serves: the Bedu is the best soldier in the world."

"But who are you loyal to?" Ephraim smiled, winking at us. "Are you loyal to Israel?"

"I am loyal to King Hussein of Jordan, ruler of the Hashimite and of all the Bedouin."

Ephraim looked around at us with mock surprise, though nothing that Bachshi said was actually new. We already understand all this. It was just never brought up; considered in bad taste, a needless airing of inconsequential allegiances, since in the field Bachshi fought for Israel as fiercely as any Jew. His dedication was as much a matter of honor and professionalism as allegiance. The Israeli Bedouin's ultimate allegiance is to himself, his gun, and his horse or camel, in that order and, of course, to his own blood. The rest is superfluous, negotiable. But the Israeli Bedouin is also unwavering in his devotion to Israel, and once we had drunk our coffees and left, that would be the end of Ephraim's ever having hope of deploying in close battle order with a Bedouin tracker to guide ever again. But Ephraim wanted to make some sort of point before we left and would not stop there.

"But here in Israel, who is the leader you give your allegiance to?"

"Arik Sharon. He is the king of Israel."

Ephraim looked around at us with a look of savage mirth. "Sharon? Some consider him to be a war criminal. Do you?"

Bachshi straightened up. "Sharon is the only one among your leaders whom the Bedu respect. He is a warrior and a king."

Even Ephraim didn't know what more to say. He should have stopped there. But some people don't know when or how to desist.

"And tell me, Bachshi," he said, "if someone fucked your sister, what would you do?"

And it got very quiet in that shack, except for the wind's howling. Bachshi stood up in front of Ephraim, who was seated and looking up now with a mock frightened expression. Bachshi towered over him with his hand on the scabbard of his short-bladed belt knife.

"Are you insulting my family?" he said stonily. "Are you calling me ridiculous?"

Whereupon I shot to my feet with a loud, hollow-sounding laugh, encircled Bachshi's steeled shoulder, tapped out a cigarette from the pack in my hand, and held it up to Bachshi's face. "C'mon," I said, "let's go outside and smoke. We need a break."

He looked at me without a word, accepted the cigarette, and followed me out of the shack. We went to the jeep, climbed inside, lit up. The gray sea heaved under a roiling sky. The wind rattled our bulletproof windows.

"He is provoking me," said Bachshi.

"I know," I said. "I saw."

"Motherfucker. Does he think I am a punk? Which?"

"No," I lied, knowing full well that probably he thought that of Bachshi, worse even; he often had said as much, in so many words, about Bachshi and the Bedouin in general.

"You are lying," said Bachshi. "You are lying like a friend, to protect me from the truth." He put his forefinger to his eyes. "But I see, man. I see. You understand?"

I nodded and lit his cigarette. He dragged on it, exhaled.

"Do you know that I can snuff out this fly with very little effort? That I can take him out with one shot at a hundred meters, from a moving jeep? That I can take him down and cut out his brain to sell to collectors of such things? And feed the rest of him to the camp dogs."

"You are speaking a lot of crap." I smiled.

Normally, he would smile back. We enjoyed that sort of bond. But now he did not smile and it was as though we were complete strangers. Even foes.

So that now, weeks later, in the tent with me and Micah, when Ephraim weakly laid claim to our ugly little combat mission out there in the wilderness, said that it must be hard — meaning, to live with the fact that one has to kill — but that there's nothing to think about, that this is what we are here to do, and so forth and so on and all that other boastful understated and heroic horseshit, neither of us argued back. In fact, Micah said "Sure" and not with condescension either but with a perfect willingness to allow Ephraim to partake of whatever imagined glory that he coveted. It was all in his head anyhow. Why not let him enjoy his delusion? And anyway, after the way he had spoken weeks ago to Bachshi, he was living, as far as we were concerned, on borrowed time. He was a dead man. Bedouin never forget.

Ali and Bachshi were not friends so much as two young stags inhabiting the same turf. Often, they hung together. But as the betting match approached, they were rarely on the same ground. Or, at least, I never saw them together but once, when Bachshi and I took a fast drive down the borderline in a recon jeep, in response to intelligence of frequent crossings at a particular outpost.

We did not announce ourselves with sirens but parked behind a rise, got out, and strolled close to the outpost and simply stretched out on the ground at a spot from which observers in the outpost would not possibly see us. We lay waiting but saw nothing. Yet neither of us rose to leave. Something between us silently understood, sensed, that we should remain, that something was up.

Dusk fell and we missed dinner and still we were there. Then the sun bled itself dry and night filled every crevice of the world with black light. Life is day and night is death, say the Bedouin. The border stretched into the distance, a string of powerful fence-mounted electric blue lights. Facing these, the outpost campaniles loomed like cyclopic giant sentries faced out to the Egyptian army's front lines.

Far out into the frontier, the main strength of Egypt's forces, stationed in Rafiah, formed a mass of pinpoint lights surrounded by an ocean of darkness. Closer to us, here and there, small campfires burned in which the silhouettes of cold and hungry Egyptian troops stood or squatted and occasionally weapons fire burst out against our lines, which did not respond but instead reported the truce infractions to our intelligence outposts. We saw Egyptian gun muzzles sporadically erupt, flicker, and crackle in the blackness. Through all this, like an immense probing finger, a great spotlight from our side prodded and scanned along the frontier.

For hours we lay there, handing the killer night-vision scope back and forth. Peering through it. Waiting.

And then we saw from down the line a single car approach with its headlights off, a small white Peugeot. Out of the darkness of the Egyptian side three men melted into view. From the car stepped two soldiers, ours. They all met at the fence. I did not recognize our soldiers. Something was tossed by one of the Israelis over the electric fence. Then the Egyptians tossed something back. Then the Egyptians vanished and the Israelis walked to the outpost, entered.

We called in reinforcements. This was heard, as we knew it would be, on the outpost's radio. Soldiers rushed out in a panic. Bachshi and I met them with raised weapons. Friend, they cried, don't do this! Sweetheart, they called us. They pleaded: No, no, oh please! My family! My mother! My girlfriend! My boss! My son, my daughter, my grandmother! And so forth. We waved them down, one by one, to the ground, to sit. We let them smoke cigarettes. They offered them to us. We declined. We had our own.

"Why?" said one of the soldiers whom we had seen at the fence. He was a broad, swarthy man with thick black eyebrows and wavy black hair, looked a little like Moshe in Jerusalem. "After all, what did we do?" he pleaded. "A little business with the cousins? What are we, terrorists? They're people too. We are just making some extra money. Them, us. This is peace. We have peace with them. Sweetie, why this? Let us go!"

"Where will you go?" I said. "What's done is done."

Bachshi said nothing, deaf to their entreaties. They weren't his people, not Bedu, so he didn't care how they had dishonored themselves.

Another, a short, lean, wiry man with an angry demeanor spit: "Motherfucking American Jew. They do everything by the book. Little fucking sheep. Like those German Jews that Hitler gassed. So now you turn in Jews, huh? You put your own in jail. You motherfucker! Do you know what will happen to us? Do you know how many years in jail we will get for this?" Another soldier began to weep. The angry one looked at him and the sight of tears stoked his fury. With a murderous expression, he began to rise.

"Sit the fuck down!" I snapped. "Don't give me that shit. I'll put a fucking bullet in your head. Sit down, asshole! Sit!"

Surprised, he sank back down. Glared at me.

"You dishonor that uniform, you fucking moron," I said. "And I don't give a shit if they put you in jail for a hundred years. My blood spills just like yours. When they shoot at you they shoot at me. So don't give me that shit. I'm Israeli just like you."

"With your American passport," he said with a sneer.

"I have an Israeli passport too, as a matter of fact."

His face contorted in disdain and he said in a mocking, high-pitched imitation of my voice: "I have an Israeli passport too! But I also have an American passport and I can get the fuck out of here anytime I want. I can come play soldier and then when it gets hard I can just pick up my ass and fly back home and eat McDonald's and watch the war on TV. Not like those stupid-ass motherfucking Israelis down there that I arrest and put in prison for four or five years of their fucking time and ruin their families and their futures for the rest of their fucking lives."

"Bullshit," I said without conviction, knowing that he was

right. And I said nothing more, though he and the others continued to alternately taunt me and plead for escape.

A small convoy of four jeeps and a Noon Noon came rumbling out of the darkness, along with the major, Yitzak, and Dedi and even some plainclothes operatives from the Sheen Bet Security Services and the Intelligence Corps.

For hours the men were questioned on-site, in the jeeps, and their affidavits were taken on the spot. In pairs they were driven away, handcuffed, in back of the jeeps. The exchange had been nominal: some gold jewelry and a brick of hashish.

By the time it was all over the sun was rising over the desert, pink in a lilac sky. Bleary-eyed and hungry, we took the patrol road to the turnoff for Rafiah and bumped along the narrow two-lane artery. Up ahead bobbed a flock of goats, crowding the shoulder of the road, and several backed-up vehicles, one by one moving slowly around them. We slowed to a stop. And then we saw the jeep and, beside it, Ali in uniform, wearing a shabby Romeo smile and his eyes burning into those of a Bedouin shepherdess with opalescent black eyes and obvious beauty, though she was concealed by the traditional black face mask and long robe-like black dress. He had taken her staff from her hands and leaned on it charmingly, his chin propped on his fists, his brown Golani beret set at a rakish angle on his head, his orange and walnut Chinese-make Kalatchnikov, prized proof of close-quarter combat with terrorists, slung jauntily from his shoulder. On his wrist, he wore a sergeant major's bracelet, though he held only the rank of sergeant.

Ali glanced over at us. His smile went sour. He quickly handed the girl back her staff. She turned and when she saw Bachshi her eyes grew wide with terror. His face had turned hard and a little crazed-looking.

"You know her?" I asked, amazed at the depth of his reaction.

"My sister," he said.

She waded in among her flock, uttering loud noises and prodding them quickly forward in an orderly stream of ratty furs and nodding horns. At no time did she look over at Bachshi or acknowledge him in any way. And Ali made no attempt to speak to her. Instead, he locked eyes with Bachshi, his own gaze mocking, Bachshi's murderous.

Twice I repeated Bachshi's name before he turned to me, his eyes cool, black, set to kill.

"What the fuck is going on with you?" I said more than asked.

But Bachshi just drove off, slowing momentarily to a crawl as he passed his sister to glare at her. She gave back a defiant look tinged with terror. On the steering wheel his knuckles turned white. Then, he slam-shifted the gearshift, almost going into a ditch as he shot past the string of backed-up cars, and took off at accelerating speed down the road to Rafiah.

Up ahead, the refugee camp loomed with its low-roofed, squalid jumble of putty-colored stone shacks and stucco cottages clustered around mosques with tall, slender minarets. Already, we could hear the muezzins calling the faithful to both prayer and holy war or jihad, against the "Israeli oppressor." But holy war or no holy war, we were determined to have ourselves a good shwarma of lamb roast stuffed into fresh-baked pita and smothered in tahini sauce. Despite the lethal looks we drew at the shwarma stand from the hostile crowd gathering around the small kiosk in a side street off the main square, we impudently stood wolfing down the excellent food at the smoky counter. But when it was time to go, it was clear that we ought to do so fast. Behind the crowd, young men darted back and forth, their red, pale yellow, and black shirt colors winking between the stationary pedestrians. Wiping our mouths in a hurry and jamming on our helmets, we climbed into the jeep and tore out with a peel of rubber as stones landed around us in the road and shouts died on the wind.

As for the encounter with his sister, I didn't bring it up, and he seemed to have forgotten about it completely. Still, I wanted to know more and later that day asked: Why are you so angry at your sister and Ali? It seems innocent enough, I said. Boy meets girl, etc.

He wouldn't answer beyond to name her for me: Batiya, age seventeen. And to nod, tersely, when I asked if she still lived with their parents. "Yes. She is at home. In fact, I'm the only one who has left."

"How many of you are there?"

He hesitated. "Five brothers and four sisters," he said. And that was all that I got out of him.

I spied them together, Batiya and Ali, several more times. Suddenly they seemed to be everywhere. Against a mauve dusk sky I saw them, she perched atop a concrete barrier, reclining on her hands, her mufti undone, her face revealed to Ali, who leaned over her knees with his hands on the barrier, laughing. They looked very much in love.

Together I saw them, just talking, he behind the wheel of a patrolling Noon Noon loaded down with dozing troops, she standing beside the road, at her feet a basket heaped with vegetables, and she looked very modest and unassuming and laughed prettily at things he was saying. They looked rather nice together, had about them that spectral, rosy glow of early courtship, and I recall smiling inwardly as I maneuvered my vehicle around the Noon Noon. Ali didn't even see me, he was so absorbed in her. The troops seemed content to sit there snoring in the sun for as long as Ali wished. It all seemed innocent enough to me.

Once, though, insanely, he brought her into Outpost Nine's mess tent, where she sat beside him, among the troops, greedily wolfing down a plate heaped with canned rations. As she chewed, Ali sat with his arm around her shoulder, face leaning close to hers, slack grin lewdly familiar, and the intimacy told me, told all of us present, that together they had crossed a line of no return.

In these days, Bachshi looked preoccupied when you spoke to him; his attention span dwindled to a fretting, ground-sweeping glance before he rushed off, leaving you to feel that everything you had just said had made absolutely no impression on him whatsoever. I never saw him and Ali together anymore. They had never been very close, but now they would not so much as enter into the same room together, and we all knew that it was over the sister.

"If he knocks her up, they'll kill her," said Micah.

We all knew about this custom among the Arabs. Israeli jails are filled with young male avengers of the family's pride who in the process of slaughtering their own sibling for sexual improprieties also butcher their own remaining time on earth. Yet I couldn't imagine Bachshi involved in anything so crazy as that.

"Not Bachshi." I said. "He's too modern. He's been around us, around the IDF, too long. He's Israeli inside and out. He's gone way past that kind of thinking."

"Bullshit," said Micah.

We let it go at that.

The betting at base camp continued to escalate, and now the bets were coming in from as far away as Beersheva. I kept the money stashed in the officers' quarters, a whole ammo box stuffed with loose cash. One day I showed it to Bachshi, who peered down into it with a tense look. "They're all betting on you," I said, "from as far as Beersheva. You better catch that fucking hare."

Bachshi nodded and that was all. His pride didn't flare up. That worried me. I took his elbow. "You can do this, right? I mean, you can beat Ali hands down, no?"

He pulled his arm away. "It's true, huh? All you Jews care about is the money."

"Fuck you. There's a lot of Druze Arab soldiers and Bedouin trackers throwing money down on this too. I'm worried about them. The odds are heavily in your favor. And yeah, I got some money riding on this too. So what? What kind of bullshit thing is that to say?"

"But it's my honor," he said. "My honor rides on this. Not no fucking money. My honor."

I half grinned. Honor. The word sounded trite. "Honor? What does this have to do with honor?" I said.

"What does anything have to do with it? Tell me," he said, "are you still fucking your friend's wife? What does that have to do with it?" and walked away.

The sad thing is, I didn't really know how to answer his question.

It hadn't always been with her and Dotan as it was now. Once, we had been close friends. But two months ago I had gone to see her and things were never the same. I had made the decision after my unit in Gaza had destroyed an enemy house.

I don't know why that particular house had hit me so hard. It was just part of the routine one carried out, day in, day out. Day in, day out, you rise in your muddy olive uniform, get up from the sleeping bag laid out on the cold cement floor of the garrison's barracks, groan to a stand from where you lay all night in a deep, stuporous, dreamless blackout, and lace on your boots. Then you hoist on your battle vest and take up your gun and with one fumbling hand snap closed your helmet's chin strap and trudge out the doorless entryway, wheezing in your lungs — the door a square hole, really, in a big clenched cement fist of a structure — and stomp down the stairs and slog through mud puddles and driving rain to the Noon Noon, which you climb aboard and roar out the gates into the drear gray wind-slashed road.

You rumble past the orchards and towns and pull up to wherever the designated house happens to stand — some suburb or hamlet or even on the edge of the city itself, the refugee camp of Khan Yunis, which is really a small surrealistic slum with its own bizarre center and here and there even ringed by expensive villas and suburbs — and already other units, troops, are there before you, at work: engineering corpsmen rigging explosive or manning a big tractor that rips out the house chunk by chunk while the family stands by wailing, pleading, shocked.

Perhaps they had had some direct hand in their son's or father's or daughter's or nephew's decision to throw a hand grenade into a schoolhouse filled with Jewish children. Or perhaps they aided and abetted the plan to enter shooting into an Israeli clothing shop or helped to set off an explosive in a crowded civilian Israeli bus. But whether yes or no, they were related by blood to killers who had either died in the attempt or vanished from sight, and so, whether they were complicitous or innocent, still their house goes down — all the same, down it goes.

And there you are, hopping to the ground from the Noon Noon, finding a spot to take up your post, guard the perimeter, have yourself a smoke. I don't know why this house. Until this house, I had never intended to turn my whole world upside down with Maya. Why this house?

Maybe it was one house too many. Maybe it made me hate all houses for once and all. Down here, I had torn down more than a few houses. And they, Maya and Dotan, with their big comfortable houselike apartment, privately owned, had the closest to a house, a home, that any of us at that time in our circle of bohemians possessed. Though all was not well in their little paradise — yes, here and there were clues left about, like that yellow flower box in their bedroom window, fronting on the street, the one in which no flowers grew, containing withered dead stems. And I, for one, lived alone in a small studio in Nachlahot, a place with a big veranda where I sat outside on a mangled sofa covered with old rugs. It wasn't so bad, but I was lonely. My neighbor, a dark-skinned old Kurdistani woman with a head bound by rags and a bloodstained apron, who used to accidentally set herself on fire at her cheap stove, would drop by with food, chicken and cakes and dried apricots that she herself had left out in the sun to bake dry and hammered with her own two hands into sheet-roll. Several times, though, I put out the flames in her dress and took her to the hospital, and that depressed the hell out of me. She was always all right, just a little singed, dazed. This was home to me, grim enough, and she the closest to family that I had, and we didn't even know each other's names or even speak. She knew no Hebrew, only Kurdistani.

I felt sorry for myself and stayed away as much as possible and spent a lot of time with Maya and Dotan, over at their place. Was there, up in their flat, all the time. So were many others. Ora and Moshe. Shirley. Barry Sheridan. Edna. Carl Perkal. Danny Ben-Ami. Evi. Laura. Bill. Uri. Danny. Roy. Itimar. The whole ever-widening inner circle rotating through on a daily basis, in and out, in and out. Artists. Writers. Dancers. Puppeteers. Actors. Stage designers. Drinking, talking, smoking, stoned, leaving, coming, crying, laughing, threatening, borrowing, promising, and, most of all, making plans! Endless plans! To be famous, rich, popular, sought after, envied. We debated the state of the nation, the constant warfare in the north and now in the territories, the Israeli arts establishment, our next program, art exhibit, poem, dance, story, play. I would come up the street in my shabby old raincoat, whistling in a drizzle, a bottle in one pocket, pack of cigarettes in the other, some book tucked into my waist to keep it dry. I'd glance up at their bedroom window, which fronted on the street. There was that yellow flower box with nothing in it. And the cold blue window mirroring the sky.

Up there at Maya's, seated or on our feet, wrapped in clouds of smoke, laughing, intense, brooding, we postured against the delicious backdrop of our own certain, imminent fame. Already the newspapers wrote about us, and it was just a matter of time before we exploded onto the international arts scene. The apartment was the hub of our energies. Dotan and Maya had a fine sense of our importance. They encouraged us to be there, to interact. It was a good place to feel special. I avoided Maya like the plague, though, always sat farthest away from her, at a remove. Told myself that secretly I didn't like her. She's a phony, I told myself. Now when I saw her in those scuffed high heels, I hated them. Yes, that's what I told myself: she's a phony. It felt better to think so. Dotan was my real friend, I told myself. He was the real goods. A great artist.

But the northern war grew worse. The territories heated up. We were all called up. And I was in that strange, lonely place that I called home, with the Kurdistani woman shuffling back and forth just outside my window, and she was humming a song. I was packing my bag, readying to go to my possible doom. There were no going-away parties. We men just went. We never knew where to next. If there was a woman, she helped us pack. If not, we packed alone. I sat on the edge of the bed, staring at the clock. When it was time, I rose. I left, bag in hand. I walked, walked, walked, and then I rode a public bus to the rendezvous place. A chartered bus waited. The others of my unit were there. In silence, we traveled, down to Gaza. We didn't know what to expect there. We'd never been. Mine was a unit normally assigned to combat duties along the Lebanese front. We weren't even serving in our own command.

Back and forth I went from the Gaza Strip to their house. He was now often up in the north with his unit, in the communications truck, under Syrian bombardment, which was constant. There were always, though, others around in Jerusalem during my leaves. I sat in the corner, in uniform, smoking, not saying much. Sometimes someone asked what it was like down there in Gaza and I shrugged, tapped an ash into the ashtray and said: "Shithole." I now often noticed her staring at me. Many told me how fortunate I was to be avoiding the madness in Lebanon and I smiled stiffly and agreed. Inside, I felt something taking hold, shooting down diseased roots, but couldn't say what this cancerous-feeling infection boded or signified. It was as if the melancholy Gazan hues of my insides — my frequent mud browns, piss yellows, grays of mood, my secret depressions, black fears, a nagging sense of despair — all were reflected in the Gazan landscape, its very skies and streets, a private morbid condition peopled with faces of infinite hatred, the teeming masses of outraged and resentful inhabitants, their interminable blames. I hid the symptoms from others, even from myself. Smoked and drank with a gallant sneer.

One time I came there and only Ora and Moshe were around. Ora said: Let's go dancing. And we all went out together, me still in uniform, to that café on Agrippa and ate steaks with chips and danced and sat around drinking brandy and arak. Word spread and others of our clique joined us there. Soon it was a whole scene. Funny how we always found each other in these places. Always some party going on.

I remember a blur of faces, gray and pink and smudged dark and white, and loud voices and lots of jostling and smoke — a lovely if temporary antidote to the Gazan crowds — and I was huddled within myself, smoking, my face lowered, chin ducked into my collar. Then, I felt her eyes on me, looked up, and suddenly, in front of everyone, before everyone, she reached across the table, stroked my cheek and said: "Darling one."

You could have heard my heartbeat thudding, framed and solitary, in that room — the way it fell silent in Gaza when our patrol moved through a crowded narrow street.

And then the noise all started up again, the cacophonous dancing clamor of our usual masked and clowning selves. That was all it was. A pause in the riotous circus. But it changed everything.

Because next, I was down there again in Gaza, at the house they were tearing apart chunk by chunk. Cinder block smashed and iron rods twisted like escaping snakes from its guts. The usual smattering of potbellied pantsless kids were about, screaming and crying as if we Israelis were devils sent to abduct them down to hell. The mothers waited, the young daughters screamed accusatorily, and no men were around, no men were ever anywhere to be seen on such occasions; all had fled into hiding to avoid arrest.

After a while, you didn't hear the cries. I just kept telling myself: This is the price you pay for blowing us up. This is the price you pay, you motherfuckers, for killing our kids. We come, we destroy you. Nodding to myself, ears stopped against the anguished cries. Smoking, smoking, smoking. Trading jokes with some passing soldiers. The rain saturating my clothes and coming down through into my skin. Shivering, cold to the bone. And when the destruction was far along, I saw, there in the grayish rubble, a spot of pink color, tiny. Went over, leaned down. A doll's teacup. I picked it up, turned it in my fingers. So delicate. And yes, I admitted to myself, this had belonged to some little one who had lived here. Pity her parents decided that terrorism was worth more than their own baby's well-being. And, turning it in my fingers, I looked around. You're not supposed to take anything away, you know, I told myself. No spoils of war or anything illegal like that. But this? So small.

It fit into the top left flap pocket of my fatigue shirt.

And from then on I carried it, a tiny, fragile bulge in the pocket, and always expected it to be shattered but somehow it never was. Not even when crushed beneath my battle vest. How can it be? I wondered. Something so small to get by like that? It was always a spot of color in the drab environs. That bit of pink against the khakis and olives and black, the muddy grays and beiges and whites and the cold blue smears of the mirroring windows. And then one night, as I shrugged off my heavy gear and lowered it to the floor, and laid down the rifle, I patted the pocket of my shirt and felt a sharpness on my skin. Delicately, I lifted out, like shards of a shattered bird's egg from a nest, the pieces of the dollhouse cup. I examined each piece coldly, turning it this way and that. I assembled them in my palm and stared at the fragments. What the fuck, I thought. What the flaming fuck. I grimaced a lopsided bitter grin and grunted to myself. Of course, I told myself, what do I think? What am I thinking? I walked to the hand grenade barrier and tossed the handful of pieces through the barbed wire. And then I lay there in the yellowish gleam of the single naked lightbulb that dangled from a jerry-rigged hanging fixture in the moldy ceiling and I thought of Maya. I looked around me, wondered, What is this fucking world anyway? Is it all in my fucking head? This? Her?

Maya.

She was not in my head. This is, all of this is, the whole world is, but she, she is in my body. She is in my rib cage, my throat, my cock, my tongue, my fingers. She is definite, the only concrete happiness I will ever know, a house that cannot be torn down. I have to tell her what I have felt over this past year, what I have denied in myself, refused to countenance. She is married, for crying out loud. She's Dotan's wife.

But what is that, a wife? A woman still. And in the café, her hand on my cheek. Everyone pretending not to see. Isn't it already too late?

And I imagined us living in New York City, in a small flat. She'll paint, I'll write. We'll forget about all this. We'll go where there's no husband and no war. We've done the war, haven't we? Haven't we been good warriors, she and I? Haven't we warred enough? And the others won't be overrun by foes if, pardon us, we leave: they'll be OK, won't they? It is very important that the others will be OK.

And I began to cry, like a fool, a weakling, a simpering jerk, some deluded pacifist who did not deserve to wear this hallowed uniform. Only I didn't care if there was peace or war. I just didn't want to be here anymore. Began to cry and to open and close my fingers where the teacup had rested and thought: What a bunch of sentimental, detrimental fucking shit. Sentimental fucking detrimental shit you are.

And I cried in despair. Quietly, to myself. I knew that they, the Arabs, were killing us, that they wanted our destruction, but I didn't want to hurt them anymore in order to survive. I knew that there were among them killers, planning our murder. But I didn't want to kill them anymore. It was suicidal, I knew, but I didn't care. There was a Palestinian baby with a round little belly and wounded eyes glaring at me in my head. Until I fell asleep. And as I drifted off I could see Maya's bedroom windowsill, the yellow wooden flowerless flower box.

I showed up the next morning in Lieutenant Yitzak's tent. He was going over his cheeks with a battery-powered electric shaver.

"Look who's here," he said pleasantly.

"Yitzak, I have a favor to ask."

"Favor for you? Anything. What do you need?"

"I need a leave. I need to go now."

He pressed the shaver into his chin, rolled it hard over his cheeks, plowing the flesh, the skin rolling up, the hairs falling under the blades, vanishing, leaving tanned smoothness. He went for his neck while I stood there like an idiot, amazed that in such small things as how one treats one's fellow man while shaving one can find the whole history of man's inhumanity to man.

"What do you say?" I said.

He rubbed his hand over his cheek, feeling its smoothness with a look of evident satisfaction. "Say?" He chuckled tinnily. "I say nothing. What can I say? You know it's not up to me. It's in the lottery. It's between the troops. You get your shot like everyone else. Draw your match from the helmet like the rest of them. What's the matter, you're having no luck? You still get a mandatory leave, no matter what. But if I remember correctly, and I'm sure I do, you already had yours. Yes, I remember. That is the weekend we caught that asshole from Islamic Jihad with all the plastic explosive hidden under the meat in his butcher shop. You weren't in on that."

"That's right."

"Well, I can't help you then."

"Yitzak, I'm asking for a favor. I've never asked for anything, have I? And I've given everything I've got."

"You're a good soldier," he agreed. "No one is arguing with that. It's just the system."

"You can get me out for forty-eight hours. That's all I ask. Forty-eight hours."

"That's all? That's all? But you're a single man. What is the emergency? Your wife is giving birth, like Itimar? Who still couldn't get out because we were on that operation in Gaza City. You remember, the sweep?"

I nodded impatiently.

"Or is it like what happened with Binny, when one of his associates, a close friend of his apparently, was found murdered in Tel Aviv? Not that I should feel sympathy for a criminal shot in a gangland slaying, but still, Binny is very broken up over that and wants to go to the funeral. But does he go? With all the protectzia in the world? No. You recall?"

"I do."

"So. Is it something more serious than that?"

"No," I say, "but I'm going to fucking blow somebody's fucking brains out if I don't get out now for forty-eight hours. I've got to get to Jerusalem."

He looks at me. "What are you saying? What do you . . . you're going to blow somebody's brains out?"

I hoisted my gun. "I mean I'm going to take this and kill someone with it. I can't take this shit down here anymore. I need a break, OK? I need a fucking break from the assholes. From our assholes and their assholes. I need a break from the fucking settler who punched that Arab bride at her wedding procession."

"Her little procession was a Hamas demonstration passing in front of his house on Shabbat, deliberately to provoke him."

"So they're bigger assholes. But he's an asshole too."

Yitzak shrugged. "Look, I'm not here to debate politics with you."

"Then don't. Let me out of here. Let me out, Yitzak. Let me out. Forty-eight hours. I'm going a little crazy."

He looked at me, studied my face.

"It's pussy. I know this look. It's pussy. For pussy, you want me to . . ." He shook his head in disgust, not at me but himself. He went to a footlocker, slammed it open, removed a book and rubber stamp, tore off a pass, stamped and signed it, and tossed it on the bed. "Go on. Get the fuck out of here. If anyone asks how you got this, tell them you're sick. Do you understand? You got a medical pass to Tel Hashomer. Anyway, it's only half a lie. You're sick in the fucking head. What happens to you? Don't tell me. Don't! Hold it in. I don't want to know. You're such a crazy lonely fuck, I can tell, that I won't stop you from . . . go on. Ruin your life. Go on. Get laid! Do you hear me? Go get it and come back here in forty-eight hours or I'll have you thrown in jail."

I left from there. Took nothing but my gun. Hitched a ride in a Border Patrol jeep. Sat back there, face a blank, I'm sure. Felt too much turmoil to admit real feelings to myself. Like shame for what I planned to do; despair at the thought of my certain rejection; rage for the emptiness I was certain to know, regardless of how things turned out.

Then Jerusalem dribbled into sight in drips and drabs of white, a slow gathering of bare stones like Chinese water torture drops slowly tapping on the iron casement of my consciousness, and the strange, almost hallucinatory feat that Jerusalem always performs upon approach occurred again. Out of pebbles and stones and rocks and occasional boulder heaps the queenly city arose tall, white-clad, with long slender arms that drew us into the bosom of her town center along sleek, curving boulevards and ever narrowing, softening, darkening jasmine-scented streets lush with bougainvillea, and I descended in Rehavia, my boots alighting in pools of dappling shadow cast by wind-stirred trees and made my way, bone-tired but with a pounding heart, to the foot of their apartment building on Rehov Aza and looked up. The shutters were drawn and the lights out. I could tell: she wasn't home. On a public telephone I called her boss, Jerry Chapman, over at Filmworks LTD, where she worked as a graphic artist. Jerry answered in his gentle British-inflected way. "Hellow! How are you? How is Gaza? We thought about you, all of us, when we heard that news report about the shooting down there."

"What shooting?"

"This morning. They killed a soldier and wounded a second. In, um, Khan Yunis, I think it is. That must be from your brigade."

"Yes," I said hurriedly, unable to handle any more lurching in my gut, to think now of anything other than her. "I don't know about that," I added.

"I'm sorry to tell you then. I hope . . ." He stopped.

"It's all right. Is Maya by any chance there?"

His tone cooled. "She's not, I'm afraid. I think she's . . . she said she'd be in her studio this morning."

"OK. I'll go check over there."

"If she calls in, I'll tell her you called."

"Thanks."

"Hopefully we'll see you soon?"

"Hopefully. I've only got forty-eight hours."

"Right. Well, after this reserves, drop in. Hal would like to see you too."

"That would be good," I agreed and hung up.

Her studio, which she shared with Dotan, Ora, and Danny Ben-Ami, was in the Katamonim slums on the western edge of the city, in a bomb shelter that they had obtained free from the municipality in return for keeping it cleaned and freshly painted, and with the understanding that in the event of a serious national emergency they must immediately vacate. It was a vast cavernous space, and they used it to both create and show art. I took a cab there. The cab traveled up and down the rock- and boulder-lined boulevards, like a marble plunging and rising through a giant pinball machine. Then the slums were on all sides, block after block of big, rectangular cement housing projects with balconies obscured by a clutter of junk and laundry, and the streets filled with tough, sullen young men in wife-beater T-shirts and with cigarettes dangling from their lover-boy lips.

"It's in that little park over there," I said, and the cab let me off.

I crossed the deserted playground, white sun-baked gravel crunching underfoot. The shelter's triangular cement entrance arose out of the ground with a big orange iron door at the entrance. It was unlocked, partially opened. I passed through and descended the steps.

"Hello?" she called nervously.

"It's OK, Maya. It's just me."

I paused on the steps, looked down into the enormous, brightly lit underground chamber where she stood at a worktable, pale upturned face lit from underneath by a powerful lamp, her red hair falling forward over her ears and shoulders, her slender, deliciously awkward body clad in a brief blue halter and light green drawstring pants. I couldn't see her feet but knew what shoes she'd be wearing: those cheap pale pink rubberized plastic sandals that buckled at her slim ankles. She had purchased them in the Yehuda Market and was so proud of them.

"Hellooow," she said uncertainly with a half smile. "This is certainly unexpected."

She had in her hands a pair of pliers and a little wire man that she had been twisting into shape. She laid these down on the workbench.

"Wait," I said. "Don't tell me. You're wearing the pink sandals from Mahane Yehuda."

She looked down at her feet as if unsure, looked up, pleased. "You know that?" She laughed.

"Of course. You always wear them with that outfit. Just like you always wear the white high heels with the green top and the mauve pants. That is the outfit you wore the first time we met."

"I can't believe you remember that."

I lowered my head. Wanted to cry. Nodded.

"What is it? You look so sad."

I laid my gun on the ground but didn't move or speak. I felt inside as fragile, as ridiculously out of place as that dollhouse cup from Gaza that could have come from the twisted wreckage of a blown-up Jerusalem bus or from the incindered shell of a gutted house or car or airplane anywhere on the earth that children found themselves caught in the crossfire of war. My feelings now were as irrational as a summery blue sky with a red balloon drifting in it; a laughing scream down a playground slide; a squeaking swing at dusk when the one you love is swinging on it. I opened my mouth to speak, couldn't even find my hands to show her the emptiness they held. Look, said my face, look what I have done. But I could tell, she didn't see. Look at the gun on the ground. I am good, I have tried, I have fought, I have won, but I have lost so much, and I'm tired. I have defended us, but in doing so, I have destroyed something that no one can replace. And I am so sad now. So broken.

"What if . . ." I said to her surprised face ". . . I told you . . . that I want you?"

Her face snapped down, to the workbench. She lifted the wire man, the pliers, began to twist, twist, twist.

"What if I told you that?" I said, to fill the silence.

Her drawn features barely contained the agitation in her. She barely resisted throwing down the man and the pliers; instead, she laid them gently down. She folded her hands in her lap, out of view, and looked up at me with resigned sadness and something like pity.

"And what if I told you that I love you?" I said. I started to explain: "Down there . . . I . . ."

"Darling," she said. "Sweet one."

We met, embraced. Her smell transformed the shelter into a sunny rural kitchen in a friendly, neutral country. And the war and the mud and the broken teacup and the ripped flesh and bone of exploded infants and the sad, unshaven dead faces of assassinated informers and the desperate shadow eyes of terrorists and the fatigued, stricken faces of soldiers and the angry glare of women in the orchards and the frightened and furious gazes of suspects as we patted them down in the roads and the sounds of explosions and of gunfire and the charred shells of bomb-twisted restaurants and gutted buses were lost in the glittering surface of the sun-dappled lake that I smelled on her and on the fresh-grown leaves of the spring greening that lay like a hint on her soft neck where my lips and nose went. I held her to me, gathered up so much of her, so silken, and yet her bones were as fragile as a cup, easily broken. I said: "I have you now, Maya. Forgive me. I love you. I'm so sorry I didn't say it sooner. I always loved you. Always. I love you, Maya. I love you, my beautiful Maya."

And she began to cry, for happiness, I suppose. But I couldn't understand what she was so happy about. To be loved by me was a curse. Didn't she understand that?

We spent that night and the next in her marriage bed, with a huge yellow moon peering in over the rooftops. The telephone rang like a madman caught in a single thought.

As Ali continued to boast of his impending victory over Bachshi, Micah and I tried to understand how the matter of Batiya might affect Bachshi's performance, but it was hard to say. Although on some level we felt we knew them well, the Bedouin people were a little unreal to us. Eleven months of the year we Jews dwelled in our flats in the cities and towns, our houses in the suburbs, our cottages on the kibbutz and in the moshavim. We worked as airline baggage handlers, college professors, sanitation engineers, writers, physicists, criminals, farmers, cooks. We drove cars and watched soccer on television, danced in discos and sat around in cafés on Shenken Street and Dizengord Street in Tel Aviv and on Ben Yehuda Street in Jerusalem, drinking coffee, watching the great parade of humanity flow past, partaking of the modern. And while we did all that our Bedouin counterparts lived in desert tents and for the most part rode on camels and little Arabian mares. They trained their sons in the use of assault rifle, revolver, and sword while their wives sat immobile in wadis for days on end, swaddled in black, tattooed faces implacable, until their periods passed and they could be readmitted to the camp.

Bachshi and Ali were anomalies — paid scouts, trackers, employees of the IDF, the best sons of their tribes. It was easy at times to forget where these men come from, to blank out, dismiss, the nature of their reality. For even though they sat at table with us and went with us into the field of battle and even sometimes died with us, and though they listened to mostly the same music and followed the soccer teams that we did and were interested in the same models of car, their world was not our world; the very moon looked and meant different things to them. The desert spelled out life to them in an alphabet and language that we could not comprehend.

One night we huddled, the three of us, around a campfire out in the middle of nowhere. To Bachshi, it was a thriving downtown district of busy impressions. To me, it was butt-fuck desolation row. I saw a small-change moon in the sky, a lot of planetarium stars that looked less real than projected ones, and small black, smokelike twists of shrubbery, and barren trees with limbs upraised like ghosts arisen from secret graves in a Bela Lugosi film.

At the fire's edge, the smoky blue crystal balls of inhuman eyes gaped and winked: jackals. Bachshi picked up rocks, threw them at their leering black snouts.

"Whore mothers," he hissed. But they returned, lured by the fire, the smell of our coffee, the scent of our flesh. Sniffing, waiting, for one of us to fall injured or die. They had stalked many men's campfires in this bleak wilderness, Israeli, Egyptian, Bedouin, and Palestinian alike, making no distinctions by our uniforms or robes, skin color or passport. We were all, equally, men and corpses awaiting our turns for extinction, just one bullet or mishap away from our inevitable end and the jackals' first delicious bite of fresh kill. They knew that a desert is full of wrong turns that lay waiting, which any of us might take, and then famine turns to feast under the sky, which holds for them neither God nor His absence: only hunger and the need to satisfy it.

I studied Bachshi's face, his mahogany skin, the thick, deep bone structure, the yellow, delicately veined eyes with irises that weren't brown but seemed several shades of black and green and yellow and sometimes red, according to the time of day and the light it held. He had a strong, hawklike beak of a nose and full, mauve-colored lips. He was tall, lean, handsome, his musculature bearing no trace of weakness or fat. He could hike a hundred kilometers at a trot with a full kit of weapons and gear on his back and decipher the destinations and even intentions of men from a mere footprint, or from even less than that. He was the beloved of his father and the adored of his tribe. It was among his clan a great honor to track for the IDF, to draw the salary and wear the uniform of an Israeli soldier. And his reflexes were unlike any I had ever seen, even among the Bedouin.

"You can't lose," I told him. "You know that, right? You've got hands as fast as Muhammad Ali. You're going to win the match."

"So you should get Muhammad Ali to do it. Because I'm out."

"Are you crazy? You started this. And you brought me in. There's been bets placed from all over Southern Command. You can't bail now."

"It is a mistake. I have no time for children's games."

"Ali has turned it into something else. You'll lose face if you back out."

The way Bachshi looked at me made me uneasy. My smile contained a hint of fear.

"I can never lose my face," he said.

"But, honor . . ." I said. "What you spoke about."

"Honor is a fool's lie. I do nothing for honor. I do because I want to do, for the love of my father."

"And you do not love to make Ali, the big mouth, look like an idiot in front of the whole brigade?"

He didn't hesitate. "No. Why should I wish such a thing? I do not hate Ali. He is a good brave. He has not done anything that I have not done at some time in the past. He is only showing his strength . . ." He hesitated an instant, then added: "And enjoying his pleasures."

By which I understood that he meant Batiya.

"I'm surprised to see you have such a forgiving opinion of Ali."

"It is not Ali who is dishonorable. A brave should have women. He is meant to."

"Even if it gets the girl murdered?"

"That is her bad luck. She can always try to escape. But she would be found, no matter where she goes."

"Like your hare. But how fair is that? It sits there terrified, surrounded, trapped, knowing it will die. You rig the game in which it fails or succeeds. And either way, it's dead."

"I told you, I don't want to do the betting anymore. I'm a soldier. It can jeopardize my job. Gambling is not allowed. I'm out."

"That's a pure pile of bullshit, Bachshi. What are you hiding? What is going on?"

We each glanced over at the jackals, who had returned and were inching nearer, shadows with smoky dolls' eyes.

"Why do you Jews always think that something must be 'going on'? Nothing has ever gone on. There is a way, and you follow or you don't. My way is known to me from birth. It is given to me by my fathers. I follow it. We Bedu have lived this way for as long as we have been in these deserts, just as the deserts follow their own ways, each different, the way of the desert as it is. And the hare, he has followed his way, since that time when Allah decreed it so. His is the life of a hare. And it is his fate that a man should be there to kill and eat him or use him for a demonstration of skills, the skills of the hunter. The hare's speed proves the hunter's hands. You Jews do not talk of these things. You do not hold them in high regard, even though you are the second-best soldiers in the world."

I smiled.

"You are not a fool, like that Ephraim. So I tell you this. Here is what you may do. You may see, witness, and then judge, condemn. Or you may behold and allow what is there to exist in you, as it is, and you may feel all that it holds, the whisper of ages, the voice of the ancients. And go then wiser. And not with an opinion but with an experience. The Bedouin is older than your ideas about things. We do not need your ideas, only your tolerance for our ancient ways."

"But what if someone is at risk of being killed? Do you just stand by and watch?"

"It depends. If they are your clan, then you fight to the death to protect them. But if they are not your blood, then you must ask yourself if protecting them is more important than preserving yourself. To the Bedu, there is no difference between the desert and life. Life *is* the desert and the desert *is* life. I have been to the city and there too is a desert. It is a desert of human beings, of species of human beings, of types and their habitations and interests. It is the dying beetle's intention to gather feces into balls that he will drag over the ground to the right spot, to bury them, warehouse them, against future need. And it is your bankers' and businessmen's intention to build and buy and sell and take his big stash of shit money to the bank against the future. And each will do what they must in order to achieve this. Fundamentally, they are the same."

"A human being is not a dung beetle."

He smiled at my naïveté. "Is he not? Have you not met among human beings the fox, the ass, the snake, the ant, the vulture, the hyena, the scorpion, the owl, the dog, the lion, and the leopard?" His eyes cornered me, awaiting my answer, which was evident before I spoke a word, in the fretting motion of my face, the half-hearted effort to conceal my grinning inner concession, for, of course, I had met all these types among human kind. Still, he waited patiently for my response, from respect.

"All right, then," I said. "Of course I have."

"And which are you, my friend Nathan?" He said this warmly and stretched out his arm and laid his hand on my shoulder. "I think," he said, "that you are a noble horse."

"Don't do it, Bachshi. I know what you're thinking of doing. Our jails are filled with your brothers, the best of your young men, the finest braves, all good sons who do their fathers' bidding at the expense of their own lives. You will never be released, Bachshi. Do you understand? Murder is a capital offense. You are a fine man, Bachshi, a great professional. You can become a commander, a leader. I have been with you in battle. You are a warrior. And you are smart. And I don't know if you've given any thought to how you would feel to have the blood of your own sister on your hands. Bedouin custom or not, Islam or not, still, you are a brother to her.

You have seen her grow from birth. She is your mother's child. Perhaps you played together. And if she has shown weakness, can she not be forgiven? Would you not want to be forgiven if you have shown weakness?"

Bachshi's face, which had grown warm, froze on the threshold of a thwarted smile. His hand dropped. His eyes fell away to a point on the ground and burrowed there, deeper and deeper, like some scorpion or ant or dung beetle. He said: "Were I to run from the battle and to leave behind my brothers, I would deserve death. She who is weak has run from the battle to keep the way of the Bedu against the temptations of the world. Courage and chastity are two virtues that have bound us as a tribe in the desert of the world for thousands of years and, Allah be praised, have held our clans together against invasions and infidels. And they have saved the Bedu from himself. It is not the man who must safeguard the honor of his daughter, but the daughter who must safeguard the honor of the men. And if she betrays that, then she must be rooted out for the poison that she is. She is a snakebite. And the man who exacts the revenge is only serving as a merciful instrument of his clan. He is a mouth to the wound, sucking the poison out and spitting it onto the sand, for his people's sake. This is the will of Allah, which no man can refuse. For he will have brought dishonor to himself, his father, his people, his God. He will be disinherited, alone in a prison of his own making, the forgotten of his mother and the outcast of his tribe. He will have lost the right to ever again behold his own father's face . . ."

"You're going to kill her, aren't you."

He rose slowly to his feet. "I see you understand nothing. I thought you are different, that you do not judge, the way others do. I was wrong."

"I judge murder, Bachshi. Don't you understand that it's murder!"

"What is murder?" he said coldly. "I said nothing about murdering anyone."

"To kill Batiya will be murder," I said, my voice shaking angrily.

"Murder by whose definition? Yours? You from Jerusalem — capital of your religion, your people — who fucks his friend's wife?"

I shook my head in chagrined amazement but said nothing. Generally, when I could help it, I kept my private life out of the army but I had told him about it once while bored out on patrol. My mistake.

"That is not justification for killing her. That doesn't make you better than me."

He glared at me in disdain. "What is the penalty where you come from for doing that? For dicking another's wife while he is in the war, the real war up in the north? Not this phony war down here. What do they do to you for this?"

I held my piece.

"You," he said. "You, from the desert of the city where men slave and cheat and lie for their big balls of dung and fuck each other's wives. Where they are the fool of their women and the mockery of their daughters and despised by their sons. Who call themselves beloved of God because twice a year they go to their worship dressed like princes of high finance and pay money to perform their empty prayers. I do not fuck my best friend's wife. I do not need to buy a ticket to worship my God. I fuck who I want when I need to, but she is free and I kneel in the desert and kiss the sands, facing east. I pray three times a day, anywhere I am. The Bedouin God is everywhere. There is no separation between the temple and the street. The desert is the temple. The Bedouin is its prayer."

"Don't be a fool," I said. "The girls you fuck can be killed for that. You are talking a lot of pretty words, but in the end, if you harm Batiya, you will leave behind the corpse of a young girl, your seventeen-year-old sister, because of a momentary weakness of the flesh that you yourself practice all the time. Does Bedu honor rest upon something so fragile, so helpless? Batiya is being Batiya. Perhaps that too is the will of Allah."

"No," he said, shaking his head self-righteously. "No! My mother, her face, it is covered with tattoos. Her ears and nose and lips they are pierced with silver and gold. Her fingers covered with rings. She is held by chains of love, self-imposed. She was a virgin to my father on their wedding night and she has borne him eleven children, of which four have died. She is old now — forty-five years, she is — and she is the queen of her tent. She would be the first to raise her hand against any child of hers who would bring dishonor to the clan. Look at the tattoos. The ones on her face."

Bachshi's open-fingered hand painted arabesques before his own face: "When I see her tattooed face, I see the mystery of God's will and God's way. She was my mother once. Now she is the desert and she is time. She has crushed out of herself every last weakness and temptation. She is stronger even than my father, who is a great man of our clan. She herself would lift the knife against any child of hers who brought dishonor to our campfire. She would even prefer to see me dead than a coward. Not all battles are fought at night against sleeping men."

"They were planning murder," I said. "They would have attacked innocent civilians."

"They were asleep."

"Beside their weapons."

"Men who are asleep, who are dreaming, who have not awakened, are not killers, no matter what they have done by the light of day or by moonlight. Men who are sleeping are in the womb of their mothers' dreaming; they are walking on the other side of night, in the meridians of God — in the worship of the true unknown — in the past of the future. It is the most merciful death, to die when sleeping, but it is the most pitiless of fates to be woken out of a dream, as they were, to their own spilled blood."

"But you led us to them. You practically ordered the attack."

"Ali opened fire. Once he did so, I joined."

"It was an ambush of filthy terrorists," I snapped. "We had every right."

"But they had not yet committed any crime."

"Bullshit! They were armed to the teeth. Moving north. In-filtrators."

Bachshi smiled. "Then why do you feel so bad about it?"

"Because I don't like killing. Because I had never killed a man before in my life. And I don't like that the first one I got was asleep. No, it didn't make me feel much like a hero."

"But they were planning to kill your people."

"Yes. But it doesn't mean I don't suffer anyway."

Then he said with a measure of disdain something in which I heard a sort of plea: "Then you do understand." And that was all. He broke off the conversation for good and retired to his sleeping bag, where he rolled himself up and lay still and was soon, merci-fully, walking in his "meridians of God."

One week later, I saw Batiya under the most musical of circumstances.

I was posted, with Micah, to a forward observation post along the frontier, a camouflaged bunker, little more, really, than a sand-bagged pit in the earth. It was covered with netting and sagebrush and camouflage tarpaulins, with a slit for binoculars or the barrel of a gun, and little more. A crawl space led into the bunker proper, which was suffocatingly hot. One man stood peering out while the other dozed off on the ground, which, oddly, was quite cool and, under the circumstances, the best place to be, for one went right to sleep there. All of us patrollers were more or less sleep-deprived and prone to hallucination. I peered out through the binoculars, a bandanna tied around my head to catch the sweat pouring off my brow. I had another bandanna knotted around my throat and was stripped to the waist. I peered through the glasses at the bright white glare of the sand-swept, pristine, bleached white view; a vista that rose in rhythmic knolls to a harshly lit sky of pure blue flame.

Against this backdrop objects stood out so perfectly that I could spot long lines of tracks and then larger and larger ones as well, belonging to ants, fire scorpions, dung beetles, dune hares, gray foxes, jackals, soldiers, jeeps, Noons Noons, tanks. We were to monitor any unusual movement. I had an intelligence book that showed in silhouette the shapes of every conceivable type of known weapon and conveyance deployed by the Egyptian army facing us. I was also to monitor the presence of UN vehicles, should any appear. But our primary mission was to watch for infiltrators.

Batiya did not fit any of these types of intruder when she appeared in her black robes, staff in hand, leading her flock, the bleating herd flowing over the dunes with bobbing heads and then wrestling to a halt, their tufted jaws ducking and bowing before the ground, seeking sustenance and, as goats will, managing, miraculously, to find something to eat where seemingly there was nothing. A rising wind lifted the top layer of powdery sand into a twister of human dimensions, a mini-tornado that spun and danced like a top. To my amazement, Batiya flung off her robes, revealing herself garbed in a flimsy, sweat-soaked blouse and skirt, and began to dance. That girl, her face exquisite, was more beautiful than I had imagined when only her almandine eyes were publicly visible, and with the staff lifted to the sky she spun in pretty, measured steps to an internal beat, slowly at first, then faster and faster as the twister danced alongside, and, throwing back her head, she ululated a song of bleached white undulating desert joy, not a single word of which I understood, yet somehow I sensed, grasped, that her song was about Ali, her love for him. And I knew that they were lovers.

Yes, I swear, I believe that such is what she sang about the very last time I saw her.

I say last, because the next time she was dead. I did not find her: Micah did. Laid out with throat cut and her life's blood poured out, her corpse crumpled in a heap behind a makeshift garbage dump fashioned from eight rusted iron oil drums bound together with thick rope and planted, absurdly, in the middle of nowhere, next to a tree and a pile of boulders that had been, apparently, carted to there for some unknown purpose and just left unused, and so long ago that it probably predated the very state.

Micah, who was scanning from the jeep with his binoculars, had seen a pair of small, tattooed bare feet protruding from behind the barrels and made for it, he later said, with a sickened feeling in his throat that he already knew who it was, though given the area any number of types were candidates for corpsehood, from informers and collaborators to settlers to innocent travelers or even soldiers, though the tattooed feet made that unlikely. As he raced to the site he speculated in that rapid-fire, calculating way that certain minds suited to danger are able to achieve under great duress that the victim's shoes or boots had been stripped, either for purpose of torture or as an act of theft, but the moment he saw her face, partly covered by its torn veil, he knew: Here is Batiya, Bedouin girl, Bachshi's sister, slaughtered by her own brother because she did what most normal seventeen-year-old girls do — fell in love.

"I feel dead inside," he said as we covered her up against flies and vultures. We used a tarp we had stored behind, under the mounted MAG, normally used to cover up our ammunition in rain, to keep it dry.

"I know," I said gently, touching his arm.

He drew it back. "We'll have to get another tarp," he said.

"We will."

"I signed on for it. I don't want to have to buy a new one."

"No," I said. He was in a kind of shock. He slid to the ground and the raised white dust swirled around him. He sat there, covered in white, head hung, hands clasped. He glanced up with a suffering, drawn look, like a kicked dog.

"Want to know the truth?"

"What's that?" I said.

"I've seen the dead before. You know that. It's always bad. But this time, I have a sick feeling — like she is inside of me, rotting — like I've cut out a piece of her and eaten it and now the cannibal taste won't go away. The taste of dead sister."

"Micah, I've got to call it in now. OK? I've got to get on the radio. You'll be all right?"

He nodded and looked away.

It was a police affair, of course: not army. And the police went after Bachshi, who, of course, was gone. Army investigators participated, as well as units from the military police, and because it was a territorial matter operatives from the Sheen Bet Security Services also took part in the hunt.

In the meantime, I had an ammunition crate full of unplaced bet money to return to men throughout the corps and did so, to the last cent, using the network of cooks and supply depot men and platoon clerks and drivers that had spread wide the betting net. It took a week. It also befell me, with help from Micah and Ali, who didn't seem overly affected by any of this, to pack up Bachshi's gear and hand it over to the boys from Sheen Bet.

It was all Micah could do to keep from exploding at Ali. I too had trouble keeping a lid on all I wanted to say to the Bedouin. Ali even grinned several times, as though he'd had no part in the destruction of these two lives: a dead young girl and a promising young man who, as good as dead, faced a lifetime of incarceration in a filthy jail.

"Tell me," I said as we left Sheen Bet headquarters. Micah was already gone, returned to the unit to look into getting a leave, which he badly needed. It was just Ali and me, at dusk, stars beginning to appear in the rose-colored sky and darkness already looming on the horizon. We were near the jeep.

"Yes? What is it, my friend?" He grinned pleasantly.

"Do you feel even a little bad?"

He looked at me, then put his hands on his hips in this jaunty way, like a cowboy, a stance he'd seen in some American film, no doubt, and now affected.

"About what?" he said coldly, though knowing full well.

"What do you think?" I snapped.

He said nothing. I heard my own voice repeating at a shout: "What do you think, Ali? What the fuck do you fucking think?"

They found Bachshi, of course. They always found them, unless they escaped into Egypt, which Bachshi was better qualified than most to attempt. Probably, he could have pulled it off. Yet he chose to stay. I knew he would. He could not be far from where his people, his family, would come pay him regular visits from their formerly dishonored tents.

I, however, had no way to murderously cleanse my own tent, which was filthy with love for Maya. On my first leave home in three weeks, I found her deep in the horrors of our disintegrating world. Dotan had returned. It was all out in the open now. Divorce in the works. He was to get everything. As an admitted adulteress, her case was indefensible.

"No one speaks to me anymore," she said wearily, lying beside me. We were in the one-bedroom cottage of her employer, Jerry Chapman. He had gone north to shoot for a new A/V show and lent her the cottage to get a respite from all the tumult. She smelled like sweat and perfume, and I drew her close as she spoke, her lips murmuring into my chest, her long slender fingers spread over my skin like a spider at rest.

"No one," she repeated. "All the people who I thought liked me are Dotan's friends, it turns out. Our whole life was him. The house. The friends. The money. The connections. The influence. I tried to meet with the director of the Israel Museum, to see about a show. I haven't heard a word back. I have the feeling I won't."

"How many times did you call his office? Eli is a busy man."

"Three," she said.

I gently moved her off me and swung my legs over the side of the bed. Naked, I walked to the record player and searched through Jerry's albums.

"What are you doing?" asked Maya.

I found what I was looking for: the Eagles. I put on the track "Desperado" and set the record player to repeat. Maya stood up and walked over, into my arms, and she let me enfold her and together we began, ever so slowly, to slow dance, naked, belly to belly, with Batiya in my thoughts, her ululating voice that carried so far over the Negev sands that it reached to me, in my lonely little hole of a life, in which I hid in the dark waiting, armed, with other creatures in their holes, the ant, the scorpion, the snake, the beetle, the hare, the fox, the jackal, the leopard, peering out of the fly-droning, airless dark for the next intruder to enter our sights, trigger our pulse, bring us out.

Three days later, I joined Ali on a short visit to his family camp. He introduced me to two men, Achmad and Magfuz, who were on the ground holding down a struggling dog. I knew what was to come. And what a fight it put up when Ali suddenly came upon it, clutching the huarti, that vicious little knife they used to cut the throats of game fowl brought down by their trained falcons. We were here only for a brief stop — an hour, no more; en route back to base — and as Ali was the tribe's finest brave, his father had insisted that Ali take care of the dog. The other men, the elders, had each nodded. I had seen all of this, not understanding what was involved. Ali explained. I stared at him in disbelief. But, it was decided. He had no choice, couldn't refuse the task. A matter of custom, of duty, you know. I saw that. Ali's lips were clamped tight and his cold eyes wore a look of grim resolve.

The dog snapped at the air with bared teeth. I had not really conceptualized what was about to occur. It barked and pleaded, growled and whined, but Achmad and Magfuz pressed down their weight all the harder. Achmad grimaced up at me, his teeth yellowish white against his coffee-colored skin, and framed by a fleshy pink display of diseased-looking gums. He was having himself a hell of a good time, and also Magfuz seemed to genuinely enjoy it all, grinning, amused, and shaking his head at the dog's pathetic struggles. The men's outstretched legs reclined like holidaying sunbathers. Each man was powerfully built. The sun beat down on us with raging fists, the desert gaped in rage. The wilderness promised to erase us very soon with its relentless glare. Just one more hour, it seemed to say, another minute and you're gone! It passed before our eyes a hand of blinding light, as if to show just how completely we would be effaced — like this white blindness, you will be gone.

In response, the men, Achmad and Magfuz, spit dryly. And beside us, the prepared fire smoked, cackling and distorting the air with undulant mirages. And then, when Ali was right upon it with the knife and the grinning men had their full weight pressing down, suddenly, the dog's struggles ceased. It lay there, tongue lolling out from a foaming grin of caked spittle, parched for thirst, its ears, velvety leaf-shaped and lined with sensitive pale pinkish skin, laid back and down.

With his free hand, almost tenderly, Ali lifted the dog's left ear, the dog's terror-bulged left eye watching all this, the creature still but for its fiercely panting ribs and Ali's face petrified into some kind of tribal mask of obsidian stone. With a shocking, swift cut he took off the dog's ear.

The dog screamed a shrill pulse beat of mournful anguish. Its whole body kicked, as though shot. Nearby, a man grooming a horse stopped brushing to witness the dog's torment; stood with a frozen grin and wide, glistening eyes. Two running little girls paused to listen to the dog's fierce wail. They met my stare with playful surprise, then continued to run. Ali's mother, by her crockpot, nodded to me, laughing. Ali's father, Beckrace, emerged from his tent, squinted at the dog and then at me, turned, and walked away with long proud strides in the direction of a cluster of men mounting camels, none of whom paused to acknowledge the suffering of the dog.

Ali's face was still impassive, his job but half done. There remained the other ear. I don't think the dog realized. Ali pinched the second ear, held it more roughly than the first, and with a single long cut sliced it completely off. I looked away, closed my eyes tight. The dog's torment was like nothing I had ever heard. Not even wounded humans made such sounds.

Ali rose with the two ears in his open hand. The dog was now frantic, but his tormentors set him loose. He struggled up, stood there with bowed head, shaking, legs splayed, clownish in his betrayed submission. Its upturned eyes looked unable to grasp the source of its anguish, see how absurd it now looked (not at all like a dog but something ratlike and aborted yet that had somehow lived anyway), and then it fell to the ground and twisted into a knot from which its head ejected with skyward nose and hideously elastic neck, and its left leg shot up and made circular scratching motions that did not dare to touch the actual bloody, gaping wounds on each side of its head.

Ali took the ears over to the fire and tossed them in. He squatted, hands clasped between his knees, watching the ears sizzle in the flame. The smell of scorched hair filled my nose. Then, a reek of burnt meat. It made me want to retch.

Only once did Ali look my way to regard me with incurious disdain, as if to say that I, as a Jew, can never cross the line to where he is, who he is, what he knows, what he stands for, what his obligations are, and I looked back as if to say that not only are you right about that but I don't ever want to understand why you've done such a thing to a poor defenseless dog. Which I believed he understood, for only then, suddenly, he smiled and nodded. "It makes them into better hunting dogs," he called out wryly. "When they lose their ears they depend more on their nose. This makes a certain sense, no?" He grinned.

I had to struggle very hard not to respond with anger. I only managed a half smile. It was enough. He looked away, plucked the ears out, and tossed them to the dog, who had lain himself down in a dazed coil of agony. The dog rose unsteadily, cautiously, and with bowed head approached the offering, sniffing the air before it as it drew near, and when it was upon the two shriveled and blackened things, its head darted forward with open jaws and gobbled down its own ears. Then it snapped its jaws several times with a gagging cough. Then swallowed one large final gulp and looked at each of us with a dull, stupefied stare of satiety, blood trickling down the sides of his head. Achmad walked over to it, gave it a harsh kick. With a yelp, it scurried a few yards away and stood there, still smacking its lips upon the taste of its unexpected snack and, no doubt, wanting more.

Ali wiped his knife in the sand, thrust it into the fire, pulled it out, wiped it on his battle fatigues and slipped it back into a small scabbard affixed to his battle vest. We had still an hour's drive back to base camp near Khan Yunis, and, hoisting our weapons, we walked to the jeep and climbed in.

"Don't you want to say good-bye to your family?" I said.

He looked over to where his father sat on camel back among the troupe of other riders. They looked resplendent in their long robes, with large curved scabbards dangling from their waists.

"You see those camels? They are stupider than dogs," said Ali. "And you see those men, those warriors?" He kicked over the engine with a sudden, angry gesture. It roared to life. "Those men there," he shouted in Hebrew as he spun the wheel and slammed on the accelerator and we surged out of the desert encampment, "they are antiques! They are stupider than camels! The hell with them!" And as he drove past, he spit out the side window, visibly, for his father and the others to see.

PART 3

THE BEST SOLDIER IN A WAR

You do not cry. This I know. Beneath the surprisingly pale, glaring sky to which I awaken at midday, jolted by the drained, crumbling pastels of Gaza City, the flecked, molting skinlike walls, I lie bathed in sweat, imagining that soon my patrol will wend through the coiling dark streets of the central marketplace in spiky formation (like some multiheaded centipede of Galil assault rifles, CAR-15s, and a Belgian MAG field machine gun, muzzles aimed at the widening portals of the way ahead and the shrinking black gates of the way back), and once more I determine, as I do each day, that though afraid I will show a tough, emotionless face to the crumbling roofs and soot-smudged windows, the doorways, the fly-buzzed storefronts, the parked cars that at any instant can take out our whole fucking squad in a loud clap of shrapnel and flames.

It is spring. For our unit, our sixth monthlong turn in four years at playing Gaza roulette with the locals, who call their ceaseless violent insurrection "Intifada." The troubles began when a settler accidentally lost control of his car and killed several locals. Rioting ensued and spread into an ongoing full-scale armed revolt that goes on year after year. We are on our guard every moment. We have no rest.

Already I can imagine unseen faces from behind watchful windows peering back at me with hatred, fear, and disdain; nut brown, hardened, unforgiving. Faces that loom like blackened guillotine blades. Already, I can visualize Pagi's blue eyes staring out of a face smudged with machine oil — covering my back as he scans the roofs opposite, the ones I can't see, probes for shooters. Up ahead, Tuli, a new man, the brusque, loudmouthed owner of a coffee shop in Ashdod, and the quiet, bearish, dependable Sergeant Dedi, step carefully, slowly, their feet moving nicely in tandem — at least this Tuli can soldier — and already I know who will be out in front of them, walking point: Yoram, of course, the oldest man in the unit, forty-five yet still a corporal, with his big brown face and nicotine-stained smile that makes one feel, ridiculously, OK, even in the worst of circumstances.

This Yoram once said, half jokingly, as a mob tossed Molotovs against the wall we cringed behind, "Soldiers never cry!" to Sayla, my friend from G-Beat days, who had tears running down his cheeks and lips. This Yoram smiles reassuringly as our Noon Noon roars down a parched backcountry road while a hidden gunman kicks up dirt around our wheels, and he winks as we creep up dark, creaking stairs to search the flat of a suspect wanted for blowing up an Egged bus. And this Yoram has a wife, Rivka (mother of five children ages nine to seventeen), who returns him to us after leaves home bearing big shoe boxes of homemade strudel, the wax paper–wrapped portions laid out in neat rows, the box bound in paper toweling and rubber bands.

Yoram — who always says that the best soldier in a war is the one who survives — breaks out the strudel at midday in the garrison, just when things feel the worst: hands around cake though we're too dejected even to bathe. The old British fort, the same as the one in Khan Yunis, only bigger, has paneless caged windows to prevent locals from tossing in grenades at us and the wind whistles through and it's winter, the water in the pipes ice cold, so why even bother to wash, and we sit, hunched, listless, around the TV in our parkas and mud-caked boots, waiting, waiting for the Noon Noon to roar into the parade grounds. Our heads are hung, eyes drooping with boredom and fatigue, our weapons and gear in piles around our feet, and the strudel crumbling in our hands.

And then comes the Noon Noon, the driver not even cutting the engine but letting it run while squads change place with dragging feet. With dread in the pits of our bellies, we hop aboard while the relieved patrollers trudge silently into the TV room to replace our listless wait, and Yoram hands them strudel too, and both squads, coming and going, assume their places with Rivka's cake kissing their fingertips.

Then Yoram jumps aboard and as the Noon Noon pulls out of the gates I stare with red-rimmed eyes at the strudel's caramelized sliced apples, the sugary raisins, the cinnamon-dusted crust, and for an instant I am not in Gaza City but in Rivka's kitchen, at her table, watching her boil coffee to go with my first helping of strudel (another portion and then another sits waiting for me on the table while Yoram admonishes, "You'd better eat at least three or four pieces or Rivka will be very insulted, won't you, Rivka-la?" And Rivka, with a warm, humorous smile: "Of course I will. Yoram knows how I am." And of course, it's all for me. Welcome home.). "Rest," says the cake to my fingers, "for a moment from your hypervigilant dread of a surprise bullet penetrating your skull from any direction or, just as bad, seeing your brother-in-arms dropped right in front of you. Instead, bite into this. It will solace you. It will lessen the pain." And I do.

Almost it feels as though I've forgotten how to eat. My teeth don't sink into the sweet confection; they gnash together, with half the portion trapped behind my lips, mashed beneath the gums. The Noon Noon vibrates, its mobile steel trembling, and hypnotically I move my jaws, note how the shredded, somewhat stale crust scrapes at the roof of my mouth. The apples taste withered, dry. How long it has been in that shoe box, I can't say. It's so difficult to swallow, dry and hard: my hand reaches behind to the canteen pouched in the web of my battle vest and shakes to feel for water. None. Forgot to fill it — how long ago? There's never really been a need.

Because right on the floor of the Noon Noon is always that big crate full of little plastic cups of Orangina that everyone drinks instead of water. The strudel might taste good softened by the sweet, watery orange drink, the crust turned a sugary mush of big crumbs and raisins, but I can't bother to rise in the speeding vehicle to fetch one. Instead, I unfasten my helmet strap, put my palm to my lips, and spit out the big mashed, fecal-looking, semimasticated mess and with a stab of despair that nothing, not even Rivka's strudel, is ever quite as good as one's imaginings of it, hurl it overboard at the Gazan wilderness as the Noon Noon takes the main road into Rafiah.

I do not cry, though I want to. Not for fear so much as for the sheer brunt of dumb heat that assails my body like a giant, fiery fist. A bullet shot at the forehead of the sun won't stop it; let alone a slingshot stone. And the Arabs' way of spreading themselves out over everywhere, seeming always to be around, with no place for privacy, makes them as gruelingly pervasive, as inexhaustible, as the relentless desert heat.

And then, there is the hatred. Neither for us Jews to leave nor simply to remain will they accept. Stay or go, we must, in their estimation, die. Neither our statehood nor their occupation is acceptable. But our destruction alone is, for them, imperative. I see myself in T-shirt, sandals, shorts, sunglasses, with short-cropped hair and an earring, at a sidewalk café on Dizengoff Street in Tel Aviv: by them, sentenced to death. Envision myself at the last stand, on the beach at Herziliya, the sea to my back and before me, stretched for miles, piles of bullet-riddled and bomb-dismembered Jewish corpses, and I am among the last survivors, with my CAR-15 and three clips of ammo left, and my parched, inchoate lips stained by a white ring of confectioners' sugar from Rivka's last, apocalyptic strudel batch, and hordes of foes armed with RPG, Kalatchnikovs, and weapons looted from the corpses of my fallen comrades, and they are descending upon me in a frenzied mob of murderous rage and some have dipped hands in the blood of the dead, painted their faces red with it, and as was done in Cambodia, Bosnia, Rwanda and of course throughout Europe in World War II, every detested inhabitant, man, woman, and child, is to be felled by bullet or bomb, hacked and exploded and decapitated — but however it happens, extinguished, each amazing miracle of us, so distinct, unique, irreplaceable. But to me the Arabs who will do this all look the same, act the same, wear, for me to see, the same indecipherable expression, until my back turns, I am past, the Noon Noon roars ahead and they melt away into their streets, yards, and fields, sworn to my death, implacably sinister under the yellowish gray Gazan sky.

But then, there is Yoram. And as I sway in the rattling vehicle I think about how Yoram always says that in a war the best soldier is the one who survives. He does not want war. He does not believe that Israel is meant to stretch to the Euphrates. His great pleasure in life: to sit at home at night on his porch with his wife, Rivka, and the neighbors Sami and Dvora, a nice middle-aged couple, playing bridge.

This Yoram is a cards champion. In his hometown of Petah Tikva, in his residence, on his cement white square porch that juts from the third floor of the boxlike white building's stone, glass, and steel — the ugly architecture softened by a crimson blood spill of bougainvillea over its facade and creeper vines wound through the very trellises that Rivka lined the porch with — stand wooden sun-deck chairs and a glass-topped wrought-iron table with a festive striped umbrella. The big porch juts into the black sky like a determined jaw. Yoram and Rivka and their neighbors Sami and Dvora sit on it and they four play hands of bridge. Yoram, handsome with graying sideburns, draws on a Time cigarette, exhales. Rivka waves away the smoke from her flustered smile of patient disapproval. Dvora, the neighbor, says in her gravel voice: "Shame on you, Yoram. You should quit those things already."

"Do you hear what Dvora said to you?" says Rivka to Yoram.

Yoram glances at Dvora's husband, Sami, winks. "Tell Dvora that Sami says it's not polite to criticize your host in his own home."

Dvora grunts to herself and laughs. "Not polite? Tell Sami I'll show him what's not polite when we get home later."

Rivka blushes: "Meaning exactly . . . ?"

Dvora raises her fist. "I don't mean what you think, Miss Sex-Starved Dirty-Minded Girl. I mean I'll give him a knock on his dumb skull, not do a striptease," and they all laugh. It smells of coffee and jasmine up there. Below the world and ahead the night. Darkness drawn over them deep blue, lovely: a bedspread crocheted with silver poinsettias. The big moon lies on the celestial bed like an ashtray and over the bed drift clouds like shredded wisps of exhaled cigarette smoke after sex. And Rivka, lovely, soft, perfumed, leaning over Yoram, her hand resting on his satisfied belly. And there in a small framed photograph on the table is the daughter, Dina, not present, a second lieutenant in the Education Corps, the spitting image of her mother's youth, on duty somewhere in the north. He sips from his coffee. He draws out a card, plays it. "Bridge." He smiles and lays down his cards.

In the Gazan night certain hues remind him, me, us, of the joker's suit, its colors: from the reds and greens that gleam in the alley to the blue and white of the mosque where the imam calls the faithful to insurrection against the Jewish infidel; the red and yellow of the marketplace cafés, their black and white jack-of-diamond floors, which we cross in our lace-up matte black boots and enter the rear — past the spiteful looks of the seated men in shirtsleeves, with their black mustaches and thick black hair and black glaring, velvety eyes with white pinpricks of light, and their yellowish brown feet in dusty leather sandals and around their necks black and white checkered kaffiyehs — and push into the back, into the spice and steam of the kitchen and storage rooms, where gray rats dart from behind enormous sacks of rice and scurry away underfoot.

Always, we are finding things in these back rooms. Yoram splits my shadow into blue and amber stripes, under a small window through which tinted light flashes as sharp as hallucinated knives; stoops among the fat burlap sacks, squatting solid and heavy in his rumpled fatigue pants and scuffed boots, his broad, sweat-stained shoulders hunched, the webbed top of his ducked helmet shown to us, his face obscured and his fingers gently brushing the floor. He looks up, furrowed brow pushed down by the chin strap of his helmet, says calmly: "Here. Right here."

It's just a hole in the ground crudely hidden by an irregularly cut oblong of wood, and the space paved with sawdust, spilled grains, and dirt. Gently Yoram's stubby fingers clear dirt away from its perimeter. Avi is already exiting the room, while Udi hurriedly gets on the radio to call in reinforcements and specialists because in the hole are what look like parts for homemade bombs.

"Detonators," says Yoram, holding up one wrapped like strudel in a wax paper that crinkles at the touch. He untwists the paper, holds up the cap, which has a red top and the rest is blue, black, and silver. Strange-looking thing. A cross between a twist candy and a battery that can detonate a million pounds of plastic. This single cap plus an ounce of plastic. Enough to destroy a bus. A house. A cafeteria. A jeep. A shelter giving shade to soldiers on leave, hitchhiking home. A crowd of celebrating mothers and children gathered for a birthday party in the bakery café of an immigrant development town.

Already we can hear our own men shouting and the scrambling and fuss, and by now we know that the sullen customers in the café have been hauled out of their chairs and thrown facedown to the floor, with hands clasped behind their necks, and all of them get frisked. Some have their hands bound behind their backs with strips of flannel gun rag and wait at gunpoint for the Sheen Bet Territorial Security Services to cart them off in the back of a Border Patrol jeep, but the owners of the café and the workers, they will go separately in the little white Carmels that the Sheen Bet drive.

Yoram has been doing this work for years, is in a war just now, and certainly he is the best soldier in it, the one who is surviving. He is nonplussed, despite the backslapping he gets after delivering his on-site report to the assembled field commanders and even sidesteps talk about a commendation and so forth. To us, the squad, he says like a real man, a good boy: "*Y'Allah!* Let's go. We still have to finish out the shift," and we gather outside to continue our patrol and are joined by Udi, our insolent radio man, who has suited up in full combat gear with a portable transmitter on his back and a rifle cradled on one arm, the handset pressed to his lips as he carries on a running chat with some girl soldier that he's fucking back at HQ.

Now, it's all changed out there: it's gotten serious, a curfew in effect, helicopters thudding overhead, the street swarming with soldiers of the various corps — Paratroopers, Border Patrol, regular police, Engineering Corps to handle the detonators, Security Services, Ambulance Corps just in case, all rushing around and some of them bursting into surrounding residences now, right through the door. Meeting a dismayed face, they shove past nonetheless; in they go, smash, crash, rip — lamps, mirrors, windows, TVs, closets, glasses, plates, cases, candles, dishes broken and furniture overturned, and in the street, shop shutters crash close and the fast-talking proprietors not sneering now from out of upstairs windows but explaining their doubtful innocence with ingratiating smiles.

This is how it goes within these high alleylike flesh-colored walls emblazoned with revolutionary calls to arms, stenciled and hand-lettered imprecations to slaughter us the Jews, the evil Jews, the Zionist invaders; to reclaim "Falastine" as they call it, all of it, to the sea, its very edge. Sand. Seashore. The promenade. The steakia. The concession stands. Cafés. Cotton candy. Falafals. Pennants. A little machine that engraves tin medallions with your name. Displayed sunglasses, postcards, T-shirts. Whole damned thing to the Palestinians. And us Jews bobbing, drowned in the salt-water surf, bloated corpses with mouths and eyes agape. Calls to butcher the young girls in bathing suits, our daughters, girlfriends, wives, lolling on their beach towels in Tel Aviv and Herziliya and Netanya in their sexy Lolita Brigitte Bardot sunglasses — these our budding Sophia Lorens who will never be as thin as Winona Ryder or as blond as Reese Witherspoon, no matter how they try, and try they do, God knows. Deserve to die, though, we do, us Jews. With these detonator caps stuck up our infidel asses.

Our eyes crawl along the walls, creep, the armor-plated, multiheaded centipede organism of our time-welded unit that has crept and crawled together through these many years from alley wall to alley wall. Before they come to us, we come to them, from out of the very walls materialize, and we do not let them escape before they arrive at our apartments, cottages, kibbutz children's houses, bus stations, synagogues, movie theaters, beaches, highways, and explode us like cheap firecrackers on the American Fourth of July. Before they dazzle the streets of Jerusalem, Tel Aviv, Netanya, Haifa, Tiberius, Keryat Shemona, with bright red splatters of our jettisoned blood, before we are sheared open, our very chests, bellies, hearts, exposed, even expelled (after one terrorist bombing an eyewitness saw on the sidewalk a still-beating heart. At another: a leg on a lamppost. Two old folks' heads landed at a pedestrian's feet). Before just one slender black gun barrel from a cracked window or a door, or slipped between bars of a gate or carried down a street or back alley opens up on us suddenly with a lead spray, or aims at the smell of Yoram's barbecue on his terrace, the burnt meat and coal smoke in his nose. And tries to slaughter his wife's finely cut, golden-skinned French fries. And the aroma of a Time cigarette.

Our black boots step carefully on rotten cabbage leavings in these curfewed alien streets. A cat's entrails, fly-swarmed, spilling out of its car-slaughtered belly. Cigarette butts. Shreds of newspaper. Wooden splinters. The nameless black mulch of urban soot universal now, everywhere, true for Jewish foot and Arab foot alike. Stink of pitiless sunlight, of Middle Eastern rot. The crumbling and disintegration of the relentless sun, that factor forever omitted from political calculation, for when all the treaties will, if ever, have been signed, all the relations normalized, the borders opened, commerce humming, still, the sun that murders our hearts and wearies our minds in this part of the world does not relent. And walls of desert grit, skyscraper tall, blow at Khamsin time over everyone and drive us all mad. For, at times, the very weather seems to impel us to war. And now as we step through the city of eyes we are burned to copper against vistas of color and space smudged with the smoke of battle, of history too old to forget and too savage to want to remember. Our skins grow darker and darker. And perhaps this *is* peace, this life with a knife at each other's throat. Perhaps this is good, the preferred version of hell.

Yoram's smile radiates even from the back of his head, from the dun-colored, bullet-deflecting helmet screened with shredded remnants of camouflage webbing, like torn nylons on an old woman's varicosed legs. Imagine it. *Look at us,* says his grin, *frightened like dogs, crowding along. Be brave, good friends, this is only one weird part of being who we are. Soon, we'll be home. Watching soccer, eating cake in front of our TVs. Sitting there is good, my friends. But for now, hang on. Watch those roofs, by the way. There's no end to these streets and night is falling. Hard to see up there. What nitwit thought up this duty anyway? Doesn't matter though. Nothing else for us to do just now. Not so funny though, is it, this place? A rotten hole, in fact.*

We are on a narrow street in the city's deserted center. The very sky itself seems under curfew as night falls, for not a star shines above, or a planet, and the moon floats hidden behind glowering clouds. Our boot soles suck at greasy cobblestones as we inch on ahead, afraid but prodded forward by Yoram's easy manner, his knowing winks. *Even here in hell, we serve with a smile,* say his winks. The very manner of this old bridge-playing veteran says: *The best soldier in a war is the one who lives, and right now we are winning.* But we are not so sure, our barrels sweeping left and right, our fingers stroking triggers, tense, ready to unload into the black windowpanes. And here and there yellow lights blink on along the alley's length. Why? *Did you hear something?* worries the mind. We stop. Listen. There is in fact some noise that sounds like scuffling feet. But when we squint at the roofs, nothing. So we walk. Forward we go, gingerly, nervously, a chill, gritty breeze whistling through our collars. We hunch our shoulders. Rub our sleepless, scratchy eyes.

Then, in a blink, Yoram's head is struck by a big white crushing cinder block and, helmet or no helmet, it explodes, though the block itself doesn't fully shatter until it smacks the sidewalk and splinters woefully into several useless chunks. I note the second chalky outer ring of bits and dust haloing his blood-soaked face. Because he's stretched out lifeless now, gone right down. In that instant, I know that he is dead. Something vital has snapped. No eyelids fluttering, his or mine.

And the steel bristles of our armed squad thrust everywhere, jabbing helplessly; poke at sky, roofs, street, windows, our faces grave, eyelids fluttering like mad, while Dedi and Avi and Tuli crouch over Yoram, Brandt performing mouth to mouth just like they show during training, in the film short about administering first aid under combat conditions. Who would have thought, though, that anyone had actually watched that dumb flick? As I recall, we were all exchanging sexual innuendos with that saucy medical corps corporal who sat on the desk showing her knees and smiling as the reel flickered and she winked like a calendar girl and probably someone fucked her that night and now Brandt is on his knees with his clasped hands raised above his head, delivering several sharp blows to Yoram's breastbone, to no avail. Dedi's ear to Yoram's combat vest, listening. Zip. Pagi's fingers at Yoram's artery. Nada. On his pulse: zero. I'm kneeling just to the right of Pagi, my hand on his shoulder. Tuli, the loud-mouthed coffee shop owner, stands up quickly, says in a flat voice: "He's gone." Then the rest of us climb wearily to our feet. Udi tears the radio transmitter from his lips, looks at Dedi: "They're coming." Dedi nods. Looks at me, face gray, haggard. Says: "Secure a perimeter."

I nod. We fan out. I station myself in a doorway from which I have a good view of the intersection of streets and from where I can pretty much spot any approach or movement from a window, door, or roof and can establish a good line of fire. Also, I have removed two hand grenades from my battle vest and placed them in the left thigh pocket of my fatigue pants, for quick access.

But there is nothing more to do than watch. It is not yet time to think or feel about Yoram. Already, life is altered. The world much lonelier. We are scrambling now like humiliated children who have shat themselves, exposed by our dirty asses as mortal hairless apes of blue and red bloody meat, diapers and daydreams, desires, cum, wetness, ache, big and motherless now and suppressing tears, soldiers' tears, which are those of men trying to make sense of the new order imposed by each fresh catastrophe, to create a brand-new fantasy about the best soldier in a war, but instead we fall back on what has been drilled into us, time and again: call for reinforcements; secure or assist the wounded/dead. Protect the area. Retain your position, if possible, for as long as you can.

We do. Not an Arab in sight. I scan the roofs. It was probably kids, who have no idea what death means. Waited for a patrol to come by. We were it. It could have been any one of us. I nod to myself in concurrence with this thought. Yes, it could have . . . yes, here. Here only, though. Here. But then I think of Buenos Aires or Fez, Paris or Berlin. These days Jews meet attackers in those cities, sure. It's no longer safe for us anywhere. Still, here, the chances of being attacked are better than good. It's inevitable.

The bleached, pocked, yellowish *shuk* walls hurt my eyes. Even their shadows cast a glare.

CAPTAIN JOHNSON

Because I wore a New York Yankees baseball cap during stints of reserve duty and was tall and very American-looking, the others sometimes called me Captain Johnson.

Captain Johnson was an American marine who, in the first year of the Lebanon war, had climbed atop an Israeli tank at a checkpoint and ordered it turned back. When the Israeli driver refused, Captain Johnson drew his sidearm, aimed, and again ordered him to withdraw. Amused, the tankist complied.

The Israeli public had liked that. It was all over the news. They had admired Captain Johnson's Clint Eastwood style.

I can just see the Israeli tankist's grin as he faced the earnest marine's revolver. Certainly, it must have been a gentle smile of affection, a more than willing deference to an American marine's spit-and-polish professionalism.

Because no Israeli takes himself too seriously when it comes to military protocol. The Israeli knows too much. He grows up surrounded by soldiers. Everyone in his family is, has been, or will be a soldier: even his mommy. There are few parades and fewer ceremonies still. Israeli soldiering is not glamorous. It is just life.

The Israeli soldier's uniform is not one to compel much admiration: no brass buttons, gold braid, white gloves, snappy tunic, fringe epaulets. The dress uniform is as drab as a work shirt.

The average Israeli reservist wears his shirttails out. He is, famously, a slob. His pants hang loose around his ankles. He doesn't wear his field hat or beret. He has sunglasses pushed back into his gray-streaked curly hair. His shirtsleeves are rolled, the shirt unbuttoned to display dog tags against a sun-scorched chest. There are on him no iron creases or folds, just bunched and wrinkled cloth. I have always envisioned Captain Johnson as assembled from sharp planes, starched angles, all pointing to a militant sense of certainty that no Israeli ever feels.

At first, I didn't mind being called Captain Johnson. When I entered a group of the men, in the garrison or in the field, inevitably someone smiled and said, "Here is Captain Johnson. We can all go home now. He will take care of everything." And everyone laughed, yours truly included.

But over time, it got to me. Even Lieutenant Yitzak, who had the sense of humor of a pit bull, began to call me by it. I can still see his young, dark, handsome face break into a playboy grin and the gold chain around his neck swinging as he swayed back and forth in the door of his tent, standing there in his bleached white BVDs and thong sandals, scratching his well-defined abdominals and bulging testicles while intoning in his version of English, "Captain John-son, Cap-tain John-son" with mirth. "Where are you going? To pull your gun and kick the ass? Huh, Captain? Kick ass. Like the Clint Eastwood!" I only shook my head with a little uncommunicative smile and did not respond. I could tell: reply and it will never stop.

By week two the joke had worn thin. I was ready for change.

I wanted my real name back. But it was too late. Nothing could reverse the tide. It was "Captain Johnson, pass the salad," "Captain Johnson, come play Risk," "Captain Johnson, turn up the volume on the TV," "Captain Johnson, come, we go take a turn down in Rafiah, there's reports of activity near the *shuk*." And so forth and so on. Israelis are that way. Once they get hold of a joke, they beat it bloody. In this regard, they surpass even the French, who hammer at a joke until it fairly crawls off to die somewhere, sick and alone.

It was inevitable that someone had to pay a price for all of this in order for it to stop. The toll on my nerves was mounting daily. Payback was going to cost a lot. But I didn't reckon on a sum as high as was ultimately exacted, for it surprised even me. Then, no one wanted to hear the name of Captain Johnson anymore.

It happened at the shooting range that we called "Little Beirut," a deserted cluster of cottages and shops in the middle of a barren stretch of wind-denuded beachfront in the Gaza Strip. It was on a rise overlooking the sea, recessed slightly back on low cliffs. We drove there in jeeps, just fifteen of us, and spent the whole day, drilling over and over to polish up our house-to-house search and fighting skills.

House-to-house was the unit's specialty. And no one, not even the officers, was better at it than I was. When I performed on a team, the others went unseen. Only I was watched. My feet, my hands. My body postures. For me, it was like playing football all over again, a sport in which I had excelled in high school as a natural-born offensive tackle and defensive end. For a time, as a semi-pro, I had played both ways. I wasn't big for a lineman either: six-two and my playing weight was only 220. But in football I had had the speed, moves, balance, and power to outperform men seven inches taller and eighty pounds heavier. I took down a lot of giants in my day.

And so it was during house-to-house. I was nimble and my gun was accurate. I was through a door blazing before you could say "jackrabbit." I fired into the cordite haze of exploded grenades in an arc so perfect that afterward the officers and NCO stood around, chins resting on their fists, pointing out the seams stitched by my bullets in the sheet metal walls of "Little Beirut." They whispered to each other in amazement, exchanged glances of naked wonder. This is not a boast but fact. House-to-house was the thing I did best in my unit, and I was proud of it and very gracious with all the compliments paid.

This is how it was in house-to-house: Your ten-man squad is on the street. Radio contact is lost. OK: now what? Investigate the village. Known hostiles. Park your asses flat up against the walls. Hug those walls. No talk. Instead, Dedi's two fingers signal twice and four men scurry across the road, duck inside a doorway. Then, hunched over, one of theirs and one of ours steps into the street, kneels, and directs crossfire to the roofs opposite. Now Dedi's hand motions "forward," and our two squads hustle down the street, hugging the walls, raised weapons scanning. When we reach our respective targeted doors one from each group drops to his knees and establishes a second crossfire, and the two men still back there, shooting at roofs, retain their posts and guard our rear.

Now a man in each squad squats up against the wall, shrugs off his backpack, and removes from it, gently, an explosive charge. He sticks it to the door, rigs wires. Then both squads retreat with mincing, balletic steps, heads ducked. A hand twists the detonator. A big blast of noise and smoke blow the door right off its frame.

Dedi's hand rested on the small of my back, just as in football, just like leading the block for a fullback as you burst through the hole in the line and spring him to daylight. I pulled my goggles down over my eyes, shouted, "Grenade!" and tossed one in and counted loudly, twenty-one, twenty-two, twenty-three. It blew.

Shouting "Me from the left, you from the right," I kicked my right boot out to catch the base of the door frame and shoved off to my left. This was like boxing where to step to the left you push off from the right foot. I skipped with dancing side steps into the room and, planting my feet, swiveled to the right, all in nano-seconds, and cut an arc of fire from the far corner of the room to the near. The blazing sweep ended by my elbow, and the flash and roar was tremendous. The smoke was too thick to penetrate. I saw, vaguely, the form of Dedi, ghostly, faint, barely discernible, and his blue muzzle flash spitting fire.

When we were done, we met in the center of the room, where we walked one behind the other, in a tight circle, firing at the floor to be sure that nothing lived. Then, I ducked, waving Dedi down behind me and duck-walked under a window and stood and waved Dedi forward. There was a door leading to a corridor. I dropped to a knee and, peering out, scanned to the left and the right. I tossed a grenade in each direction. I swung out my weapon, firing to each side. I led Dedi down one end, alert that, hypothetically, no gunfire opened on me from my rear, though Dedi covered my advance. We were both vulnerable. We duck-walked under windows, pretending that corridor was a death trap. We traversed stairwells, flats, roofs. It was all an exercise. We walked our way through the whole village, never leaving the skein of houses. We crawled, jumped, ran, slid our way forward, tossing grenades, firing, changing out clips, firing. When we reached the end, we reassembled, switched sides to the other street, and started the whole thing all over again.

At night we set up a perimeter, made camp, and heated up cooking oil in a big drum, using a huge acetylene torch on a tripod stand. Into the pot we tossed buckets full of sliced French fries that our unit cooks had prepared. We boiled coffee and ate the fries with bread and washed it all down with strong mud coffee and had big bars of Elite chocolate for dessert. It was a great meal, and we slept like stones that night until Gil awakened me. Stretched beside me in our two-man pup tent, Gil had been roused by sentries to go perform guard duty.

"You were in the police in the USA, Captain Johnson. I'm sure of it," said Gil with a yawn. He was tall and wiry with a head of black macaroni curls, and wore tortoiseshell horn-rimmed glasses with magnification so powerful that his eyes seem to bulge at you like goldfish. In the real world, he made big bucks as a computer engineer, was some kind of genius at writing code.

"Don't you have to get to your shift?" I said.

"Captain Johnson," he said with a sneer.

"Don't be stupid," I said crossly, too exhausted to tolerate such discussion now.

"Yes, you were some kind of cop. A weapons expert. Maybe Interpol. I am sure of it," said Gil.

I blinked wearily at the tent's roof, which hovered just inches from my nose. "Man, I hate that you say that. I never touched a gun before I came to Israel."

Gil laughed. "So. You were a SWAT cop."

"You're being a real asshole, Gil. You know as well as I do . . ."

Gil sighed. "OK, OK. Hey, don't get so fucking nervous."

"I'm no fucking policeman," I said, my voice trembling.

Gil grew still. After a long pause, he said: "We are all policemen here, Falk. We are not soldiers anymore."

"We are soldiers, Gil."

"So, you be a soldier, Falk. I don't know what I am anymore. I just want out of this fucking hole."

We lay there in the dark, breathing. In the far distance, a patrol peppered a perimeter with preemptive machine gun fire. Gaza nightcrawled with dark shapes, inching, lumpy forms that crept toward you with primed hand grenades, Molotov cocktails, full bullet clips. Take Gil and me. To torch us in our tent would be a cinch. A lighter's flick, a casual toss, and just melt away. Our sentries would not see you. How could they? They are as tired as worms, worn out — their uniforms smell bad. They taste mud in their mouths, their fatigued eyelids barely stay open. Some of them may be sleeping. All the guards are sleeping now as we lie here, exposed, killable. And why wouldn't they want to kill Jews? Isn't it a point of honor for them? To say, *I killed a Jew, with a grenade. He died screaming. I slipped right past the guards. They were all sleeping. The Israelis are asleep. We will kill them in their dreams. They will die of their dreams.*

"Falk," said Gil.

"What?"

"This Captain Johnson, though. He is a soldier, no? A real soldier?"

"He is a fool," I spit. "A deluded, self-centered, grandiose fool who knew damned well that no Israeli soldier would shoot an American soldier, under any circumstances. And I do not want his name. He is not a soldier. You and I are soldiers. We are not policemen. We are soldiers. No matter what they say about us in the world, we are not cops. We are not John Waynes. We are soldiers. Do you hear me? We are soldiers."

"OK."

He crawled out and the sound of his departing boots faded away.

But next morning, it started again. Not from Gil but from Tuli, with that jeer that I now recognized as self-hatred. This is what has been done to us, I reflected. Fine soldiers, the best in the world, made into swine by a Circe of a world that never loved us anyway.

"Captain Johnson," Tuli's bass voice rumbled out of his enormous frame. "A real soldier. A marine. Hey. This is where you learned to shoot like that, up close, huh? Only commandos do that good. You were a commando, Falk, an American commando in the American army, hiding out here in Israel, huh? Maybe they sent you to spy, huh? To spy on the IDF?"

"Motherfucker," I whispered under my breath. And I knew that Tuli, no one else but Tuli, would have to be the one to whom I publicly made my point. So later I said, to Dedi, nonchalantly: "Put Tuli on our squad today. He likes to watch me shoot. So, let him come behind me."

"He wants to stick it in your ass," said Binny.

"So let him." I smiled.

"You see," Binny said to Dedi, "We have turned Falk into a whore. He comes here a Zionist idealist and now he's just an ass-hole like the rest of us."

"Well, isn't that the point of Zionism?" I said. "To level the playing field so we can be just like everybody else?"

Binny grinned and nodded. "But the goyim, who *are* every-body else, don't like that."

Dedi looked at him. "Tell me, Binny, when you are out there in civilian life doing your gangster thing in Tel Aviv, are you this dumb? Or is this behavior of yours saved especially for us? Is this your own special gift to Israel, which took in a jailbird from Siberia and gave you rights equal to the prime minister himself? What kind of rights did you have under the Reds, huh?"

Now Tuli joined us, towering over us in height. "Captain Johnson," he said, nodding at me.

Binny wagged his finger at Dedi. "You are naughty, Dedi! But I like you too much to kill you, bad boy, but please, don't hurt my feelings. I'm too sensitive to be talked to like that!"

"Where did they get this psychopath from?" Dedi asked of the grinning faces around him.

"He's not a Jew," said Tuli, delivering it with a clowning smile down at Binny. "Isn't that true, Russki? You're not even circumcised. I saw it myself in the shower. And besides, there's not enough down there to cut off anyway. Or maybe you are just a goy who pretends to be Jewish so you can stay out of Stalingrad Penitentiary."

The Russian moved faster then I would have thought possible for him. It took us some effort to drag Binny off of Tuli, who was laughing the whole time that Binny attempted retribution. Tuli was enormous, whereas Binny was heavyset, stocky but short and mainly all mouth and sweat. It's not what he himself could do to you that made him appear deadly, so much as the knowledge of what he, as a known associate of the Russian mob, could have others do to you when you weren't looking. And yet now he quit the scene with a curse. And we had no fear for Tuli and Tuli had none for himself because there was an unwritten code among IDF soldiers that what happened here did not come home with you. Here was here.

It didn't matter what you did out there, gangster or professor. Here you were a soldier, nothing more.

And when you were not here, you lived as though here, wherever it is — Gaza, the West Bank, Lebanon — did not exist; was only something you saw on the news, like anyone else.

Though of course at home in civilian life, at night before sleep or when you awoke at dawn and lay there, your mind addled with nameless terror, it came back to you, even just over dinner or out in the park, or at a barbecue, for one instant of eye-shutting dread you heard the roar of heavy armor, the clank of treads, smelled the hot, dry dust that coated your mouth and feet, nose and skin; you saw the nutmeg-colored skin of sun-scorched men in their faded olive green field fatigues, the dull matte gloss of assault rifles and other infantry weapons — the MAG, the RPG, the TOW, the mortars, the rocket, the bazooka, the M-203 grenade launcher, and atop the APCs the big .05s and .03s. And the clumsy radio helmets that were worn by drivers and officers in the tanks and

APCs; and the jeep reconnaissance troops in their baggy desert dust–proof suits and the goggled eyes and the shouting mouths of flesh-tone beige lips and white teeth.

And now we were moving down the ghostly street in stages, our deadly ballet a football fullback draw running in slow motion for daylight into a black hole door, behind which, someday, might lie a muzzle barrel pointed at your knees or loins or belly, chest or head, that blows you off your feet and down you go, bleeding anguish, your mouth maiming the air with hopeless screams. And he was behind me, Tuli, still talking Captain Johnson this, Captain Johnson that, and I was amazed, for under all conditions, he talked.

You see, I had never worked with him before — he was in another squad, one that exists at the other end of my platoon. Tuli's negating voice I had heard only in the mess hall, or in another tent, his loud mouth and grinning face always remote, removed from me. One simply moved in different circles: a platoon is a world, and there are men in it you never speak to even once. Your paths don't cross. Intentionally. That's fine. But ours had crossed now.

And he was speaking. He was saying, "Captain Johnson, why do you wear that stupid baseball hat? New York. New York is Sodom, I hear. It is Gomorrah. Why do you filthy the IDF uniform with your Yankee hat?"

Dedi, who was alongside me with the explosives backpack, looked at me and rolled his eyes. I shrugged. From my face you'd never know what I now intended to do. If Dedi had known, he would have stopped me right then. But I was good. Better than good. I was best at this. My trigger finger hovered near the trigger guard, and the gun barrel balanced in my left hand felt like an electric guitar on which I was about to play a Jimi Hendrix solo in hot lead.

Dedi blew off the door. I'm from the left, you from the right. Tuli's butting head bumped me forward. I shoved off the door frame, bounced to the left. Smoke in my eyes, jumbled snatches of wall space. My weapon's barrel swung at Tuli's corner. He was just to my right, planting his feet, poised to shoot.

I shot in a hot stitching blaze of automatic fire that cut ninety degrees and ended up just at Tuli's elbow, our lines of fire cutting parallel swaths from his corner to his near side, my bullets just left of his.

When it was done he stood in the deafening aftershock, his hands fumbling at his helmet; frantic, he tore it off his huge head. Now the goggles came off. He started to stumble out but paused to gawk at me and shrieked: "Maniac! You fucking . . . you fucking . . ." and he exited into the sunlight.

I was calm now. It felt nice in the room. The smell of the cordite smoke mingled with that of explosives, not unpleasant, wafted around on the slight breeze leaking in through the door.

Outside, the world was glaring bright, but in here it was dark though hot, so hot — the sheet metal absorbed the heat like a sponge — but still there was shade here, there was shelter; it was, after all, a house. I leaned against the wall. My weapon burned. I looped the gun strap off my shoulders and lay the still smoking weapon on the cement floor, which, I noticed, was cool.

Leaning against a wall, I slid down to sit in a kind of Zen meditative posture, and Dedi, slow, powerful, filling the doorway, gingerly stepped across the threshold, his weapon shouldered but on his face an expression alert, receptive, unsure. He no doubt had only just seen Tuli stumble out, his big face in his hands, and didn't know what to expect to find in here. Maybe me dead on the floor in a pool of blood. But there I was, to his left, seated, quite calm.

"What gives?" he asked, with a second, sweeping glance of professional scrutiny, assessing the room with a mental checklist of possibilities now that he knew I was OK.

I shrugged. He nodded. Looked at the wall to where we had

fired. And when he saw what I had done, his body posture changed, drew tight, and he walked to the wall and with two extended fingers traced the almost perfectly parallel bullet tracks that ended only six inches short of each other — the six-inch margin I had allowed for in order not to kill Tuli, only send him a warning: a message from my gun to his mind that I'd had enough of his fucked-up Captain Johnson jokes, that the next time my shot nerves might keep going till I'd cut his motherfucking torso in half. Or maybe one clean shot right to his head. *I am on edge,* said my bullet holes, *the very edge of the last limits, not just with you but with this whole Gazan nightmare, from Rafiah to the sea.*

Dedi's extended fingers rested on two bullet holes, the last of my gunfire. Without turning, he said, his voice flattened by the battered acoustics of the room: "Since when are you so angry, Falk?"

I didn't answer.

"There are other ways to make a point."

"Not down here," I fired back.

"I could have you put into prison for this."

I shrugged.

"I'll talk to Tuli. He's not the kind to squeal. But I wouldn't blame him if he did."

"Next time he calls me Captain Johnson or starts with his fucked-up sarcasm I'll put one in his head."

"Hey," said Dedi angrily. "This is not Vietnam. We don't shoot our own."

"No," I said. "We shoot ourselves."

"That would also be stupid."

I nodded. "I feel stupid," I said. "I don't understand anymore what we're doing. Do you? Do you know what we're doing?"

"No," he said, and his hand fell to his side. "No," he said again and stepped into the sunlight.

BATTLE OF THE BANDS

This is the record of a fantasy conversation, held one day in my head while standing in the miserable rain, guarding a perimeter as my squad searched the house of a wanted terrorist in Gaza. The suspect's immediate family, a mother and a boy, stood outside, drenched to the skin.

In the fantasy, I walked on a sunny day down a dirt road into a grove, and in a nice spot I threw down my kit bag. I jammed a loaded clip into my Galil assault rifle and, folding back the stock, laid it down close by. I removed my boots and reclined in the sweet-smelling place between two small grapefruit trees with thick, snaking trunks. It was cool on the ground, and moist. I lifted buttery petals and leaves, rubbed them between my fingers, put them to my nose, sniffed, pressed my lips together, studied the sky. Now what kind of clouds are those? I wondered. Those small, curvy puffs are nimbus, I guessed aloud. Yes, nimbus. I didn't know for sure. Still, it felt nice just to say the word. Some ants crawled up my shirtsleeve. I brushed them off.

Suddenly there appeared a barefoot Arab boy squatting on his haunches, materialized from thin air, watching me from a distance of about ten feet. I looked at my rifle and his eyes followed.

I'm not a fighter, he said.

I looked quickly around to be sure we were alone. You speak Hebrew, I said, appearing to be nonchalant as I rose to one knee and leaned with pounding heart toward the Galil.

Yes, I do, he said.

I lifted the rifle, laid it down right beside me. He was a winning, tousle-headed lad with nut brown skin and almond-shaped black eyes. His lips were cracked from the sun. I noticed my thirst, ran a tongue over my lips.

You work here, I said, looking around.

Yes, he said.

You are an Israeli Arab.

He hesitated an instant before answering: I am me. If one has his way, he would tell you that I am a Palestinian Arab. And yet another would say Israeli. And a third would say just Arab. But finally I have decided that I am none of these. I am fourteen years old. And you, you are an American.

Yes, I said.

So, why are you in the Israeli army?

I looked at him skeptically. You really want to know?

Yes, he said.

When I was home in New York City, watching on TV what was going on here, I'd realize that Israelis are Jews just like me. And that terrorists from your people, or else armies from big Arab states, were dead set to kill them. But I did nothing. It was like standing by at a slow-motion-unfolding genocide, paralyzed. I felt like a shitheel. I wanted to let Israelis know that they're not alone. That other Jews care. But Israeli soldiers, and civilians too, take more hits than I ever guessed, and it never stops. It's a way of life, a condition of mind. It changes you, fucks with your head, makes your life a war where every second something feels like it could go wrong. And now, I feel fucking alone too. I'm punch drunk with it. And so crazy. War has split me right in two, and the more I want to get away from it, the harder I go to it. I can't see a way out. I've become an Israeli.

But you are also an American, he mused thoughtfully. He smiled, showing rotted teeth like a fence of bones.

So, what does that mean?

The Beach Boys, he said.

The Beach Boys. I grinned.

He extended his clasped hands before him. And what else?

I tried to think of what else, but there was so much to choose from. It depends.

From where you come, who was really big? he said.

For me, it was always Marvin Gaye, I said.

His brow furrowed. I do not know this one. He is rock-and-roll singer?

Old school soul singer, I said. A great one.

What did he sing?

He sang a song called "What's Going On?"

The boy considered the title, then shrugged. What else?

When I said 2 Live Crew, it drew a blank for him. So did Lou Reed and Talking Heads. Now other old-time names marched back into memory. The Jefferson Airplane, I said. From San Francisco. Also, Janis Joplin was from there.

Yes, Joplin. I know this.

How about Jimi Hendrix?

Hendrix! he exclaimed. The name turned his smile into a floodlit stage in a packed stadium. It draped an American flag over his narrow shoulders, and a Fender electric guitar burst into flames in his hands. Purple Haze on my mind! he sang.

You got it, my man. I laughed. Get down!

That made him happiest. He exclaimed, GET DOWN! and jumped up, stamped his bare feet on the rocky soil, shook his shoulders in a boogie step and rapped out: GET DOWN! Yeah! GET DOWN!

I came to my feet and dusted myself off. What's your name? I said. Hey! Yo!

He stopped dancing. Get down! He chuckled.

I asked you, what's your name?

MY name? My name, soldier, is my name. And your name is your name. I am Jimi Hendrix and you are Marvin Gaye. That is my name: Jimi Hendrix.

Makes sense to me, I said, liking him very much for his answer.

I stood with the rifle in my hands and shouldered it. I nodded with a smile and started to go. He didn't say anything. Squatted back down, clasped hands extended before him. If his parents or his friends or maybe his relations or neighbors knew what he was doing, it would go badly for him. At the outside, a bad beating. Even broken legs. Possibly death. Better for me to leave before we were seen, for they dealt pitilessly with "collaborators," who were those who socialized with the "occupation forces." I turned around. Hey, Jimi Hendrix!

He grinned and swept the hair from his eyes. Yes, Marvin Gaye?

Do all you people hate us?

His face hardened into reflection. A long minute passed. He looked up and said: Many hate you — most — but some, a very few, don't. Not because they think you should live but because it is not easy to hate. Some don't have any strength for this. They just want to have a good life. But if they could I'm sure they would hate you too. There is no forgiveness for what has been or what is or even for what is to come. But you know what, Marvin Gaye? It is not a matter of hating but something much deeper that I have no words for. There is no word for it. My people will fight yours for as long as there is memory. This is our pride. And there is no way out of this but by your own door, because my people will not leave.

I nodded. Still, I don't understand, I said.

I thought you wouldn't. Good-bye, Marvin!

Good-bye, Jimi!

GET DOWN!

I grinned. RIGHT ON!

"WHAT'S GOING ON?" he shouted.

But I didn't come back with a fatuous song title. I left it behind to float on the silence, went on my way, puzzled and sad.

And the real-life counterpart of the fantasy boy, standing right there across from me in the rain, soaked to the bone, encircled by his wailing mother's arm, glared at me with a look that promised a death someday that would be slower, more brutal, more excruciating, than anything I could ever imagine.

THE SPOKESMAN

Due to a damaged elbow incurred while carrying an injured man on a nighttime foot patrol, I was temporarily reassigned to serve as an "escort officer" in the offices of the army spokesman. I spoke English and was combat trained, which made me an ideal candidate for the job. I was a phony officer with decorative temporary insignia, and my job was to escort foreign correspondents into "hot zones." I jockeyed them up to Lebanon and over to the West Bank.

It was great fun, and the correspondents, some of them quite celebrated, were mostly awful drunks, and I got ripped with not a few of them. Since I was with the spokesman's office, they assumed that I was privy to all sorts of secrets, which they tried to pry from me with booze. They bought me drinks and asked me questions, the answers to which I pretended to know but regretfully could not divulge.

"Don't, then," they would say. "Just tell me if I'm close."

To which I'd reply with an enigmatic, lip-sealed smile of good-natured all-knowingness.

In truth, I didn't even know what was on the menu of the base cafeteria that day, let alone whether or not the IDF possessed such and such a missile or intended to attack somewhere. I didn't even know when I'd get my next leave. I didn't know, even, when my immediate superior, Lieutenant Colonel Amit Gilad, was regularly scheduled to visit the military optician, though I was the one who, unfailingly, he leaned on to set the appointment.

"You are my eyes and ears, literally," Amit would say with a chuckle, "which is why most of the time I feel like I'm deaf and blind." I had to think hard even to remember his rank. Sometimes I called him "Captain," which made him furious, as he felt passed over for the higher ranks out there. Among his peers, lieutenant colonel was low as ranks went. His pals were all full colonels and generals.

I was not a very observant person and had poor memory skills. I didn't even remember what I was told that I could and must divulge: all sorts of facts about numbers of Katyusha rocket rounds falling per week on the Galil; troop deployment sizes of the South Christian Lebanese militias fighting with us against Fatah in Lebanon; the distinctions between Shiite and Sunni Muslims; who is suspected of funding the terrorist cells in Khan Yunis and Rafiah; or even the names of the general staff members themselves.

I was useless for the dispensing of information of any kind. My chief virtue appeared to be, in retrospect, my quite reckless willingness to blindly go anywhere I was ordered to, and also the especially pleasant and important quality of "cheerfulness."

"You have a nice, cheerful smile," said General Dror Raviv, the head spokesman of the combined armed forces, whenever he saw me. "A smile like that is a serious weapon," he added, though how much such weaponry is deployed he never divulged. Of course, probably that too was top secret, so I did not ask. I only smiled.

Once, though, I was summoned with solemn gravity to the chief spokesman's office for a meeting, the purpose of which was shrouded in secrecy. Even my immediate superior, Amit, did not know why I was requested.

"No, really!" Amit protested, spreading his great meaty hands and densely furred forearms. "He hasn't given me a clue about what he wants. Yes, I asked. Of course! After all, as fucked up as you are, Falk, you're still my soldier. I'd want to know, to see, if there is trouble, what I can do to help you out. But, nothing. He won't say."

"How serious is it?"

"He's a general. The spokesman of the whole army." He shrugged. "If he's calling you, it must be serious. Though what the fuck he wants with you is beyond me." I thought I detected not a little envy in his voice.

The meeting was set for the general's headquarters in the sprawling base at Tel Hashomer. The general's aide-de-camp, Major Orli, a drop-dead gorgeous blonde who was also universally known to be the married general's mistress, rose from her desk in the outer chamber to the general's office and said very solemnly: "Wait. I'll let him know you're here."

"Orli, what is this?" I said. "Do you know?" I offered my best cheerful smile.

She looked at me with an expression in which I thought I read enormous pity and said: "Come here."

I moved closer.

"Come right here to me," she said. I came up to the foot of the desk. She rose, leaned over, her cleavage tugging at my attention, and brushed the hair out of my eyes. "You should have gone to the barber before you came. Didn't Amit tell you? Dror's a stickler about haircuts. You look a little bit like a hippie. I'll go tell him now you're here."

I heard the general's deep, resonant voice command: "Send him in . . ." and Orli held open the door for me to enter. My arm grazed the tips of her breasts as I passed.

General Raviv was bent over a map spread open on his desk. He wore thick black horn-rimmed glasses, and he studied the map very intently. When he looked up, his dark, intelligent eyes took my measure in a glance, and I thought that he had a truly wonderful face: deeply tanned, large, very carved-looking, with dark pockets around the eyes and many folds about the corners of the mouth, and those deeply scored cheeks. It was a very turbulent, vividly alive face, and very authoritative. His eyes at first seemed brown but then I saw the hazel and green tint in them. He waved me into a seat with a gesture of his huge hand. He was an immense man, taller than I, or seemed to be, though perhaps it was only the authority he radiated that made him seem colossal. And he had a sensuous mouth, a tough, hard upper lip but a full, almost Italianesque bottom lip. A terrible white scar ran down his chin that made him seem toughly handsome yet also told a story others might not really want to know about, involving helplessness, explosions, unendurable pain, reconstructive surgeries, and as such the scar discouraged curiosity, inspired tact, and put him at an even further remove, for there it was, whitely glaring at you, vicious, disfiguring, unavoidable.

He slid a newspaper over the map as if to hide it from me and said: "I don't know why they make me privy to these operations of theirs. There is nothing that I can ever say publicly about any of them, except the standard cryptic bullshit that drives reporters to look even harder at the henhouse for the golden egg. But I can't give up the golden egg. No, not ever. I can't even show them how it shines or tell them what karat it is. And most of all, I must pretend that I don't know where we've hidden the magic chicken that produced this marvelous thing that I am forbidden to do anything but hint about. No, this chicken does not exist. You won't find it in the coop, no, even though there it is in plain view."

He smiled. "You don't know what I'm talking about, do you."

"I think I do."

"No, please: don't tell me you do or I'll think you're an even bigger idiot than Mr. Fried of the *New York Times,* who said that he knew exactly what I meant. 'That is very good, Mr. Fried,' I told him, 'because it happens that I am talking completely out of my ass right now. So, perhaps you will translate back to me in logical English what I am trying to say.' And do you know what?"

"What?" I grinned amiably, as I had already begun to like him, though never forgetting for a single moment that before me sat a general, the most dangerously unpredictable of all creatures in the military world, for the powers they possess are of a god, and, famously, they enjoy them with cruel gusto.

"The son of a bitch did it. He spit back at me a coherent interpretation of everything I had said about eggs and chickens, gold, and all the rest of the bullshit and gave it to apply to the entire Middle East situation — and did so in a way that was not only completely logical but even compelling. For this, I not only expressed to Mr. Fried my unqualified awe but bought him several rounds of the best scotch whiskey over at Finks bar, downtown, in Jerusalem. Do you know this joint? A funny little place, off King George Street. Famous place, actually. Many writers go there."

"I know it very well," I said. "I once met the British novelist Allan Sillitoe sitting in there, and we had a nice chat."

"He is well known?" asked the general respectfully.

"Used to be. He wrote *The Loneliness of the Long Distance Runner.*"

"I have heard of this," said the general, pleased with the breadth of his tangential knowledge.

"That's a funny story about Fried," I said, "though I am a little unsure of the point."

"Ah, this is what I wanted to see. So, you are a bright person after all. That is the correct remark to make. And here is the point. 'Fried,' I told him, after many drinks courtesy of the Israel Defense Forces, 'Fried . . .' and I slapped his back as I said this: 'I will let you in on the greatest military secret of all time. Do you know what it is?'"

The general leaned his marvelous face close to me. "'It is not only that we in the IDF General Staff religiously read the *New York Times* and especially your articles about us, on the military situation here. But it is also this.'" And here, the general leaned even closer. "'Tom,' I told him, 'Tom, the secret is that it is as your American painter Barnett Newman — who was a Jew, by the way — what Newman once said about the relationship of the abstract expressionist painters to art criticism . . . it applies, you see, to the relationship of you reporters to what is going on here, what the Israeli army and the Israeli people experience here first-hand from war and terrorism. And that is, Tom, that the *New York Times* is to our situation in Israel as ornithology is for the birds.'" And here, he drew back quickly, fell back against his chair, crossed his hands over his belt buckle, and waited.

I stared at him, and then I burst out laughing. And he burst out laughing. And there we sat, belly-laughing loudly. And it was wonderful!

"And that is my job," he said, laughing so hard it brought tears to his eyes. "It is to remind the reporters that they are to Israel as ornithology is for the birds!"

He then sat back again, hands clasped over his belt buckle, nodding, still chuckling. "Yes, I told him that. And then I told him, I said: Mr. Fried, you journalists don't even realize that you, not us, no, but you, are the very magic chickens who lay the golden eggs — you, Tom, are that magic chicken you search for so frantically here, in Israel. What is the army? I asked him: nothing! Who am I? I asked: nothing! But you, you and Claybone from the *Washington Post* and Tessman from NBC and of course, the great almighty Poppel, yes, even Poppel himself, are the true miracle workers. You take the molehill and make it into the mountain. You make the wolf the lamb, the lamb the wolf, and Little Red Riding Hood into a venereal slut. I don't know how you do this! But it fills me with such wonder. What a power to have, to completely rearrange the face of reality into your own ideas of things: why, into something that does not resemble itself even a little! Journalists make China into Canada, the Pacific into the Baltic, Russians into leprechauns! Two hundred million Arabs attempting to crush and annihilate five million Jews, and guess who comes out the bully and the bad guy? That's two hundred Arabs for every Jew. Imagine: one Jew faces two hundred Arabs and the *Times* reports that we commit massacres, oppress people, and I don't know what else. The Arab landmass is six hundred times that of Israel, but we are the land-grabbing, greedy conquerors. Journalists! Truly, they are the magic chickens. Perhaps it is only my job to show them how magical they truly are, since nothing in my arsenal is of a magic to equal theirs. Nothing." He shrugged. "After all, all I have is the truth." He made a funny frowning, sourish face. "What is that against magic chickens? Not a lot."

"I see," I said.

"Yes. I can see that you see. That is why I called you. Because Amit tells me that you are of an above-average intelligence and even something of a poet. Tell me. You are knowledgeable of the poet W. B. Yeats?"

"Yes, of course," I said.

General Raviv raised his thick eyebrows in mock amazement. "'Of course,' he says. 'Of course.' Why is it that to all you poet types the knowledge of another poet's name and work is *no big deal*. But do you know what a *big deal* it is to me that *I* know such a thing? It is the biggest deal in the world. It is a much bigger deal than the top secret military horseshit that is in that map on my desk, which I covered over with this morning's edition of *Ma'ariv* because it is such a big deal that not even you can see it."

"I would imagine," I said, "that I would be very low on the list of those entitled to see it."

"And you would imagine correctly." The general laughed amicably. I could tell that he liked me and wondered if I could somehow parlay his fondness into a forty-eight-hour leave for myself. We'd have to see.

He leaned back in his swivel chair with his large hands interlaced over the brass buckle of his forage belt and gazed up at the ceiling, musing on something with a smile. He wore an olive green "A" dress uniform with insignia on his epaulets connoting a brigadier general, and had a chest full of campaign ribbons, the significance of which I could only imagine. And he had paratrooper wings and maroon jump boots but also wore the brown beret of the Golani Brigade mountain troops. That he had seen hard action and was something of a war hero was not only probable but absolute. You do not rise to the general staff without having seen your wars up close and desperate. Everything about him spelled a fighter.

"So, what about Yeats, sir?" I said gently, to remind him.

"Yes! Yeats! Where do these lines of his come from? 'The dogs of Europe bark at the disgrace on every person's face'?"

"Those are not the exact lines, sir. Close. But not the lines. It goes:

'*In the nightmare of the dark*
All the dogs of Europe bark,
And the living nations wait,
Each sequestered in its hate.

'*Intellectual disgrace*
Stares from every human face,
And the seas of pity lie
Locked and frozen in each eye.'"

Moved, the general allowed a pause for his emotions before saying: "He is a great poet, this Mr. Yeats."

"Mr. Yeats did not write it," I said.

The news stunned him. "No? Who, then? I have been misled. Misinformed. You are sure? I was told . . ." He seemed very embarrassed.

"The poem is not by Yeats but rather *about* Yeats. It is 'In memory of W. B. Yeats' by the British poet W. H. Auden, who wrote it to commemorate Yeats's death."

A great light of comprehension spread over the general's face, and I don't think he could have looked happier.

"So, the author's name, it is a W Something Something, isn't it! I wasn't that far off, then, was I? I was close. You'll grant me this."

"Closer than most would get."

"Tell me. Do you know the whole poem? Recite it for me."

I did. When I was done, the general's eyes looked misty. He sat there for a long time with his gaze fixed on nothing in particular and then rose without comment and walked to a cabinet from which he removed a bottle of bonded scotch and two shot glasses. He put a shot glass down before me and unscrewed the cap slowly, the whole while his misty eyes fixed on mine, and poured me a shot and then one for himself.

"Take it," he said, nodding at the shot glass.

"Sir, I . . . regulations."

"Fuck regulations. Take it. I order you. I am your general. We must drink to Mr. Yeats."

I hoisted my shot glass. "To Yeats," I said.

"To Yeats!"

We knocked back our drinks. He filled the glasses. We hoisted them.

"To Mr. W. H. Auden."

"To Auden," I toasted.

Again, the glasses filled.

"Who is this for?" I asked wetly, feeling the effects.

"This is for your British writer in Finks."

"Mr. Sillitoe."

"Yes. Let us not forget him."

"Indeed not," I agreed. We drank. The whiskey felt wonderful. I had not had anything this good for the entire length of my service in the combat unit or, for long stretches, not even so much as a single beer. But the three drinks awakened my body's memory of all the wonderful and also not so wonderful drinks I had imbibed of late since my reassignment to the IDF spokesman's office in Jerusalem and made me wish very much to get completely wasted now. He did not look drunk, though, and by the time he tightened the cap on the bottle, I knew that our pub crawl through poetry was over.

"I will tell Amit to give you a nice leave," said the general, rising, his hand outstretched. Truly, a man who understood his fellow man. We shook. His hand was large, cold, and dry despite the whiskey, very dry. I had begun to feel a moist film of sweat break over my skin from the alcohol. But it didn't affect him that way.

I stepped back, saluted.

"None of that," he said with a dismissive gesture.

"Shall I go, then?"

"Yes."

I turned to go.

"You know . . ." he said at my back. I turned.

"Know what, sir?"

"You know, I was going to say that . . . I don't really understand . . . someone like you. Many years older than eighteen. How old are you?"

"Twenty-eight, sir."

"Ten years older than a recruit. And educated. Who knows Auden and Yeats and I don't know what else. So, what brings you to here? To serve in the army? You are a Zionist? You love the Jewish State?"

I thought. "Yes, sir. I love the Jewish State. And I would do anything to keep it alive."

"But why? You, from America. That's a nice place. Why so much love for this place?"

"Because loving it is like loving oneself. At least for me it is."

"Now you are getting sloppy. I gave you too much to drink." But I could tell by the catch in his voice that he was moved.

Good to his word, he called Amit that day and recommended me for a three-day leave.

"You made quite an impression on Dror," Amit remarked wryly. Evidently he didn't like my big success with the general. "He asked me to give you a three-day leave. So, what will you do on your own for three days? You have a woman someplace?"

"I have nobody," I said truthfully.

"Why don't you ask the South African in Zev's office. What's her name?"

"I don't know. The one with black hair?"

His face reddened. "What am I, your pimp? I don't know. They all have fucking black hair."

"No, there's a blonde in there someplace."

"So, then fuck the blonde!" he shouted. "Get out of here. I'll see you in seventy-two hours. Come late, I'll have you court-martialed, Dror or no Dror. This is a fine thing. I have that paid flunky of the PLO, Claybone, from the *Washington Post* coming at three. He wants to go up to Metullah to see Haddad. Who will take him?"

"He should go out of Tel Aviv. Let them take him."

"Listen to the big shot friend of the general. Now you're running both my office and the general's. But I'm telling you: fuck the South African."

"Why?" I smiled. "Why not Irit?"

Gilad paused and winced at my presumption.

"Irit? You, a lowlife like you, will fuck Irit Arella? First of all, she is Asher Yaron's girl. Second, she is the sister of Israel's most famous novelist. And third, she is too beautiful for you."

"Lieutenant Nurit told me that I remind her of Israel Tal, the tank general. She said he was legendary for his handsomeness." I smiled my most winning smile.

He gaped at me in disbelief. Then said: "Get out of here. Get out of here now, this minute. You are this close from jail." He checked his watch. "Seventy-two hours from now. One minute late, I have you shot by firing squad."

"There are no firing squads in the IDF. There's no capital punishment in Israel."

"No, but we hung Eichmann. So don't be too sure of yourself.

Also, when you come back I want you to take that fucking French photographer from Gamma up to South Lebanon, to see Major Haddad. There's another one you made a big impression on. He asked for you specifically."

"Haddad's a good man."

"Why do you want to make so many friends in high places, huh? You are selling dope?"

"Yes," I said. "Now I've got the general hooked. You're next."

"Get out," he said. "Go fuck the South African. I feel sorry for her. She looks so miserable. She's a pretty girl. Look at her tits. Tell me what you think. Leave Irit alone. She'll fuck your head up. She's fucked up many men. I need you to take the Frenchman north. Don't get ruined. Irit will ruin you."

"I thought you considered me ruined already."

"Yes," he said. "You are ruined but still usable."

"I think you're worried about me, Amit. I'm very touched."

It was true that behind his overcompensating gruffness lay a very tender man who loved his mother, paying her regular visits in the old age home, and was a devoted husband and father. He was a dedicated officer who doted on me and Nurit, the two soldiers under his immediate command. We had the best of everything and more liberties than were usual for soldiers. Observance of military protocols in the office was almost nonexistent.

Amit grunted with irritation and said: "Look. Get out of here before we start grabbing each other's asses. And you drink too much. You think I don't see? Lay off the drinking. Fucking is healthier. One hour late: court-martial and death!"

I shrugged. Court-martial in the Israeli army was not a big deal. You were court-martialed for anything. Loss of your beret was a court-martial offense. You could be court-martialed for pissing on another man's boot in the latrine. You appeared for it in combat fatigues, if that's what you had on. Someone clapped a dress beret on your head. Your commanding officer ordered you to stand at ease. He read the offense. You pleaded guilty. Always, you did that. It was a given. The outcome, regardless, was the same: a small fine. To go to jail you had to do something really dumb, like sock your sergeant. All soldiers were expected to serve some time in jail at least once. The legendary general Moshe Dayan had said that an Israeli soldier who did not serve time in military jail was not a real soldier. I was not a real soldier, then, since jail held no attraction for me and I used my wits to stay out of it. I played by the rules, socked no one, stole nothing, and kept far from trouble.

"You know I'll be back right on the button, boss."

"'Boss,'" he snarled. He never knew what to make of me. His hand waved me out the door.

PART 4

HORSE SALE

In 2000, Arik Sharon took a stroll up to the Temple Mount in Jerusalem, the Palestinians objected, and in no time, Intifada II raged out of control. It was a new kind of war in which big numbers died on all sides, fighters and civilians alike, and nothing was gained for anyone. We were now up against Arafat's Tanzim militia, also Islamic Jihad and Hamas. The Palestinian Authority also privately fielded their own death squads. Things had come a long way from the early days of masked Shabab with slingshots, rebels with hand grenades, and hit men with handguns. The old Fatah Hawks still roamed the refugee camps and back alleys with axes, hacking suspected informers to death. But they mainly terrorized their own folks. The militias, including the Palestinian Authority, were armed to the teeth with every kind of ordnance, and they attacked our troops at every turn. But their most dreaded weapon, the one we feared most, was the suicide bomber.

In what now seemed like quainter times, attackers left their bombs behind and split. Now they strapped them to their ribs packed with plastic, ball bearings, nails, paid a fare, and rode one-way to God's house. The bomber's family got twenty-five grand, and if the bomber was male he was also promised a harem in heaven of seventy virgins. I don't know what dead female bombers got. Nothing, probably. Our unit, still consisting of many of the same veterans who had been working together for years in Gaza and Hebron, now conducted joint ops with members of the Border Patrol in all sectors of the administered territories, in both Southern and Central Command, switching back and forth between territories to stop teams of infiltrating bombers.

I patrolled in an armored jeep with Uri, Semel, and Trok. Uri was an Israeli Jew; Semel, an Israeli Druze Arab; Trok, an Israeli Bedouin Arab. A real stew. One afternoon we were out cruising over a part of the new fence that runs between 120 and 180 on the other side of Palestinian Authority–controlled territory, in a sector designated by us the operational code name "Ireland": a hot, dry, reddish place of baked rocks and shimmering blacktop road. We had entered the PA's turf to have a look around.

Semel drove. Uri commanded. I was the weapons backup. And Trok, our tracker, could tell by the pressure of a footprint how tall a man was, what sort of guns he carried, how far he had traveled and had still to go — even how tired he was. Trok was a trip. His eyebrows, so thick you could drive a tractor over them, joined at his nose in a straight, unbroken black line of bushy hair. And he had troublemaking, mischievous eyes. You could tell: Trok was a hard-ass. A bad boy out for himself. Nothing wrong with that.

As usual the jeep's air conditioning flatulated blasts of sputtering warm air. Uri, the corporal, seated up front next to Semel, slammed his big fist against the dust-caked dashboard panel, where the cooling system's dials were all turned up the highest they could go.

"Fucking piece of shit," he cursed, giving voice to all our feelings. He jiggled the dials futilely, for the thousandth time.

"That won't help," said Semel wearily.

"Then the hell with it," muttered Trok, and his boot shot out at the rear door handles that were supposed to keep us safely encased within the bulletproof hot box of the armored jeep, and the doors exploded open. The angry reddish terrain burst in — and a glancing sword blade of sunlight hacked at our eyes. I threw my hands up, blinded, and saw in the white flash the hallucinatory figure of an Arabian mare horse come bounding into the road. Its regal head possessed the unreal comportment of a chess piece knight. Its chestnut brown trunk was compact, shapely, and powerful. Its tail, in the manner of the best Arabians, formed an omega-shaped curve that swished and floated behind its prancing ass. Beside it walked a tall, lean Palestinian burned copper by the sun. His short-cropped white hair and beard powdered his leathery skin like dust. He had long bony wrists and hands and wore sandals.

Uri shouted: "What the hell!"

Semel slowed down. We stopped, Uri watching the horse in his passenger mirror.

"Where do they come from?"

"From Um El Fahel," said Trok. It was an Arab village from which Palestinians frequently infiltrated, either seeking work or to kill Israelis.

"He's not a terrorist," Trok added.

"How do you know?" said Uri, watching the horse high step absurdly alongside the electronic fence. The fence was only motion sensitive, not electrified, and the horse came ridiculously close to it, maybe even brushed it.

"I know," said Trok with a snide look.

The radio sputtered on. Avi in the command room: "501. Where are you?"

Uri spoke into the receiver. "In Ireland. Right at 172."

"What is that hitting the fence?"

"A horse," said Uri.

"Horse?"

"A horse. A Palestinian horse," as if the horse would have a nationality and an ID card to prove it.

There was a little boy too now, and farther down the slope, climbing up slowly, a woman — his mother — in a long dress and her head covered by the bright kerchief they wore.

"There's others," Uri reported. "A woman. A boy. And the man."

"Find out who they are. Over."

"Will do. Over."

Uri leaned out the window. The bulletproof glass was down. He stuck out his face and elbow and shouted in Arabic: "Hey. You. Come here."

The horseman nodded, smiling benignly, and approached. When he was twenty feet off Uri made the motion with his hand that everyone understood. The horse owner stopped in his tracks and lifted his shirt, exposing his stomach. Uri made the circle motion and slowly, a little self-consciously, the horse owner made one complete revolution in place to show that he did not bear any hidden explosives strapped to his body for a suicide bombing. It's not unusual for suicide bombers to appear at the fence with live-stock, which they pretend to graze until, at the right moment, they find a place to slip past the fence, which is, after all, still just wood and wire in most places.

He was clean. Uri waved him forward and the horse owner advanced with a casual saunter. He had a lean, mustached face.

"That's what my horse looks like," said Trok, gazing out the back at the prancing horse.

"Your horse?" I asked.

"It's with my mother," he said. "Mine holds its tail like that."

"What is it? A racehorse?"

"No," he said impatiently, "it's a riding horse. But not for just anyone."

The horse owner was now at Uri's window. Uri motioned for his ID card. He gave it.

They spoke in Arabic. The horse owner pointed in the direction of Um El Fahel. Now the wife was on the road, standing off at a distance with the boy. They watched the horse gallivant outrageously along the fence. Then Uri's Arabic rang out. He couldn't speak that well, apparently. He turned to Semel. "Tell him his horse is hitting the electronic fence, setting off the motion sensors. This cannot be."

Semel told the man, who listened intently and, when Semel finished, nodded that he understood and said something to Semel, who translated it back to Uri. "He'll take him off the road, back down into the canyon."

"OK," said Uri.

"Wait. Ask him . . . wait!" Trok jumped out of the jeep. Semel glanced back, scowled, since you're not supposed to leave the jeep suddenly like that due to the possibility of ambush. "Nathan, go with him."

I jumped out, my CAR-15 at the ready, and followed Trok around the jeep to the horse owner. Trok stood before the man with a sarcastic grin, greeted him with a sly nod. The man nodded back with a stiff smile, sensed Trok's hostility. Trok glanced over his shoulder, saw me standing behind him, weapon ready; smiled and winked at me. "My horse," he said, "it sells for three thousand shekel. Let's see what he wants for this one, OK?"

I shrugged.

Trok said: "You'll see. My horse is cheaper and better."

"I'm not in the market," I said.

"Why not?" Then, to Uri, whose head hung out the jeep window: "What about you? Buy a horse?"

Uri considered. Semel watched all this with interest, his arm wrapped around the steering wheel, his face resting against his forearm. It was hot. You could hear what sounded like stones cracking in the furnace heat. Or were those hoofbeats of the horse, trotting this way and that, back and forth across the road? The woman shouted something, clapped her hands. The horse ignored her. The boy threw a stone, which struck the black tar in front of the horse and dribbled away. The horse kept on.

"Your horse," I said to Trok, "its head and tail look like that? Its tail does that?"

"Just like that. But, handsomer!"

The horse owner watched all this with a frozen white smile. In moments that he saw us stare admiringly at his horse, he nodded knowingly. The horse careened near the fence.

"Take him down to the canyon," Uri shouted, irked at the horse owner.

The boy signaled "OK" and threw another rock at the horse, which trotted in a beautiful, unconcerned figure eight, and Uri shook his head and got back on the radio:

"501 to 30."

"This is 30."

"It's just the horse."

"Well, isn't it time then, Dudu, to get the horse out of there?"

In the field, we soldiers call each other by the name "Dudu" so that the other side can't ID us and target our families.

"I'm trying."

"Roger that. Out."

"Take him down to the canyon now."

"Wait," said Trok, still wanting to cost-compare horses. I had the feeling that he actually believed that if he persisted either Uri or I would end up purchasing his horse. And indeed, to have a horse seemed, at that moment, in that place, like the finest thing in the world.

The horseman, with his long wrists and affable, somewhat blank smile, looked at Trok, then glanced at Uri, uncertain what to do. There was no wind. The sun slammed down on everything, all of us awash in bleaching light. Figures moved with a quality of furious struggle made all the more comic by their determined expressions. Trok, the horse owner, the woman, the boy, moving from here to there, stopping, the colors of their clothing — khaki, red, yellow, blue, dark blue, against the light — leeched sienna red from the surroundings. And the horse still galloping brown and immense and absurdly beautiful on spindly legs, its coat brushed with fire and body poised with that prancing and imperious attitude of a carousel steed. Trok came up again to the horse owner, his thick black eyebrows knitted, his haughty eyes narrowed fiercely as he spoke in Arabic to the man, who nodded, all lanky and with an expression of frozen amusement, while Uri half hovered out the jeep window and the radio to his left cackled. Then, with a noise like a ball-peen hammer smacking steel, a bullet struck the jeep's armored hide, and the echoing clap of the gunshot spread in a widening and appalling radius over the flat red hills. We hit the deck, all of us, soldiers, horse owner, family, on the ground, motionless, terrified.

"What the fuck!" I shouted.

Trok was crawling on his belly, elbows, and knees to the jeep, fast. Uri was down behind his jeep door. Semel too. The woman was a long, brightly colored form on the ground. The boy leaned against the rock he had found to crouch behind. The echoes reverberated among the rock beds from which the shot had come. The horse cantered unfazed between the jeep and our motionless forms.

Trok reached the jeep and climbed inside. Now all of our

weapons thrust out through the bulletproof windows' sniper slots, but the gesture was absurd, for we had nothing visible to aim at.

The horse's high legs stepped, hooves crunching on gravel. The boy whistled for it but the horse ignored him. It needed no one. The boy's face was calm, even a little happy. The horse owner did not stir, but his wife was on her knees now, climbing heavily to her feet. The horse cantered. It tossed its head, its mane flailing at the heat, its nostrils snorting, demonlike, its bulging eyes haughty with pride.

Uri spoke into the handset, calmly: "501 to 30."

"501, this is 30."

"The firing is from their side. We're still in Ireland."

Beyond Ireland lay Florida. And beyond that, China. And beyond China lay the border with Jordan.

"We're sending units in. Are you pinned down?"

"We are pinned down."

"Over. 501, this is 30. We're right to you." Meaning that the Golani Brigade would rush to us in a now turretless Russian-made tank captured during the Lebanon war from the Syrians, converted into a troop transporter, and mounted with .03s and .05s. In that, we'd be extracted.

"501 to 30. Understood. We're waiting. There are Arabs on the road, that family and their horse. Over."

"30 to 501. Order them to take cover with the jeep. Get them out of there. Use your loudspeaker. Over."

"501 to 30. Understood. Over."

She was hunched down and waddling toward the horse owner's motionless form. He lay with his long hands folded over his head, like a prisoner, to protect his skull, as if that would somehow shield against bullets. There was still a chance of another shot. Semel looked back at Trok and me.

"OK?"

We nodded.

Uri threw on the siren and also the caged blue revolving light. The siren wail-whooped eerily. He lifted the handset, spit breath at its receptor holes. The noise scratched the white hot air.

"People on the road: come to the jeep. Lady, get down. Get down! Your husband is OK. Get down and come to the jeep. Get behind the jeep. This will give you protection. Boy, get behind the jeep. All of you. Help is coming."

But she kept toward her husband.

"They don't understand you," said Semel. He grabbed the handset and told them in Arabic.

She stopped, melted uncertainly to one knee, then clumsily lay down and stretched out in the dirt. The horse gamboled past, tossing its head in a maniacally happy way, tail swishing.

"My horse is better," muttered Trok jealously.

"You're fucking nuts," I told him.

He looked at me with a weird smile. "You should have a horse," he said. "You don't know how good it is. It's the best thing there is." The Bedouins really believe this, that in life there is no better thing than horse ownership. But also, there is nothing worse, not even the prospect of death, than seeing another horse superior to yours. Jealously, Trok watched the horse prance.

Uri's voice spoke out again to the people on the road. But they did not move, just lay there, exposed, as if stillness were a form of armor, as if in lying there they were not more perfect targets than if they moved. And the horse gallivanted, stepping prettily.

"Out of the road," Uri's deadpan voice commanded. But they lay there. And now the next shot rang out. Came unannounced by rung steel. Instead, it struck invisibly with a soft thud into the horse. The horse went down in a rout of brown tumbling flesh, legs crumpling, head twisting impossibly, and I saw its teeth scream and its glaring eye explode like a hawk out of a tree.

But it didn't just crash down during this highly organized ambush but fell onto something bad. A mine, I thought. Some concealed detonated bomb that lifted up the horse on a geyser of smoke and dirt and the head sheared by thunderclapping flame followed the corpse's gigantic slam into the ground and what lay there now was bloody entrails spit from jagged exposed bones white as teeth, the torso ripped wide to make of it a kind of mouth, like a gaping grin of mangled red. Its head, a short distance off, was not on its side but propped improbably at an awkward tilt on the reddish road, with its disgorged tongue snaking out. And the woman screamed; she crawled, though her husband never budged. His foot twitched, the side of his face a red smear. Uri and Trok were already firing single-shot. But then I saw Semel open the top of the jeep and let loose a raking burst of automatic fire at the hillside of the village opposite, down among the rocks and dust puffs drifted up like wraiths into the pale blue sky.

Then an armored car came, stopped, and opened fire with its .03 at a range that reached to the very foot of the village, at an abutment of low stone walls from which the sniper probably had shot. I joined my fire to theirs and then fired to the right, where I thought another shooter hid. I was wrong. Nothing there. My unfocused eyes blinked, blurred with sweat. I could see the cusp of my own left cheek larger than the view, and it was so bright, rimmed with titanium. The boy yelled, I noticed. His clenched fists waved. He cried, his little brown face twisted in anguish for the horse, whose carcass burned in the road, the scorched-flesh smell awful in our noses.

One week later, I am perched in night ambush high upon a bluff overlooking an as yet unpaved portion of the so-called separation fence. My camouflaged face is hidden behind rocks as I peer through my night-vision killer scope, and the radio beside me is on squelch so as not to disturb poor Avram, the Ethiopian, who lies behind me wrapped in a blanket like a sausage in a bread roll, his face and hands painted with mosquito repellent, for here the little vampires by the hundreds whine in your ears, and despite the army-issue repellent, we have both been stung senseless.

It is quiet still. I scan the milky green landscape with the killer, my gun beside me at the ready. But no bushes move, no rocks grow hands and feet. It is the sky that changes suddenly, that becomes a plain of thundering hooves. In gravelly sky stampedes into view a sudden mustang herd of flying horses, our own peculiar Israeli kind, Apache helicopters — only three in all, yet they sound like a whole squadron. Their thwooping blades chop like hoofbeats at the atmosphere as they dive over the roofs of Um El Fahel, to a particular broad flat building used by the ones who had planned the attack on us a week ago, and now the structure lights up in fire, with swift pointed thuds and claps of light like a knocking fist, as if a rider with a message had jumped off a steed's back and stood there at the door, pounding, pounding, eager to deliver the answer personally, face-to-face.

FISHING

With a motion of Shagram's hand, the three Palestinians standing in the road lift up their shirts to expose their bellies and perform that absurd, awkward pirouette that I have seen so many times, whenever we pass through the gates out of Israel proper to the area of the Palestinian Authority–controlled territory that we have designated by the code name of "Ireland."

They slowly spin with a variety of expressions and very different kinds of bellies. In fact, I have come to see that no two Palestinian bellies are quite alike. In fact, they are as distinctly different from each other as faces can be. It is so strangely intimate as well, and the unfairness of it is that on their side, they have no real intimacy with Israeli bellies. Perhaps if we all saw one another's bellies, how pathetic they are, we'd stop the war.

When they lift their shirts their faces wear the shy innocence of disrobing teenage girls, their fingers holding up the bunched shirts with touching delicacy. Their faces, with one or two hardened exceptions, look surprised and vulnerable as they turn under our scrutinizing gaze.

Shagram, a Druze Arab in the Israeli army, is in calm command of himself. Behind him, mottled blue space lies across the sky like a wine-stained shirt on an unmade bed. The clouds move their fat white thighs suggestively, and the wind pleads to be noticed. But Shagram, who is a corporal, has signed on to serve one extra year in the Border Patrol and goes about his business with calm professionalism, ignoring the elements, boots planted in the dirt road without a trace of dust on them, his casual open collar baring a columnar neck and the sleeves of his olive green uniform rolled over sinewy forearms. He has a full head of wheat brown hair and his eyes are bluer than those of some of the Russian Jews with whom he serves. Also, he has left behind his helmet on the fender of the jeep. The rest of the unit lingers close by, with guns poised, standing behind the armored doors or within the boxlike vehicle's bulletproof walls.

Shagram's raised hand, like a magician's, opens and closes with a minimal gesture. One of the Palestinians, an angry-looking man with a fierce black mustache and unruly hair, shuffles forward in the road, ID card extended; stands there looking mussed with his shirttail out and his sandaled feet coated in dust. Shagram waves him over to the jeep. I am just to the right of Shagram, my raised weapon with the muzzle pointed at the earth and the stock abutted into my shoulder, so that, in a flash, I can lift it to fire. Also, my helmet is on my head. I am no hero.

I watch the man advance. His two companions are still waiting in the road. He looks back at them, trying to make eye contact as he hands Udi his ID card through the jeep window, but his friends look away. He is on his own now.

The drill is slow but simple. Like anyone we encounter, the man is a possible suspect. We have gone "fishing." Ireland is our waters. There are good spots, favorites. But the other side knows them. So, now and then, under a smart commander like Shagram, we travel spontaneously to remote places where something good might turn up. This is such a place, on the outskirts of Jenin, the capital of Palestinian suicide bombing. In fact, so unknown to some of us is this particular stretch of road that we can hear from over in the jeep Udi speaking on the radio now, tapping the Palestinian's unchecked ID card against the steering wheel as he answers a sudden urgent call from 62 — code for the operation commander's jeep — to please reveal where the hell we are.

"This is 502," says Udi. "62, I read you. Over."

"502, I know you read me: state your position, goddammit. Over."

Udi glances inquiringly at Shagram, who nods to go ahead, comply.

"We are due west of the main road to Jenin," says Udi, "about six kilometers' drive southwest of Jenin, at the intersection of coordinates 93 and 84. Over."

"502, this is 62. Received. What the fuck are you doing there?"

I have never heard the operations commander, whose name is Samir, use the word "fuck" before. Typically, he uses "shit," "goddammit," or "hell."

"We're fishing. Over."

"For what? Over."

"We've got fish. Over."

"You have. OK. 502, this is 62. We're on our way. Keep your fish right there. Over."

"Affirmative."

The mustached Palestinian looks exasperated. Udi nods at him sympathetically, indicating that he understands. He waves the man's ID out the window for Shagram to see and shrugs as if to say: So, what do I do? Shagram nods to go ahead, call HQ, check the man's ID for clearance. This in contravention of Samir's order to wait. Udi nods, radios details of the ID, name, residence, resident number, and so on, to HQ. They will either clear the guy or else order that he be detained as a suspect.

Time passes. The checkers back at HQ are in no hurry. Impatiently, the man looks again at his two companions, who remain in the hot sun in the middle of the road, averting their eyes from his. Nervous, desperate, he asks Udi a question but Udi waves his hand impatiently and puts a finger to his lips: be silent. We are waiting for 62's arrival. What possible interest the commander might have in our little dragnet would need a Yemenite dream interpreter to decode.

It is hot, dry. Up ahead, yellow and orange taxis pull into line, mix with vans and crappy-looking cars. Palestinians mill around their vehicles, ID cards in hand. Big flies bounce off your face, and if they land your heart skips a beat. The temperature is suffocating. The backed-up column steams and grows in shimmering waves of listless heat. The two Palestinians waiting in the middle of the road are becoming a blurred mirage. Still more cars add on. No one dares pull out or we'll be on them, blue siren light spinning like a burning meteor, weapons cocked.

We no longer require specific intelligence to know with complete certainly that somewhere among these people, if not in this batch then another, is someone rigged with an explosive belt, set to blow. Man, woman, or child, we can't say. We're fishing. Our traps are set. The lucky one who gets through will blow one of our civilian buses to hell. Each day another bus goes up or a restaurant or a roadside hitchhiking station for troops. The militias call it "The War of the Buses." The bomber slips aboard a crowded bus in one of our major cities, dressed as a Chasid or a student or a nanny, then triggers an explosive belt and *ka-boom!* Whoever falls into our net is checked, but we can't snag everyone. That someone will get by us is a mathematical certainty. It will mean the loss of ten or twenty or thirty or one hundred civilians to either death or wounding. We soldiers tell ourselves before sleep that it's not our fault but never believe it, and blame ourselves.

Still, better only one to get through than two, three, or four. We are not searching for number one, who is a guaranteed success. We seek numbers two, three, and four, whose odds are less good, and whom the militias send only in order to better the odds that one will get through.

In the white-hot glare, steam rises from the road. The waiting vehicles seem like an optical illusion. Undaunted by the heat, Shagram stands squarely, facing the two men with IDs in their hands. I am right behind him. The radio hisses. Udi answers. Headquarters reports. "He's clear." Udi hands back the mustached man's ID. Exonerated, relieved, the man saunters back up the road to his car, his face passive. He passes his friends with a fierce glance of disapproval. Shagram summons forward the next suspect: a portly, balding, nattily dressed man in a blue sports jacket, pinstriped shirt, black trousers, and white canvas sneakers. His shirt is soaked through with sweat. His neck and hands display gold jewelry, and he walks down the road with a slow, dignified gate. He strolls past us. Shagram nods, and the man ignores him and glares timidly at me, astonished at the way I hold my weapon on him, my readiness, at a moment's notice, to open fire. Deadpan, I watch him pass. He has actually grown brave and furious. His hands shake with rage as he hands Udi his ID. Udi peers at him with interest. Accepts the proffered ID. Keeping one interested eye on the man, he puts the handset to his lips, presses the button to transmit, and calls in the man's ID number and name.

And so it goes, one after another — they approach and they return: Shagram summons them to suspicion and Udi sends them back acquitted. In such a war as this, they are all guilty until proven innocent.

Suddenly, 62 appears, followed by a second jeep, and they pull up at the side of the road in a thick cloud of dust. Samir, the operations commander, a major in rank, appears, jumps out, looks around, calls to me, "You! Get back behind your jeep. Take protection. Why do you stand in the road like a cowboy? If they shoot, where will you hide? Take a jeep door for cover. Go now!"

I retreat to the jeep, stand behind the passenger door.

"Dudu," he barks. Shagram turns.

Shagram looks at him with lazy scorn.

"Back up. You're too far in the road. Stay close to the jeep."

Shagram nods but doesn't move.

Muttering a curse, Samir heads for the line of cars up ahead. He stops to survey them. He is short but built like a bull and is spit-and-polish, down to the snug fit of his helmet's chin strap. Now out of the second jeep steps Corporal Demetri, a tall, blond, blue-eyed, husky Russian. He approaches Samir, his strut stylish, affected, a parody of authority. From his sneering mouth dangles a limp cigarette.

Together, they wade in among the Palestinians and order one of the Arabs to collect ID cards from all the rest and bring them back to Samir, who hands them to Demetri, who turns his back on them all and strides away. Demetri climbs into his jeep, flips through the IDs. He gets on the handset and calls in something, waits.

"Did I tell you," says Shagram, who has wandered over, "that not so far from here they shot one of ours?"

"No," I say.

"Over there," he says, pointing to the west. "Maybe less than half a kilometer."

"I didn't know."

He nods. "Shot him in the fucking chest. Handgun. Pulled it out of their dashboard and shot him. It took a long time for him to die. Two weeks."

"I think I heard of this."

"Maybe," said Shagram. "So, yesterday he died."

I wait. Up ahead Samir stands doing exactly what he had just warned Shagram and me not to do — waits alone and exposed before the Palestinians, even closer than we had been. Just stands there. As if daring them.

Then Demetri lunges from the jeep with the handful of IDs and strides halfway up the road and, stopping, calls out to Samir: "They're cleared."

Samir nods but doesn't move. He stands there looking at the Palestinians, eyeballing each one. There is one, a woman, dressed in a white head covering and a white dress adorned with imitation pearl beads. Beside her stands her husband, thin and unshaven with a bushy black mustache and a rumpled white shirt, gray slacks, and sandals. Samir seems particularly intent on them, though I don't know why.

Then, suddenly, he spins on his heels, his back to them all, and walks off.

Now Demetri comes up to the Palestinians. He too looks hard into the faces of every last one of the suspects on the road.

"The shot man," comes Shagram's voice to me, "was from 62's unit. He was Samir's cousin."

Then, with a look of unmistakable contempt, the Russian corporal holds the IDs aloft for all to see, and with a theatrical flourish flings them into the dust, shouting, "You can try to kill us all you like! But, still, you mean nothing to us! Do you hear? Nothing!" and strides away.

BLAME

The match flared against Corporal Brandt's camouflage-blackened face. His skeptical blue eyes crinkled with anticipation and his dirty-blond hair fell forward boyishly as he lowered his cigarette to the match. The flame gleamed against his tar-colored brow. Unlike the other soldiers who had blackened their faces for the coming operation, he didn't seem like a commando so much as one of Israel's most famous sports figures, a legendary soccer referee, which he was. And he was the famous ladies' man who could have any woman he liked even though tonight, for some absurd military reason, he just happened to have silly camouflage stain painted on his face. That was his attitude and it's why we all admired him. He puffed the cigarette to life. By the flickering light of the teardrop flame his eyes gleamed brilliant, warm, but when he pursed his lips into an amused sneer and blew sharply once and the match went out, his eyes turned cold again, and bored. He flicked away the dead match and drew deeply from the fag, eyes narrowed shut in concentration, his thumb and forefinger pinching the filter, squeezing it. When he exhaled, he nodded at me; with his forefinger tapped the pack of Marlboros laid on the jeep fender.

"No thanks," I said.

His head tilted back once, resigned to my quirks. "What is this? A health thing?"

"I've got my own," I said, slipping mine from my shirt pocket just enough for him to read the brand name: "Time."

"How can you smoke that shit?" he said. "You prefer that to Marlboros?"

"All bad for you," I said.

Again his face tilted back once as though rebuffed by a truth.

"You're a philosopher," he said.

I nodded and then we went back to saying nothing. The others were on the ground stretched out on their backs, their torsos propped up by bulky ammo vests, or else with backs leaned up against the wheels of the armored cars. There were four and all had dings from bullets.

"If I had my way," said curly-headed Reuvi, the newest and youngest man in the unit and only recently married, "I wouldn't wear this fucking vest."

"Wear it, wear it," said the bearish Sergeant Dedi wearily.

"The terrorists don't," said Reuvi. He was very earnest, this his first time going out with us on a full-scale operation, and we all liked him a lot, maybe even felt overly protective, since he had only just tied the knot a few weeks ago, the poor kid. No sooner had he returned from his honeymoon in Crete than his summons came to serve. "You know how they go, those terrorists?" he said. "I've seen them up in Lebanon. They carry just two clips. And a few grenades in their pockets. That's the way. In sneakers. That's the way. You can't move in these vests."

Lieutenant Yitzak stared at him, his wiry black hair speckled with sweat drops, the back of his neck streaming with perspiration, the gold bling chain gone. Even he knew that you didn't wear gold for the kind of shit that we were about to do on militia turf, or anything that jiggled or made noise or gave reflection. Your canteens were filled to the brim and wrapped in cellophane and rubber bands so that nothing splashed, and anything iridescent on your gear, like buckles, was wrapped in flat black electrical tape. Just one missed shiny surface could get you sniper-dead. He slapped his own cheek. Mosquitoes, eating us alive.

"Avi," he said.

Avi, the taxi driver, looked up, his deadpan face black. I could tell: he was mentally preparing for the job ahead of driving the armored car that would carry me, Brandt, Reuvi, Uri, and himself into the riot zone — not quite the same thing as cruising easily in a six-passenger Mercedes back and forth between Jerusalem and Tel Aviv, his main taxi route.

"Give Reuvi the camouflage."

Avi tossed a smudged white plastic squeeze tube into Reuvi's lap.

"Paint your face," he said with a hint of affection.

Reuvi sat up. "Sayla, you do it for me."

With a big joking smile, Sayla said, "For this cute groom, anything!" and went to it like a professional beautician. It looked like he was giving Reuvi a pricey facial massage. He worked very carefully, deliberately, with the four fingers of his right hand spreading the black color over the white surface of Reuvi's face. When he was done, Reuvi's face was completely masked.

"Thank you," said Reuvi, humbly, in respect for the effort and thought that Sayla had put into making his face invisible. "I wish my wife could see this."

But no one said anything to that.

After a time, to break the silence, Binny said, "You know what I think? I think maybe this little Reuva-la has a good point."

The Russian mobster had grown as fond of Reuvi as the rest of us had. "Think of it. How much gear do we carry? Sixty kilos each. More, maybe? Who needs so much shit?"

"With the MAG is more," said Pagi, our mechanic, who didn't really require camouflage; he already wore a perpetual thick coat of black engine grease on his hands and face but had on some camouflage anyway. "With the two hundred rounds for the MAG, is much more."

"What do we need all this for in a city? We're going into a city. We'll be on militia turf. A gun and ammo is all we need to mix it up with those pieces of shit," said Binny.

"Keep it on anyway," said Sergeant Dedi, frowning wearily. "When they run out of ammo the militias go home to their TV sets. But we have to stay. We have work to do. They have no work. Their work is to disrupt, to make chaos, to murder. To do this you don't need more than a gun and a few clips. To be a soldier, you need more."

"You hear?" said Pagi sarcastically. "You are a soldier!" He leaned over and clapped Binny hard on the shoulder. The Russian's mouth turned up in an annoyed smile.

"If they want to see what soldiers we are they should let us go out there in jeans and T-shirts with a few clips and then watch what happens," said Reuvi.

"Happens nothing," said Dedi. "Happens your head gets shot off just the same."

Everyone's mood changed then. Everyone grew very quiet and sat or stood with blank looks on their camouflaged faces. Again Brandt tapped the pack of Marlboros inquiringly and I shook my head no and he shrugged at the ineffable mystery of my refusal, almost as though it were something too rare for one as lowly as himself to appreciate. I smiled, drew a Time from my own pocket, and leaned it into the match that flared in

Brandt's cupped hands and floated to my face, where its light burnished our blackened, almost touching faces with a kind of bronze hue.

Then I heard the voice of Avi in a hoarse, furious whisper tell Dedi: "It's forbidden. Forbidden to say such a thing at a time like this — forbidden! You bring us bad luck!"

"Forbidden?" Dedi's unshaven face screwed up incredulously. "Did you say 'forbidden'?"

"Yes!" came Avi's harsh, low whisper — almost a wheeze now: I had never seen the taxi driver so upset. "You don't mention death as though you wish it on us, at a time like this."

Behind him, on the ground, swaddled in a mud-caked, unzipped sleeping bag, a soldier named Yona yawned, turned on his shoulder, threw off the bag, shifted onto his back, and pillowed his head on a helmet to better see the arguing men. He lazily waved mosquitoes away from his blackened face and peered with smiling interest at Dedi.

"Don't be a fool," said Dedi. "A time like this? What does luck have to do with a time like this?"

"Luck?" hissed Avi. "Everything to do with it."

"It has nothing to do with it."

"You are talking too much, Dedi," called out Lieutenant Yitzak. "You are making even me nervous. Why do you want to make me nervous at such a time?"

"That's right," hissed Avi indignantly.

Reuvi's curly-haired head twisted from side to side and his young face wore an uncertain smile. He listened intently to what the veterans said.

"You can clam it up too," said Yitzak. "Both of you are having a bad fit of nerves."

But nothing could erase that exchange from our thoughts. In a very real sense it was out of the bag and among us in the night

like something vast and dark and shingled with the leaves of calendar pages torn from an undertaker's daybook. I glanced down
at the soldiers seated on the ground in disportive postures reminis-
cent of my own misspent youth, their weapons like absurd toys,
and it seemed insane to ask any of us to go out and face a chance of
getting shot on such an evening.

Yona lay there with his head propped against his helmet, but
now suddenly he was glaring with hatred at Dedi, still flicking his
hand at mosquitoes, though much more sharply now.

Brandt and Dedi came together. They stood side by side, leaned
up against a jeep. Brandt offered a Marlboro; Dedi accepted. A
match flared. Dedi leaned his cigarette into the rosy bowl of
Brandt's cupped hands. But Yona continued to glare like a Buddhist
demon mask at Dedi. And who was this Yona? A tall, slender,
lanky boy with looks that fell just short of movie star's: he would
never be that. But a great hit with the girls, yes. Potentially a Brandt
in the making. And his face had that familiar expression I have seen
before, of being too young to die and knowing it to a painful degree.
His jet black bedroom eyes were locked on Dedi's face. A breeze
stirred his brown curls like a mother's adoring fingers. Everyone
had his collar fastened to the last button, but not him — his battle
shirt was open to the breastbone, his sleeve cuffs also undone. A
lover, even in war, he was now up on his boots and shouting with a
fierce, ugly expression twisting his confounded dreamboat face:
"You shouldn't command. You put the wind up our asses. You dis-
courager! You disfigurer! You depressed fuck! I think *positive!* Pos-
i-tive! I visualize what will happen. And it all turns out great."

"So visualize this," said Dedi. "Visualize the elevator shaft
where the Hamasnik hid, who shot Gabi."

So, that was it! But even I thought this was going too far. I
looked down at my boots to avoid Yona's face. They had been
roommates, Gabi and Yona, very close friends. And it happened

only a month ago, in Jenin, when they went to arrest Abu Massa, though it wasn't Massa who blew off Gabi's head when he poked it from the top of the elevator shaft for a peek around but one of the terrorist chieftain's lieutenants, a nameless gunman who briefly kept us pinned down as we struggled to extricate Gabi from the shaft and finally got him out. Then Brandt led a group to the roof, where they found the motor room, broke it open, and tossed a hand grenade down into the shaft. That got the son of a bitch. There was little of him left to identify. Later, though, the security forces guys got from one of the Hamas survivors the killer's name. I don't recall it. Saw it published in the newspaper *Haaretz,* in an article about Gabi's death and the operation. It made no impression on me, on anyone, this terrorist, his nameless name, or that he was not from Jenin but a small village nearby. Veteran Hamasnik, said the article, gunman. Not on the radar, though; not one of the wanted fugitives, the dangerous hunted. Instead, he was a surprise, insignificant, a nobody who shot Gabi through the head, our Gabi who was well known for his beautiful grin, that kid — you should have seen it. You don't cry, not after the funeral. Wipe your tears and go on. Soldiers must. But here now was Yona, sobbing on Avi's shoulder, and a few of the guys gathered around him and Lieutenant Yitzak looked ruefully at Dedi, who shrugged, and Brandt had two cigarettes going at once and handed one over to Dedi, who flicked the ash with a thoughtful expression but didn't drag on it yet, and Brandt looked at me but I said nothing. Instead, I buttoned my shirtsleeves. The mosquitoes were whining in my ears like tiny demons. And the boy Reuvi didn't know what to do and sat there by himself, looking afraid.

And then, all at once, Major Barak was among us, enormous, suited up in full battle gear, his blackened face framed by short-cropped red hair. His CAR-15 assault rifle looked tiny in his hands. He stood flanked now by Major Samir and Lieutenant Yitzak. We all came to our feet, indifferent, shattered and consolers alike to receive his briefing, which was short.

"You know about last night's suicide bombing of a Jerusalem bus. Thirty more are dead, and I just heard from my wife who, you know, works there at Beilleson Hospital, that it's a good chance that more will die, which makes thirty-one. It wouldn't be better if it was six or three. But with thirty-two is a good chance that among them are more than a few babies and children and their death is not a soldier's death, nor are they the death of young willing martyrs like some of those twelve- and thirteen-year-olds from the other side who blow themselves up or shoot at us or kill civilians. The ones who die innocently are Jewish children, not fighters. They do not run to the war; in fact, they hide from it but the war comes to them anyway, brought to them by terrorists, and this makes their death something I cannot, I refuse, to get used to. So now, we will go to find their killers. We think we may know where they are. Tonight we go to find out if our info is right, and if it is we will go get the bastards, dead or alive. I don't make a speech here. I only say, I want to see, out there, professionalism. And discipline. Is that clear?"

Glumly, we nodded.

"One more thing," he said.

We waited.

"We lost Gabi on a mission just like this. He did his job and he was killed. It was nobody's fault, do you understand? We are soldiers. Soldiers die. Even the most careful, even the bravest, the best. We die. When one of us dies we all die a little. This is how it is among brothers. So remember that before everything we are brothers. Is that understood?"

He scanned our faces with grim intensity, met each and every one of our eyes with a searching look, to find the answer to his question. Some turned away shyly. Others returned his gaze. Finally, someone, unable to bear it, squawked out: "Yes!" in this raspy, dry-throated voice.

"Good," said Major Barak. "Because brothers do not hate each other. They love. They work together. They do not harm one another. Yes?"

From the ranks the word "Yes" was mumbled and proclaimed in a dozen different ways.

"Mount up, soldiers!" Barak trumpeted, and we poured between the armored cars, pulling open doors, climbing in, slamming them shut. I sat in back with Reuvi, who looked a little pale, and smiled at him reassuringly, and Avi and Brandt took up seats in front. And Avi said as motors roared to life: "Except Cain and Abel."

"What?" I shouted above the roar.

"Cain and Abel. Barak says true brothers don't hate or kill one another. But I ask: 'What about Cain and Abel?'"

"I don't understand," I shouted.

The radio set cackled on, the voice of Udi, from the ops room, requesting, "501, 501. This is 30. Over."

And Avi scowled at me in the rearview mirror as I turned away to squint through the circular firing hole of the bulletproof glass at the armored cars peeling out, one after another, in a thrumming harp of dust.

ACKNOWLEDGMENTS

I wish to thank William Clark, my literary agent, for his superb efforts on my behalf. I also wish to thank the Little, Brown team for making *Matches* a reality: Geoff Shandler for seeing the possibilities, Judy Clain for her deft editorial guidance, and Molly Messick for her invaluable assistance. Also, a special, heartfelt thanks to Israel's great writer Etgar Keret, for his friendship and encouragement, and to Thane Rosenbaum, the novelist, for his inspired example and unflagging support.

ABOUT THE AUTHOR

Alan Kaufman is the author of the acclaimed memoir *Jew Boy* and coeditor of *The Outlaw Bible of American Poetry* and the *The Outlaw Bible of American Literature*. He has served as a combat infantry solder in the Israel Defence Forces. He has also covered the Middle East conflict as a correspondent for the *Los Angeles Times* and *Partisan Review*. He lives in San Francisco and is a member of PEN American Center.

Back Bay **Readers' Pick**

A Reading Group Guide

MATCHES

A NOVEL

ALAN KAUFMAN

Alan Kaufman
on the Origins of *Matches*

Many readers who know me only as a poet and memoirist may be rather surprised to learn that my first full-length fictional effort is about Israeli soldiers serving in the West Bank and Gaza Strip. How, they might wonder, did I come to write about Israeli soldiers?

I am a binational, Israeli and American, and an Israeli army veteran. I touched on this briefly in my memoir, *Jew Boy,* but did not discuss then that I have an Israeli daughter from an early marriage. Isadora is seventeen years old, living in Israel, and just a year away from her own army service. A Hebrew-speaking beauty with dirty-blond bleached hair and mischievous blue eyes, she is an accomplished actress and sometime writer who has already appeared in several important stage productions. She is also a highly skilled equestrian (her dream is to own her own horse someday) and in every way a typical Israeli girl — her mother's best friend and in perpetual contact with her posse on her cell phone. She dates boys and listens to Israeli punk bands and, despite her mother's protests, wears a ring piercing above her eyebrow. It was my fears for her safety that started me on the road to writing *Matches.*

In 2002, Intifada II raged, and suicide bombings of Israeli restaurants, buses, and soldiers' hitchhiking stations were daily headlines. Due to my strained relations with Isadora's mother, my daughter and I had been out of touch for three years. But in 2002, each time a bomb went off in Israel my heart stuck in my throat and I became frantic with worry over Isadora.

My state of mind was not something that I felt I could share with my friends in San Francisco, Jewish and non-Jewish, who tend to lean politically to the left and are not especially sympathetic to Israel. They all knew that I had served extensively in the IDF, but we never really spoke about it. Although my friends were receptive to my concerns, I felt very alone with my memories of military experiences and with my anguished worry for my daughter. Also, I felt that the general discussion about Israeli soldiers in the public and media was fraught with misconceptions.

At a reading I gave from *Jew Boy,* an audience member declared that Israeli soldiers were little better than those who had hunted my mother, a Holocaust survivor, during World War II. The audience applauded her as she took her seat. On another occasion, at a bookstore appearance, a woman angrily insisted that Israel's leadership should be tried in The Hague for "crimes against humanity." It was evident to me that, when it came to the subject of Israel, these otherwise perfectly nice and undoubtedly intelligent people — some of them Jewish — had lost all perspective; they could not be more divorced from the realities of life there or grasp the reasons for and experience of actual military service.

Let me then pause here to say a brief word about the Middle East conflict.

At the turn of the twenty-first century, Israel is perhaps the only modern Westernized state whose very existence remains the source of ongoing speculation and debate in the forums of the world. This, and countless wars, have produced in Israel a status quo of existential crisis so deeply rooted, so profound that Israelis are no longer even aware of it.

The modern Israeli cannot find his or her own reflection in the mirror of the outside world. When he glances that way, he is greeted by looks of inimicable hostility and, as often, the barrel of a gun. Surrounded by foes, yet she longs for friends. Proud of their achievements in creating an enlightened modern state out of desert and swamps, Israelis feel like democratic heroes yet are treated by the world as pariahs.

It is a condition painfully familiar to Israelis, for it echoes, with relentless irony, the predicament of their pre-State forebears at the turn of the last century, when Jews were also universally despised — a condition that the Jewish State was intended, in part, to remedy.

Israel's most well-meaning critics cannot seem to grasp that modern Jewish history, culminating at Auschwitz, has taught Israel a fearsome lesson; one that constitutes her very raison d'être, as well as that of the Israel Defense Forces. It is that in the modern era, a people without a state and an army are fair game for certain annihilation.

Therefore, Israel's tough and sometimes unpopular diplomatic and military stance reflects, in part, a knowledge of the consequences of failure to defend oneself against attack. To fail to respond — or be unable to — spells, simply, the end of existence itself.

What many Westerners — bred on political and philosophical paradigms untested by so rigorous an experience as the Holocaust — do not seem to fully grasp is the extent to which, in Israel, sheer survival is the ultimate litmus test of social and political policy. If we are surviving, then the strategy is succeeding. Whichever policy assures the continuation of safe life for Jews in the tiny sliver of land that is the Jewish State wins the day. Whichever leader fends off the peril that has stalked Jewish history in various forms is the best leader.

While this does not make for much public relations capital in the world at large, it means, for Israel, that a nation of Jews can rise to breakfast one more day and then one more day again.

This is something I learned as a soldier in the IDF, when, in basic training, our sergeant told the unit: "In a war, the best soldier is not the hero but the one who survives." I was to hear this view repeatedly throughout my army service. Later, I would grasp how this very same idea permeates Israeli politics.

To make diplomatic breakthroughs often requires a people to altruistically stake their very necks for the sake of an idea, a principle, a condition, a vision — one usually fostered by third parties. This Israelis are unwilling to do. We know too much. For Israel arose from the ashes of every cherished principle held dear by that very same world which today militates for its concessions; governments and moral codes that utterly betrayed us Jews before, during, and even after World War II.

Yet there is also a kind of lofty pragmatism imbedded within this relentless Israeli impulse to survive at all costs, regardless of how unflattering it looks. For in order to live, a people, no matter how gravely tested, must also be able to dream.

Therefore, twice now, first with Egypt and later with Jordan, Israel, in sometimes glaring contradiction of everything that is thought about her, has proved quite willing to make extraordinary concessions for the sake of establishing peaceful relations. And when, at the Camp David Accords, on the White House lawn, before the entire world — including many stunned Israelis — Yitzak Rabin shook hands with Yasser Arafat, who personified, for most of us, the perennial foe, we Israelis proved that we too could make such a leap into the unknown; on the other side of which might lie — equally, in our imagination — a swimming pool or a mass grave.

The Israeli survival mechanism is thus far more complex, more multifaceted, than any of her indignant detractors at those bookstore readings might care to admit. And yet there remains the matter of the seeming intractability of the Israeli-Palestinian conflict.

Palestinians have been called the Jews of the Arab world. Like us, they are an exilic people rooted by heritage to a particular ground. Whenever I meet a Palestinian, I feel a sharp pang for how alike we are in certain respects. Our nimble wit and deft handling of adversity. Our aptitude for science, culture, and commerce. Their grandmothers in their scarves look like our grandmothers in their babushkas. We should be friends, not foes. The Palestinian right to a homeland is genuine and unarguable. Theirs has been an aspiration rooted equally in *culture and memory and pride*. Though they do not look back over a diasporic history strewn with the corpses of brethren slain in country after country in genocidal slaughter, Palestinians, like the Jews, have been socially and politically brutalized as the odd man out. Though support for Palestinian aspirations is de rigeur among Arab states, few have extended to them any genuine assistance or substantive guidance. Twice now, in 1948 when the UN partition granted to them a state of their own, and decades later at Camp David, when they withdrew from the Clinton peace process, the Palestinians have retreated from the prospect of a state. Senior Arab governments of the region should never have permitted them do so. But perhaps these were only tough lessons to be learned along the road to eventual statehood. After all, it took us Jews nearly two thousand years to relearn them.

Here is what I fear. I fear that the Palestinians have forgotten what their dreams are. For of late, they have undergone a large-scale radical change from a nationalistically driven people possessed of a legitimate vision of self-determination to a religiously inspired one, running aground on a campaign of furious genocidal jihad.

Hamas — an implacable militant religious movement sworn to the destruction of Israel — controls a far greater majority among Palestinians than is generally known. Islamic fundamentalism has been steadily spreading throughout the Middle East and not only in such hotbeds of poverty as Gaza but in greater portions of Egypt and Jordan as well. In Israel's former administered territories, the by-now old school Palestinian Authority, who seem to be in charge, are in fact not in control, and are barely holding on by their bloody fingernails.

The Palestinian Authority wants a state for the Palestinians. This, Israel desires.

Hamas, and so Islamic fundamentalism, covets Israel in her entirety, and encourages a perpetual state of destabilization, for the eventual triumph and glory of radical Islam. This, Israel will not permit.

Here is my hope: that the Palestinians will gain a state, and that it will be enough. But so long as hostilities proceed, the Palestinians remain troubling and oppressed heroes to many people in the West, and in a sense, this encourages them to prefer a violent glory to an uneventful peace. For perhaps the Palestinians grasp too that once peace is attained, the world will quickly rush to forget them.

Two parties, faced with an insoluble dilemma, may remain locked in belligerence that, like Maya's bad marriage to Dotan in *Matches,* eventually explodes. Israel and the Palestinians today are like a marriage in which no partner has been willing to leave, and that has become, over time, strangely, awfully, a way of surviving.

In 2002, Western perceptions of Israel deeply concerned me, but it was not until much later that I decided to write a novel about being an Israeli soldier in the territories. For, like many others, I was yet in a state of paralyzed disbelief at the sudden tailspin of the peace process that had culminated in the assassination of Israeli Prime Minister Yitzak Rabin. I had supported Rabin's dreaming gamble on peace. One moment there was every reason to hope; but then, in the next, none whatsoever. When Rabin was assassinated, gradually the dream gave way to a ceaseless round of attack and counterattack that I knew only too well.

Night after night I found myself at the computer, reading in the online Israeli newspaper *Haaretz* about the latest terrorist attack on Jews and the inevitable retaliation against Palestinians. Each time I read of a new suicide bombing, I selfishly prayed that the incident had not occurred in an area that my daughter frequented. For a while, such locations seemed magically exempt. And then a suicide bomber struck too near. I made frantic calls to her home. No answer. It was one of the worst moments of my life.

When I called friends, tried to explain my worry, I could hear by their voices their real inability to grasp what I was talking about. I don't blame them. How can they know — even given the events of 9/11 — what it is like to have buses blow up daily on major urban thoroughfares; to have crowded family restaurants explode in a fireball? It's not your average sort of human experience.

It was the attack on Isadora's immediate vicinity that persuaded me to do something, anything. I could not stand feeling helpless for long. Unable to bear inaction, I sought recourse to journalism. I persuaded a major daily newspaper to accredit me with the Israeli government as a foreign correspondent. I flew to Israel at the height of the suicide bombings and covered the war that had come to be known as "the War of the Buses."

In 2002 I found a country steeped in terror and gloom. Jerusalem, my old hometown, was deserted. Walking its streets reawakened in me many, many memories of events that are portrayed in *Matches*. I saw the sprawling house in Katamon where I lived in a rented room with a wide veranda, next to the old Kurdistani woman who would accidentally set herself on fire. In its large courtyard still sat old Iraqi Jewish women making apricot leather in big metal pans. I saw the steakias on Agrippas Street where so often I went drinking and dancing late at night with fellow artists and writers. I walked alone with press badge prominently displayed in the Old City of Jerusalem, in the Arab Quarter, where, in happier days, my friends and I would move in a lively shoulder-to-shoulder crush of tourists, shopping for bargains in the crowded stalls; this was followed by sumptuous dining on lamb and rice in a Palestinian restaurant. But now there was not a tourist in sight. I was advised by a squad of militant young Palestinians to return to the Jewish Quarter or else. At the Wailing Wall, normally aswarm with festive visitors, the only people in evidence were armed soldiers and a handful of somber old religionists.

I also saw something I'd never seen before. In the town center, on Ben Yehuda Street, the most popular party street in Jerusalem (and so, the hardest hit by suicide bombings) the sidewalks were eerily quiet, the shops empty. But on the street corners were musicians — violinists, cellists, and flutists, young and old, figures out of a Chagall painting — who stood there serenely playing classical music, Mozart and Brahms and Bach, serenading the desertion. Their playing, they explained, was an affirmation against death. Everywhere I went in Jerusalem, armed guards frisked me at the doors of coffee shops and restaurants. In the streets and on buses people looked anxious, shell-shocked. I had never before seen Israel like this.

I hadn't been in touch with the military side of life for some time but now I visited IDF units in the West Bank and interviewed settlers, Palestinians, and also the families of Israeli teenagers who had been killed by suicide bombers. One of the

Jewish mothers I interviewed showed me albums of photographs of her sixteen-year-old daughter, a talented guitarist, who died in the bombing of the Sbarro Pizzeria in the center of Jerusalem.

The suicide bomber had entered, she said, bearing his nail bomb in a guitar case. He had stood, according to the forensic reports, right next to her daughter, who also bore an instrument case, though hers contained a guitar. The bomber, she explained, had detonated right next to her daughter. She showed me a photo taken of her dead daughter's face as it looked after the blast. It was completely flattened. "You know," this mother told me, "you don't stop loving your child just because her face looks like this in death. Even this face you love. And I look at this photo with as much love as all the others."

All this reawakened in me traumatic memories of my years serving as an IDF soldier in the territories, in Gaza and the West Bank. Out of this trip came articles, most notably a large spread on suicide bombers and their victims, that I coauthored and that appeared in the Sunday *Los Angeles Times*. The experience also reawakened in me an interest in the woman's side of war, her experience, as I interviewed many mothers and other women and generated two articles about women in the war. This is why women's experience, Jewish and Arab, forms one main nucleus of *Matches* in the book's long middle section.

While reporting on the war I visited my daughter. It was the first time we'd met in years, and she had grown into a lovely young woman. We circled warily around each other, seeking an opening. The breakthrough came when I hung out with her friends and answered their questions about what girls wear in San Francisco and also about the rock scene. They oohed and ahhed, visibly impressed. They chattered happily about Isadora's new boyfriend, a tall basketball player, and asked, shooting secret glances at each other, for tips about boys. Clearly, my answer was make or break. "Always keep them off balance," I said. "Women are the mystery that men should spend their lives trying to solve . . . never let them succeed." They liked that and laughed and laughed. My daughter threw her arms around me and gave me a big kiss. I had passed the all-important best girlfriends test. Now I was accepted.

Isadora talked about the books she was reading: *Prozac Nation* (in Hebrew translation) and *The Collected Poems of Dylan Thomas*. She no longer rode the bus into Tel Aviv for her theater rehearsals, she told me, but took taxis each way. Buses terrified her, and also bus stations. When we traveled to Tel Aviv together, she slid down in her seat as the cab passed the Central Bus Station. "You don't have to worry here," I said naively. "Not a whole block from the bus station." "Of course you do," she said. "After they blow up one bus, then they blow up a car somewhere nearby just as the ambulances are coming to help. That way they kill the rescuers." She also said that each time she rode the taxi to and from Tel Aviv — about twice a week — she worried about a terrorist attack. She worried about an attack when she went to the beach. When she sat in a café. When she walked in the center of town. When she shopped for groceries in the supermarket. She worried about an attack when she sat in school, learning. Sometimes she dreamed about an attack.

Gradually, we attained intimacy, mended fences. She is a budding poet, and when the Israeli author Etgar Keret staged a reading for me in a Tel Aviv club, I brought her on stage with me and we performed together, she in Hebrew and I in English, each reading our poems. It was a miracle moment! The audience gave us a standing ovation, and Isadora told me that she was proud to have me for a daddy.

One week later a suicide bomber targeted another club close to where we had performed. He tried to drive his car bomb through the club doors and kill everyone inside. Luckily, an alert armed guard at the door opened fire and stopped him. That it could easily have been Isadora (and me) in that club was plain.

In the way of such things, like grim cosmic karma, I was contacted not long after this by an old IDF buddy who told me that because of my experience in the IDF I could be reactivated to a front-line unit. I agreed without hesitation to go. I felt that I had to do something to protect my daughter, and Israel, against suicide bombers.

In 2003, I was reactivated and served in the conflict in a front-line unit, alongside young soldiers. During the rigorous retraining, I discovered that my eyes were less sharp than they had been. I hadn't handled an automatic weapon in some time, and I found it hard to hit the longer-range targets, some of which were a hundred yards away. But the young soldier beside me, a marksman sniper, offered to shoot my target for me, so that when the officer in charge came around to grade performance, he was dazzled by my skill. My target bore several direct bullseyes. The grinning young sniper and I exchanged winks.

To the troops I served with in the IDF in 2003, I was like an older brother, the experienced veteran, and we got on famously. It was a tense time. IDF soldiers were being kidnapped and murdered by militants. My unit was engaged in operations to prevent infiltration by suicide bombings, and I felt satisfied to be able to take a direct hand in protecting Isadora. Naturally, I didn't tell her that I was serving until my tour of duty ended. She would have been sick with worry, and with good reason. Days after I returned to San Francisco from my service, one of the boys on the base, a twenty-one-year-old sergeant, was killed by militants.

By this time I was actively engaged in the composition of *Matches*. Some of the material in the novel was developed directly from notes taken on the front lines of the conflict, during lulls in the action and even, at times, in the midst of operations, hurriedly scrawled into a little notebook that I kept in one of the ammo pouches on my battle vest. Naturally, certain details were later changed, but the feeling — the urgent sense of things — is very much retained.

After my years of service in the IDF as a soldier in the territories, I began to exhibit certain clear symptoms of post-traumatic stress disorder as the direct result of the sorts of events portrayed in *Matches*. And it occurred to me that in writing this book I needed to faithfully portray the psychology of a soldier engaged in such service — not only as an act of personal expiation but also as a guide to understanding the anguish of soldiers, Israeli and American both, who are currently engaged in antiterrorist operations in the midst of hostile civilian populations. I felt it important that I compose a novel that would avoid the polarities of the heated political discourse and remain faithful to the soldiers themselves, the challenges posed to their decency and humanity. I wanted to show the personal consequences of such warfare. Therefore I tried, to the best of my ability, to create a work that is neither left-wing nor right-wing but an honest account of the experiences of Israeli soldiers.

Questions and Topics for Discussion

1. Part of Alan Kaufman's aim in writing *Matches* was to provide an evenhanded and unbiased account of the day-to-day life of Israeli soldiers, and to illuminate the human toll that such a conflict takes on those at its front lines. Do you think it

is possible to write a balanced account of such a controversial conflict? Do you think Kaufman succeeds in this aim?

2. Given that religion and politics are so closely entwined in the Arab-Israeli conflict, were you at all surprised by the (arguably small) role that religion plays in the daily lives of the soldiers in *Matches?*

3. Consider the large-scale effects that war has on the fabric of Nathan Falk's social and artistic milieu in Jerusalem. Identify and discuss some of these effects. Do you think that American-fought wars have a similar impact on the American home front? Explain why or why not.

4. How do trust and friendship figure in the novel? Who are Nathan Falk's friends? What about his friendship with Bachshi — how is that different?

5. In general, how is ethnicity handled in *Matches?*

6. How would you describe Nathan Falk's moral sense? He's pushed into a kind of gray area by the extreme conditions of his life as a soldier. Did you consider the problems in his relationship with Maya a reflection of his true character, or a manifestation of the effects of war?

7. What understanding of women's experience in the Middle East did you derive from *Matches?* Thinking of both Maya and Bachshi's sister Batiya, how would you characterize their experience of the Arab-Israeli conflict? What is Kaufman's point, do you think, in describing so thoroughly Maya's imbalance and breakdown?

8. According to your reading of *Matches,* does Falk ever empathize with those on the flip side of the conflict? If so, at what points?

9. How does *Matches* inform your understanding of the ongoing struggle between Israelis and Palestinians? How does it affect your thinking about the IDF, and about this conflict?

Alan Kaufman's
Suggestions for Further Reading

Red Cavalry by Isaac Babel

This Way for the Gas, Ladies and Gentlemen by Tadeusz Borowski

Herzl by Amos Elon

Blood Meridian by Cormac McCarthy

Selected Poetry by Yehuda Amichai

Heart of Darkness by Joseph Conrad

The Bus Driver Who Wanted to Be God by Etgar Keret

Hunger by Knut Hamsun

Waiting for the Barbarians by J. M. Coetzee

A Farewell to Arms by Ernest Hemingway

The Jewish State by Theodore Herzl

Dispatches by Michael Herr

Absalom, Absalom by William Faulkner

Madame Bovary by Gustave Flaubert

The Letters of Gustave Flaubert (1830–1857), edited by Francis Steegmuller

Last Exit to Brooklyn by Hubert Selby Jr.

The Arab-Israeli Wars: War and Peace in the Middle East from the War of Independence through Lebanon by Chaim Herzog

A History of Israel: From the Rise of Zionism to Our Time (Second Edition, Revised and Updated) by Howard M. Sachar

A History of Zionism: From the French Revolution to the Establishment of the State of Israel by Walter Laqueur